THE CRUX

Charlotte Perkins Stetson [Gilman] in 1900. Portrait taken in Los Angeles, California by Charles Fletcher Lummis. Courtesy of the Schlesinger Library, Radcliffe Institute, Harvard University.

THE CRUX

A Novel
by Charlotte Perkins Gilman

Edited and with an
Introduction by
Jennifer S. Tuttle

DELAWARE

Newark: University of Delaware Press
London: Associated University Presses

Associated University Presses
440 Forsgate Drive
Cranbury, NJ 08512

Associated University Presses
16 Barter Street
London WC1A 2AH, England

Associated University Presses
P.O. Box 338, Port Credit
Mississauga, Ontario
Canada L5G 4L8

PS1744
.G57
C78
2002

0 48013351

The paper used in this publication meets the requirements of the American National Standard for Permanence of Paper for Printed Library Materials Z39.48-1984.

Library of Congress Cataloging-in-Publication Data

Gilman, Charlotte Perkins, 1860–1935.
    The crux : a novel / by Charlotte Perkins Gilman ; edited and with an introduction by Jennifer S. Tuttle.
        p.   cm.
    Includes bibliographical references (p.   ).
    ISBN 0-87413-771-3 (alk. paper)
    1. Women pioneers—Fiction.   2. Massachusetts—Fiction.
3. Colorado—Fiction.   4. Sex role—Fiction.   I. Tuttle, Jennifer S., 1967–   II. Title.

PS1744.G57 C78   2002
813'.4—dc21   2001053420

Contents

The Crux

Editor's Acknowledgments

There are many individuals who deserve my acknowledgment for their contributions to this project. I would like to express my appreciation to the reference and interlibrary loan librarians at the Geisel and Biomedical Libraries at the University of California, San Diego, as well as to Sarah Phillips, Reference Librarian at Harvard University Widener Library, for patiently helping me to locate obscure materials and information. Karyl Klein at the Colorado Historical Society, Marie-Hélène Gold at the Arthur and Elizabeth Schlesinger Library on the History of Women in America at the Radcliffe Institute, Walter Stetson Chamberlin, and Gary Scharnhorst have earned my considerable thanks for their help in locating visual images for the frontispiece. I am extremely grateful to Karen Connolly-Lane, for her inspired suggestion to use Gilman's Soapine illustration on the novel's cover; to Patrick Scott, Associate University Librarian at the Thomas Cooper Library, University of South Carolina, for helping me to acquire the image; and, especially, to my brother Geoff Tuttle, for doing me the honor and the service of adapting Gilman's image for the book jacket. I would also like to thank Deborah Evans and Frederick Wegener for their generosity in sharing what was then their unpublished work on *The Crux* and related topics. My introduction to the novel was enriched greatly by my lively conversations with Susan E. Cayleff, about women healers in the American West, and Nicole Tonkovich, about what an editor's introduction should do. I also extend my appreciation to the anonymous readers selected by the University of Delaware Press for their enthusiasm for and comments on the edition, and to Christine A. Retz at Associated University Presses for her superb editorial assistance. Finally, I wish to express my deep gratitude to

Catherine Golden, for her constant encouragement of my work on this project, and for her friendship and faith in me; to David Kuchta, for his close reading of the manuscript, his sage editorial advice, and his unflagging intellectual, emotional, and technical support through every stage of this work; and to Denise Knight, for the inspiration to begin the project, for valuable editorial suggestions on an early draft of the manuscript, and, most profoundly, for her truly boundless generosity as a friend, mentor, and advocate, which has sustained me from the first.

THE CRUX

Introduction to *The Crux*

Speaking about her collection of poetry *In This Our World* (1893), Charlotte Perkins Gilman explained in 1896, "I can't call it a book of poems. I call it a tool box. It was written to drive nails with."[1] Expressing both practicality and passion, this statement exemplifies the ethos behind Gilman's entire body of work. Throughout her career she would reiterate the sentiment: she saw herself not as a poet, but as a preacher, a calling for which the metaphor of driving nails was often apt.[2] Looking back in her memoirs upon the reception of her work, she revealed that she was "most agreeably surprised by the acceptance of so much of what I had to offer. One cannot undertake to alter the ideas, feelings and habits of the people and expect them to like it."[3] In all of her work—poetry, fiction, and nonfiction alike—she set for herself no less a task: for Gilman, the measure of "good" literature was not so much its aesthetic qualities as the extent to which it induced positive social change.

At the root of many of her calls for change was the fundamental conviction that women should be recognized primarily in terms of their humanity rather than in terms of their sex or gender. In Gilman's words, the problem lay in "[m]en having been accepted as humanity, women but a side-issue." As a consequence, fiction "has not given any true picture of woman's life, very little of human life, and a disproportioned section of man's life."[4] In *The Crux* (1911), a novel that frankly examines the issue of sexually transmitted disease, Gilman set out to remedy this literary misrepresentation as well as the social ills and gender inequalities of which it was a symptom. She did so by seizing upon supposedly masculine prerogatives and redefining them as human, and thus equally accessible to women.[5] Such prerogatives, all radical for women in her

11

day, included sexual self-determination; frank discussion and knowledge of medical topics affecting women, particularly sexually transmitted disease; freedom from domestic drudgery and economic dependence; entitlement to do socially meaningful work; a central role in American Manifest Destiny; and the opportunity for heroism and adventure. Such freedoms, Gilman argued, would allow women to fulfill their human potential as healthy, vibrant members of their community—all for the social good, since she asserted that the health of women was directly related to the well-being of society as a whole. These, then, are the nails Gilman drives in *The Crux*. Categorized by one of her contemporaries as "more an argument or a sermon than a piece of art" (a designation with which Gilman likely would have agreed), the novel preaches a bold message that adds new dimensions to our understanding of Gilman's life and work.[6]

Coming from a family of preachers, Gilman laid hereditary claim to the role.[7] She professed to have inherited from her father, Frederick Beecher Perkins, the "Beecher urge to social service" (*Living* 6). Through him she was related to the distinguished Beecher clan, including her great-grandfather, the renowned preacher Lyman Beecher, and his daughters, novelist and abolitionist Harriet Beecher Stowe, educator Catharine Beecher, and suffragist Isabella Beecher Hooker. She was born Charlotte Anna Perkins on the third of July, 1860, in Hartford, Connecticut, and was raised by her mother, the emotionally distant Mary Fitch Westcott Perkins, after her father left the family in 1869. Despite growing up steeped in traditional New England conservatism, she was precocious and independent-minded, shunning the constraints of conventional women's fashions, exercising regularly, and studying at the Rhode Island School of Design. Though she identified with New England blue bloods, she was raised in genteel poverty and struggled financially throughout her life.[8] Earning her own living as an artist and teacher, the young Gilman aspired to greater accomplishment, desiring to "help humanity" (*Living* 70). She would devote the remainder of her life to this purpose.

Throughout her career Gilman wrote close to five hundred poems, a number of plays and dialogues, nearly two hundred short stories, and several novels. She was equally prolific as a writer of nonfiction, publishing scores of essays, six book-length studies, and an autobiography. For a short time she edited the *Impress* (organ of the Pacific Coast Women's Press Association) and, from 1909 to 1916, she single-handedly wrote, edited, and published her own magazine, aptly named *The Forerunner*. She later contributed a regular column to the *New York Tribune*. Despite such literary output, Gilman earned her living mainly from lecturing, for which she traveled throughout the United States and Europe. She identified herself not as a feminist, but rather as a "humanist": in print and on the platform, she advocated for women's rights as a means toward a reorganization of human society as a whole.[9] Among her best-known agendas were socialized housekeeping and child care (advocating kitchenless homes and the professionalization of child care), woman suffrage, and women's economic independence. By the time of her death, however, Gilman, once considered the leading women's rights advocate of her day, had fallen out of favor. As Ann J. Lane explains, after World War I, "Gilman continued to espouse her communitarian, socialist commitment to a life of productive, social purpose, whereas young women of this time sought a different kind of womanhood, one stressing personal, emotional, and sexual satisfactions."[10] Nevertheless, she is recognized today for being in the vanguard of American feminism, a dedicated reformer whose progressive ideals would prove to be relevant to social debate throughout the twentieth century. Suffering from inoperable breast cancer, Gilman calmly took her own life in 1935. She ends her autobiography (completed shortly before her death) on a characteristically optimistic note: "My life is Humanity—and that goes on. . . . The one predominant duty is to find one's work and do it, and I have striven mightily at that" (*Living* 335). Too long neglected, *The Crux* is a significant part of this life's work: it is a novel that espouses all of Gilman's major tenets, sometimes in quite an original manner, and it is a story that was wrenched out of Gilman's own life, in ways that are only beginning to be recognized today.

The Crux was first published serially in The Forerunner in 1911, after which Gilman brought it into print as a single volume through her own publishing house, the Charlton Company. Since that time, however, the book has been out of print and largely unavailable, both to students and to scholars.[11] The novel is of a piece with the aims and strengths, as well as the limitations, of The Forerunner as a whole. Gilman initiated The Forerunner out of necessity when she found that, "if one writes to express important truths, needed yet unpopular, the market is necessarily limited" (Living 304). Finding it harder and harder to place her work, Gilman proclaimed finally, "If the editors and publishers will not bring out my work, I will!" (Living 304). She fittingly labeled the magazine a "literary tour de force" (Living 308): in its seven years of print, it comprised what Gilman estimated to be twenty-eight volumes of writing.[12] Though the pressures of time and space necessarily limited Gilman's ability to polish and develop this work, such a large output did have a profound purpose, clearly evident in the novel: to "stimulate thought; to arouse hope, courage, and impatience; to offer practical suggestions and solutions; to voice the strong assurance of better living."[13] Likely modeled on the feminist reform magazine the Woman's Journal, each issue propounded Gilman's ideas in a variety of forms in conversation with one another, ranging from essays, serialized nonfiction books, reviews, and other commentary to short stories, satires, serialized novels, poems, and fables.[14] The magazine treated an array of topics important to Gilman, and can, in fact, be read as a "complete microcosm of her themes and theories."[15] Though The Forerunner did not pay for itself, having only approximately fifteen hundred subscribers (some from as far as Australia and India), Gilman considered it a worthwhile enterprise (Living 305). She claims that it gave her the opportunity to record her "heresies" without censure, "to say exactly what I had to say, fully and freely" (Living 310, 307).

The Crux exemplifies this uncensored expression of Gilman's "heretical" vision. The novel tells the story of a

group of women who leave behind the stagnant and outdated New England way of life to migrate westward on the
advice of a woman physician, finding growth and establishing an enlightened community in Colorado. Whereas
in their hometown of Bainville, Massachusetts, with its
repressive traditions, excess of unmarried women, and
scarcity of marriageable men, such women languish out
of duty to the old ways, in the West they form the heart of
a thriving new world founded on many of Gilman's principles for progressive social change. Central to this multigenerational cohort of women is the heroine Vivian Lane.
The novel presents Vivian's struggle to reject outmoded
ideologies of gender that render her an object, voiceless
and defined only through her relation to others. Such ideologies not only deny Vivian the opportunity to develop
her talents and to pursue rewarding work; they also
threaten her health and well-being. The ideal of female
innocence they prescribe deprives Vivian of bodily self-
determination, as she discovers when, because she is
kept ignorant of sexual and medical matters, she nearly
contracts syphilis from her earnest suitor, Morton Elder.
The novel is thus a strident critique of cultural imperatives and medical policies that leave women and their
children vulnerable to what was then called venereal disease. Significantly, Gilman sets her heroine's quest for
knowledge, power, and self-determination in the West,
which brings the book into conversation with national
discourses of health, renewal, and Manifest Destiny. The
novel is not subtle about its arguments: Gilman was dedicated to effecting social change through her work, rather
than to simply providing entertainment. Though this self-
conscious commitment to didacticism has likely contributed to the novel's being so long out of print, it is also precisely the reason the work is so important, for it engages
powerfully with a number of compelling social issues,
cultural phenomena, and literary forms from the turn of
the century. As Ann J. Lane explains of Gilman, "It is the
imaginative demands, not the literary skill, that make
reading her fiction informing."[16] Although at the height of
her career Gilman was recognized as an important social
theorist, all of her work was out of print by 1930;[17] it has

only been through the prescience and dedication of
teachers and scholars later in the twentieth century that
her writing has been rediscovered and studied for its important contributions to American social and literary history. *The Crux* is yet another important work that offers
much to our body of knowledge about Gilman, her writings, and her time.

"THE DUTIES OF A DAUGHTER": IDEOLOGIES OF WOMANHOOD

One of the most salient characteristics of *The Crux* is its
engagement with competing ideologies of white, middle-
class womanhood.[18] Like much of Gilman's work, the
novel posits that women's possibilities for self-definition
and self-determination are directly related to the welfare
of the community, the nation, and the human race as a
whole. Thus, cultural debates about women's nature and
their proper place are fundamental aspects of her plot.
Vivian Lane must navigate among conflicting models of
womanhood in her struggle to define herself and to find
her place in the world. As Ann J. Lane notes, she is "torn
between" two womanly ideals represented by women of
her acquaintance.[19] In the end, she must forge a new
model of female identity—one that Gilman suggests is
necessary not only to improve women's lives, but also to
reform American society. Gilman's main target in the
novel is the gender ideology of old New England, which
espouses a constricting ideal of womanhood conceived
through an array of duties to family and tradition. Resem-
bling what Barbara Welter has called the "Cult of True
Womanhood," this ideology demands that Vivian define
herself through her functions as daughter, wife, and
mother: her destiny is to serve these duties selflessly, to
exhibit the virtues of piety, purity, submissiveness, and
domesticity.[20] The story begins with the young heroine
trying to contend with such an ideal. Well trained, she
seems on the surface to be "restrained and courteous,"
yet "inwardly [she was] at war with her surroundings"; indeed, like the young Gilman, she finds herself "boiling
with rebellion" against the traditional ideals and atti-

tudes of her culture.[21] Prohibited by her father from attending college, Vivian "longed for occupation," explains
the narrator, "but she could never hypnotize herself with
'fancy-work,' " the supposedly feminine tasks of ornamen-
tation and homemaking. Convinced that "[h]er work must
be worth while," Vivian feels that her strong mind is
being "held in dumb subjection" (*Crux* 106). Traditional
New England women, Gilman suggests, are denied both
voice and subjectivity—the agency granted to human beings—and Gilman uses Vivian's predicament to illustrate
the intellectual and emotional costs of such a role.

While Vivian bristles under the overt domination of the
novel's patriarchs, however, she is seduced into a certain
yearning for a traditional female role when it is modeled
by Adela St. Cloud, a former Sunday school teacher who
is the sister-in-law of the town's minister. Dressing always
in "soft, clinging fabrics, always with a misty, veiled effect
to them," Mrs. St. Cloud dazzles Vivian with her gentle
beauty (*Crux* 98). Saintlike, she preaches complete self-
abnegation, and the conscientious Vivian is drawn to
what she perceives as the nobility in such a role. Through
the character of Mrs. St. Cloud, Gilman illustrates both
the attractions and the ultimate dangers—to both individual women and society—of this model of traditional womanhood. As the novel begins, Vivian is on the cusp of a
youthful romance with Morton Elder, who is her long-
time neighbor. But in the first chapter, Morton, as tired as
is Vivian of the stifling way of life in Bainville, leaves for
the West, which as a man he is free and encouraged to do.
Vivian proceeds to pine for him for nine years, at length
encouraged in this pursuit by Mrs. St. Cloud, who
"stirr[ed]" within Vivian "the depths of romance. . . .
From her [Vivian] learned to face a life of utter renunciation, to be true, . . . true to the past, to be patient; and to
wait" (*Crux* 107). Ironically, of course, this is precisely
what the New England traditionalists had pressured Vivian to do. As Gilman notes in the novel, such "dumb patience" (*Crux* 98), a silent, passive, and childlike role that
Mrs. St. Cloud claims to exemplify, was often undertaken
out of necessity because of the small ratio of men to
women in the Northeast.

Though this passive model of womanhood, Gilman suggests, creates a tragic waste of humanity as well as a stagnant way of life, it also has more dangerous effects, since it nearly leads Vivian to marry a man infected with syphilis. Morton, having sown his proverbial wild oats in the West, renews his acquaintance with Vivian and undertakes a determined courtship of her after her move to Colorado. Yet Vivian is torn between her remembered feelings of some nine years past and her present distaste for Morton's rough and discourteous demeanor. Too innocent to truly understand what is at stake, however, she has only a vague sense that all is not as it should be. Mrs. St. Cloud, the novel's patron saint of traditional gender relations, attempts to intervene at this moment of uncertainty, appealing to the True Woman's duty of positive "influence," a term that was invoked widely in the nineteenth century: "you can make a new man of him! A glorious work! . . . . Oh, my child, it is the most beautiful work on earth!" (*Crux* 170). As Gilman argues, the blind innocence and self-sacrifice so admired in a True Woman would endanger the health of Vivian and her prospective children, not to mention its emotional costs, and Vivian is ultimately warned off. Yet the perils of True Womanhood are made quite clear.

Mrs. St. Cloud embodies, in fact, the worst result of what Gilman called women's "sexuo-economic" relationship with men. In her groundbreaking work *Women and Economics* (1898), Gilman argued that women's economic dependence upon men had reduced them to mere consumers who were forced to develop sexual (and hence maternal and domestic) attributes as "a means of getting [their] livelihood."[22] The "sex parasite" Mrs. St. Cloud serves to illustrate, then, the destructive effects, on both women and society as a whole, of women's need to participate in their own objectification (*Crux* 229–30). As her name and her veil-like garments suggest, Mrs. St. Cloud's beauty masks a coquettish, acquisitive, in fact destructive parasitism that proves to be as destructive to her love-struck male conquests as it nearly is to Vivian. As Aleta Cane explains, "Mrs. St. Cloud becomes an egregious example of the women who live only for themselves, and not for the larger community."[23] Ultimately, Gilman makes it quite clear that such a model of womanhood has no place in an enlightened society: the novel ends with the revelation that St. Cloud, who has come out West to hunt a husband, will leave this group and return to the East, where she belongs—to a society driven to decay by its devotion to outmoded traditions of the past.

Diametrically opposed to Mrs. St. Cloud is the character of Dr. Jane Bellair, who advocates those values Gilman associates with a progressive future and exemplifies the early generations of what were called "New Women."[24] Eschewing St. Cloud's fragile, passive, and childlike beauty, Dr. Bellair is "strong, cheerful, full of new ideas, . . . and radiating actual power" (*Crux* 108). She rejects fashion for practicality, sporting low-heeled, comfortable shoes and several convenient pockets (*Crux* 109, 115)—sartorial choices that were particularly dear to Gilman's heart.[25] She is also an educated, independent, and professional woman whose rejection of conventional femininity is symbolized in her physical removal from Bainville and all of its expectations; she seeks new opportunities in the "masculine" West despite New England's cultural imperative to stay put and wait for a man to lead her to her destiny.[26]

Though in her heterosexuality and her support of marriage and motherhood Dr. Bellair is by no means the most radical example of New Womanhood, her status as a woman physician nevertheless represents a significant challenge to traditional orthodoxies of gendered behavior. As a female doctor she is pursuing a profession that was both male dominated and culturally coded as masculine. The second half of the nineteenth century has been acknowledged as the period spawning the simultaneous rise and "masculinization" of professions such as law, medicine, and literature.[27] Characterized by the "institutionaliz[ation of] values of rationality, objectivity, specialization, and authority," this trend had the "net result" of "plac[ing] . . . limitations on women's participation."[28] Not surprisingly, these calls for masculinization came at a time when women were seeking higher education and entering the professions in record numbers. Women physicians justified their pursuits in a variety of ways, ranging from claims that, as intellectual beings, women were entitled to be doctors without respect to their gender, to assertions that women, as feminine beings, had unique traits and values that would uplift the profession.[29] Dr. Bellair might be seen to represent a combination of these two positions, in that while she claims the male privileges of mobility, practical dress, and intellectual inquiry, she also, as we shall see, espouses essentialist notions of women's character and capabilities (that is, she bases her theories on traits she claims are essential and unique to women). Historically, of the two extremes, the latter appeal to domestic ideology, and, indeed, to "True Womanhood," was much more successful: in the face of male physicians' attempts to claim the role as inherently masculine, women's strategic appeals to maternalism, among other sacred cultural values, made their pursuit of the profession more palatable.[30] As a result, the late nineteenth century saw a steady rise in the number of women medical professionals.[31] By the time Gilman wrote her novel, however, the situation was beginning to change for women practitioners: though the year 1910 represented a peak in the number of women physicians at 6 percent nationally, the backlash against them was already under way by the male-dominated medical establishment, curtailing opportunities for women as well as for others not from the dominant group of white, Protestant, privileged-class men.[32] With her own appeals to maternalism (discussed presently), Dr. Bellair clearly invokes the New Woman doctor, who both appeals to traditional femininity and espouses feminist ideals that challenge such tradition. She is also a heroic figure: as Frederick Wegener has argued, "the determination of such persevering women to establish themselves as doctors in the face of concerted and typically degrading antagonism came to epitomize, in Gilman's eyes, the larger struggle for professional acceptance and economic parity" so central to Gilman's life work.[33]

The anxieties and changes presented by the woman physician (and, by extension, her status as a New Woman) were explored in literary trends as well as educational policies and professional regulations. By 1911, the woman physician had become an increasingly popular character type in American literature, having her own unique literary conventions. Among the most common were the notions that she enters the medical profession as a displacement for a failed love affair, that she finds a medical career to be incompatible with marriage, that she becomes "unsexed" by medical study (that is, she loses her "feminine" characteristics and takes on "masculine" attributes), and that she undertakes medical education to begin with because she is in some way unfeminine or "mannish."[34]

Gilman inverts such conventions in her novel. Certainly, she invokes the ways in which women physicians were associated with the rejection of traditional femininity in favor of characteristics coded as masculine; but in Dr. Bellair (as well as in the doctor's prescriptions that her women patients leave behind New England's constraints upon their aspirations) this is figured as a positive, progressive quality: such *human* characteristics, the novel suggests, should not be gendered.[35] More important, perhaps, is the way that Gilman handles the presumed relationship between a medical career and romance. Though Dr. Bellair was married previously, she had left her husband—not out of "mannishness," but because he gave her gonorrhea, thus destroying any chance she had to become pregnant. This is particularly distressing for her because, as Gilman's mouthpiece for a progressive, "new" kind of New Womanhood, she espouses motherhood, performed in an enlightened manner, as the highest duty a woman can perform for a reformed society. "When I found I could not be a mother," she admits to Vivian, "I determined to be a doctor, and save other women" (*Crux* 190). Thus, to say that she becomes a physician because of disappointment in love, or to say that her career is "incompatible" with marriage, is only to state the case in the most literal sense. More accurately, she has lost her opportunity for what Gilman considers to be the highest social service because she has been victimized by her husband's decadent sexuality and her culture's Victorian insistence that as a woman, she remain innocent of sexual and medical knowledge which could have prevented such infection. Denied the opportunity for motherhood, Dr. Bellair cannot shine as the star of the plot, but she can protect other women from the same fate, thus serving the higher good.[36]

In such a role, the doctor also follows a familiar convention in Gilman's body of work. In her relationship with Vivian, she is part of a team of Gilman's stock characters. Ann J. Lane describes the formula: "The young girl-woman, restricted by her traditional view of parental obligation or social place, or endangered by an innocence that does not protect her from a cruel libertine, is offered the model of an older woman, frequently a doctor, who presents her with options she never knew existed and knowledge she did not have."[37] The innocent and dutiful Vivian is indeed threatened by the syphilitic Morton Elder. She is saved from a fate similar to the doctor's by the doctor herself, who breaks the Victorian code of silence about such matters and tells Vivian of Morton's condition. In light of this new knowledge, Vivian is empowered to make informed decisions about her body, her sexuality, and the course of her life. The "new options" offered her by Dr. Bellair, then, are many. In giving Vivian these powers of self-determination, the doctor models an assertive female voice where True Womanhood had urged silence and ignorance. For a whole group of Bainville women, including Vivian, she provides the opportunity to break away from the sterile devotion to an irrelevant past in which they wait indefinitely for marriage, urging them to move to the West, which she associates with growth and fertility. Part of Vivian's growth consists in meaningful work for the good of the community, for in Colorado, Dr. Bellair provides her with the opportunity to run a kindergarten, where her independently attained education is socially valuable.[38] Even more important, according to Gilman, the doctor preserves Vivian's health, so that she will one day be able to fulfill her highest aim: to do "something for the world" through enlightened motherhood (*Crux* 190). For Vivian and all of the Bainville women who travel west, she preaches that marriage—and the motherhood that, she claims, is its

main aim—is a "duty." Though this invocation of duty is
still a problematic appeal to women's biological destiny
which resembles precisely those repressive Victorian
values Gilman detested, it is meant as a liberatory prospect. The duty no longer is owed to the family or to tradition; rather, it is invoked as a way for women to serve the
community as a whole.[39] And it is a duty that should be
carried out not in the old New England way, but in a manner that nurtures women's health and fulfillment as
human beings. Appropriating the language and many of
the tenets of True Womanhood, then, Dr. Bellair prescribes a new kind of New Womanhood for Vivian and her
cohort. As the text's resident New Woman, she herself is
not the heroine of the story. Exhibiting a worldview common among New Women reformers like Gilman, who "envisioned themselves as chaste yet maternal heralds of a
higher race," the doctor is a sort of midwife: she turns her
literal lack of childbearing ability into an opportunity to
birth a new, enlightened ideal of community and womanhood.[40] It is into this new world that the new Vivian—
symbolizing, as her name suggests, the powers of life—is
born.[41]

"WHO SHOULD KNOW BUT THE WOMAN?": WOMEN, MEDICAL DISCOURSE, AND VENEREAL DISEASE

Like her fictional character and many women of her
day, Gilman herself wrestled with conflicting ideologies
of womanhood. Full of power and optimism about her aspirations, the young Gilman met artist Charles Walter
Stetson, who proposed marriage to her in 1882. Though
she was in love with him, Gilman declined, fearing that
the roles of wife and, eventually, mother would threaten
her independent identity and prevent her from achieving
all she hoped to do for the world. "[A]s much as I love you
I love *WORK* better," she wrote to Stetson in 1882, "& I
cannot make the two compatible."[42] Ultimately, however,
due to Stetson's persistence, Gilman entered reluctantly
into an ill-fated marriage with him in 1884. Though he
loved her deeply, Stetson was too steeped in the tradi-

tional expectations of his day to provide Gilman with the kind of marriage that would nurture her individuality and her devotion to work. Calling her commitment to women, humanity, and social change her "monomania," he expected Gilman to embrace domesticity as her new "work," supporting his career over her own.[43] In some ways, Gilman did attempt to fulfill this role: she learned to cook, took up housekeeping, and strove for True Womanly self-sacrifice, writing in her diary before her marriage that she aspired "to be uncomplaining and unselfish" and "a pleasure to *some* one, no matter what I feel myself."[44] Such a role proved, however, to be not only impossible for Gilman to fulfill, but also a threat to her health and sanity. Having buried her own identity and aspirations, she felt trapped and overwhelmed, especially upon learning that she was pregnant; after the birth of her daughter, Katharine Beecher Stetson, in 1885, her depression increased greatly. As Walter Stetson reports, Gilman explained to her doctor that "her whole usefulness & real life was crushed out of her by marriage and the care of the baby."[45] Thus began the nervous breakdown whose effects would stay with Gilman, on and off, for the rest of her life, and whose causes would move much of her most compelling writing.

Suffering from unbearable physical and emotional pain, Gilman eventually sought the help of a physician, yet she found that the medical theories and treatments of her day were based on the same conservative assumptions about gender that had made her ill in the first place. Though she had many experiences with the medical profession throughout her life, it is her treatment by the renowned Philadelphia neurologist Silas Weir Mitchell, from whom she sought help for this nervous breakdown in 1885, that is best known today. While Gilman's experience with Mitchell has been discussed widely in writings on her life and work, it bears repeating briefly here because it raises a number of issues to which Gilman would later return in *The Crux*. The treatment Gilman received from Mitchell was his (in)famous "rest cure," which Mitchell prescribed for patients suffering from neurasthenia, or nervous weakness. Though many women adored Mitchell

and praised his treatment, he had some vocal critics in
his time, and his cure has been widely disparaged by late-
twentieth-century feminists as an attempt to discipline
unconventional women into their "proper" place as passive, domestic beings.[46] Given in its most extreme form
most frequently to women, the cure consisted of extended
bed rest, seclusion, excessive feeding, and forms of passive exercise such as electric shock and massage. Before
meeting Dr. Mitchell, Gilman reports that she wrote a
case history for him explaining the course of her illness,
a document that she claims Mitchell promptly dismissed
as "self-conceit" typical of the Beecher women (*Living*
95).[47] Still trusting in his medical expertise despite this
implication that as a woman, she could not possibly contribute anything of value to a discussion of her own body,
she took the cure for one month. Separated from her family and gender role obligations, Gilman recovered enough
strength that Mitchell sent her home. Upon her departure, he gave her a prescription to embrace what he saw
as her "natural" roles of wife and mother, for this, to him,
represented healthy femininity: "Live as domestic a life
as possible. Have your child with you all the time. . . .
Have but two hours intellectual life a day. And never
touch pen, brush, or pencil as long as you live" (*Living* 96).
Not surprisingly, such a remedy, contrary to Gilman's
being in every way, only made things worse, driving her to
"mental torment" that bordered on insanity (*Living* 96).

Her most highly acclaimed short story "The Yellow
Wall-Paper" (1892) was inspired in part by this experience. The narrator, a new mother who undergoes a rest
cure prescribed by her loving yet paternalistic physician-
husband, is driven to madness by the cure and the stifling
domestic ideology on which it is based. Denied the authority to speak about her condition, the protagonist is
forbidden to do any creative or intellectual work, while
all of her attempts to resist this childlike and passive role
are pathologized. The story is a scathing critique of dominant ideals of femininity, which denied women intellectual stimulation, fulfilling work, and the authority to
understand and control their own bodily experience. It
simultaneously condemns the medical discourses whose

definitions of health and illness were used to naturalize such prescriptions.[48] For Gilman, writing this story was part of her recovery, not only in its content but in that it represented a return to her work using the very pen Mitchell so feared. "I cast the noted specialist's advice to the winds and went to work again," she proclaims.[49] Separating from her husband by mutual agreement, Gilman moved to California with her daughter in 1888. She and Walter would eventually divorce, and she would give custody of Katharine to Walter and his second wife, causing much public scandal. Though she would struggle against her culture's prescriptions for gendered conduct, as well as her depression, for the rest of her years, however, Gilman ultimately devised an independent, work-filled way of life that fit her own definition of health and propriety.

With its condemnation of the rest cure and the repressive domestic ideology behind it, "The Yellow Wall-Paper" is one of Gilman's most powerful articulations of the perils medical theories and treatments held for women in her time. *The Crux* advances a similar critique, focusing not on neurasthenia and Mitchell's cure but on sexually transmitted disease, or, as it was called then, venereal disease. Gilman makes a compelling argument in the novel that women must be granted complete knowledge of the symptoms, communicability, and consequences of venereal disease, for it is only through such knowledge that they can exercise bodily and sexual self-determination. Such openness requires, of course, a rejection of the outdated model of True Womanhood and its imperative of female innocence of sexual and medical matters. Instead, Gilman suggests, women should be given a voice in decisions about their health and sexuality; they would therefore be equipped to perform what Gilman saw as their most important role: to bear and raise healthy, vigorous children.

Diseases like syphilis and gonorrhea were troubling social and public health problems in Gilman's lifetime. As in the present day, reliable statistics measuring the percentage of the population that was infected were impossible to obtain. At one extreme, some studies from the turn of the century reached the alarming conclusion that, in

selected sectors of the population, up to 80 percent of
men had at some time been infected with gonorrhea.[50]
Though 1906 saw the development of the Wassermann test
to detect syphilis, and 1910 marked the discovery of Salv-
arsan to treat it, the latter was too expensive and involved
too lengthy a regimen truly to be of use on a wide scale,
and there still existed no simple test to detect gonorrhea.
An effective cure for venereal disease would only come
in 1928 with the discovery of penicillin.[51] Furthermore,
when *The Crux* was published in 1911, it joined with the
voices of feminists, social reformers, and some medical
professionals already engaged in a complex struggle to
change long-held cultural beliefs and practices that
needlessly helped to spread the disease. These reformers
invoked one particular model of disease transmission repeatedly, tracing infection "from prostitute to unfaithful
husband to innocent wife."[52] While the accuracy of such
a rigid model was clearly questionable, it was extremely
powerful, and widely used, as a rhetorical strategy. Gilman and other reformers invoked venereal disease as a
symbol of women's powerlessness and victimization by
men, decrying the sexual and economic exploitation of
the prostitute and the "innocent wife" alike.[53] Though
some reformers and physicians, believing prostitutes
were the main source of venereal disease, urged that
these women be regulated by mandatory examination,
many feminist activists opposed such policies because
they held that "prostitutes were not the perpetrators of a
crime, but casualties of an economic system that left
women without choices": it was men, not women, who
were the root of the problem.[54] Tracing the common economic dependence on men of both prostitutes and wives,
some feminists, such as Emma Goldman, wrote that
though both groups of women were equally victimized,
the prostitutes were the less hypocritical of the two. Yet
by and large, it was the wives who inspired the strongest
sense of pity and outrage among middle-class reformers
(including Gilman), who blamed what they saw as a foolish and outdated Victorian value system for making
women so vulnerable.[55]

Certainly, there was a general lack of information about

venereal disease at this time: despite its preoccupation
with sexuality, American society of the nineteenth and
early twentieth centuries maintained "a conspiracy of polite silence" about syphilis and gonorrhea which prevented frank discussion of the problem.[56] But women's
situation was generally still more disturbing: as the supposed moral guardians of the home and family, white,
middle-class women were taught to uphold an ideal of
both sexual passionlessness and "innocence"—a lack of
all knowledge—with regard to sexuality.[57] "According to
many reports," says Allan M. Brandt, "women often entered into marriage with no knowledge about sex," and
"some doctors . . . suggest[ed] that sex education might
disrupt marriages, because women might come to understand the cause for many of their gynecological ailments."[58] Feminist reformers decried such ignorance,
which might lead to infection by profligate husbands, "as
an illustration of women's oppression."[59] Even the American Medical Association concerned itself with the problem, holding a symposium in 1906 on the "dire effects of
ignorance of the consequences of venereal disease on
married women, marriage, and the family."[60] Many feminist reformers proposed as a remedy the rejection of innocence as an ideal in favor of women's education about
sex and its dangers (many proposed children's sex education as well). Gilman was especially partial to the nurse
Lavinia Dock, whose 1910 book *Hygiene and Morality* suggested, in Gilman's words, that since venereal diseases affected "both wife and child, it is specially necessary that
women should be informed about them."[61] Gilman recognized that such knowledge and discussion were associated with masculinity in her culture. In *The Crux*, when
Dr. Bellair broaches the topic of Morton's syphilis with
Vivian, she explains, "I am going to talk to you 'as man to
man' " (*Crux* 189); frankness about such things is something that could only be conceived of in masculine terms.
Yet Gilman asserts in much of her work that such a "masculine" prerogative should belong equally to women, particularly because of their duties as mothers. In a speech
before the American Society for Sanitary and Moral Prophylaxis (whose main aim was to combat venereal dis-

ease) in 1910, she argued that "through her children [the mother's] suffering is more than doubled, and she certainly should understand all the facts in the case, and should have the knowledge and the power."[62] Not one to sacrifice her message to subtlety, she made sure that her position on this topic was clear in *The Crux* from the outset. In her preface, she acknowledges that "[s]ome will hold that the painful facts disclosed [in the novel] are unfit for young girls to know. Young girls are precisely the ones who must know them, in order that they may protect themselves and their children to come. . . . If some say 'Innocence is the greatest charm of young girls,' the answer is, 'What good does it do them?' " (*Crux* 81). Clearly, Gilman believed that innocence was in fact ignorance, a "virtue" that women should leave behind with the other vestiges of True Womanhood.

Of course, the ideal of female innocence not only kept women completely in the dark about the dangers of venereal disease; it also formed part of a sexual double standard that made them even more vulnerable to infection. Contrary to women's supposedly natural lack of sexual desire, the theory of "male sexual necessity" held that men's physical and mental health were dependent upon sexual intercourse, a doctrine that provided a justification for male sexual promiscuity, even in marriage.[63] In response, reformers called for what was dubbed a "single standard of morals," though they did not all agree on what that standard should be. While some urged women's adoption of men's standard and free expression of their own sexuality, others, like Gilman, asserted that sexual activity, noble and sacred, should be confined to procreation. Carl Degler has argued that despite its repressive tendencies, this position was more of a "feminist strategy" than "Victorian prudery," since it presumably would provide women with more control over their sexual and reproductive lives.[64] "Young men may now be taught," wrote Lavinia Dock, "that the same virtue which is desirable for their sisters is good for them."[65] In addition to a new standard of sexual morals, however, Gilman points out that many men needed to be taught more of the facts about venereal disease. Though it was culturally accept-

able for them to have this knowledge, Gilman suggests
that they, like women, were sometimes not made aware of
the consequences of infection. "[Y]ou mustn't feel as if all
men were Unspeakable Villains," says Vivian's grandmother, consoling her over the broken engagement with
Morton. "They are just ignorant boys—and nobody ever
tells them the truth" (*Crux* 202). It was the entire population, reformers argued—including children and men, but
especially women—who needed to be educated about
sexuality and sexually transmitted disease.

Supported by the sexual double standard (and in general by the gender ideology of the time) was the "medical
secret": a "collusion between physicians and male patients, either husbands or prospective husbands," in
which the physician would invoke confidentiality, refusing to inform the wife or fiancée of the male patient's infection. "[D]eeply entangled in the psychology of male
power and loyalty," this phenomenon resulted not only in
women being denied knowledge that would have pro-
tected them from being infected with venereal disease,
but also in their being prevented from understanding the
nature of the illnesses that befell them as a result.[66] If it
did not lead to sterility, of course, it also led to the afflic-
tion of children conceived in such unions.[67] Feminist reformers pointed out that this ignorance of both their own
bodies and the disease's symptoms, transmission, and effects was profoundly disempowering for women. Elizabeth Temkin summarizes their position thus: "Men's
ability to harm women was physically manifest in venereal disease," and, "Physicians who sanctioned the act
with their silence symbolized the social institutions that
ignored and fostered women's suffering."[68] There was
considerable debate among medical ethicists in the early
twentieth century about the medical secret, much of
which invoked the rhetoric of "protection of the innocent."[69] Gilman took a strong stand on the issue, asserting
that "to voluntarily inoculate an innocent loving wife and
even the unborn child with a hideous disease is a plain
crime and should be so treated, so punished," including
the recognition of physicians as " 'accessories before the
fact' . . . . The heaviest burden of responsibility so far lies

at the door of those who know most fully the terrible consequences of these diseases, and yet connive at their perpetuation."[70] *The Crux* presents this problem in equally vivid terms through the argument between Dr. Bellair, who knows that the syphilitic Morton plans to marry Vivian, and Morton's physician, Dr. Richard Hale. When she asks him if he intends to "sit still and let that dangerous patient" marry "the finest girl in town," he responds that "[i]t is a matter of honor—professional honor. . . . I will not betray the confidence of a patient." "A man's honor," Dr. Bellair responds, "always seems to want to kill a woman to satisfy it" (*Crux* 185–86). Attempting to prevent such a "killing," Dr. Bellair tells Vivian the truth when the male doctor will not. Though, as Ann J. Lane points out, this conveniently avoids a "direct challenge to medical protocol" because Morton is not Bellair's patient, it does present a sharp critique of masculinist medical practice, contrasting it with the feminist medical philosophy of Dr. Bellair.[71] In doing so, it is a powerful indictment of the male-dominated (and male-serving) medical establishment that had caused Gilman herself so much grief.

In addition to their direct calls to end such confidentiality policies, reformers who supported women's right to sexual and bodily self-determination attempted to prevent collusion between male patients and physicians by advocating mandatory reporting of cases of venereal disease as well as requiring examinations for the disease as a prerequisite for marriage.[72] In 1915, Gilman took up the cause, praising Ohio for making venereal disease "notifiable."[73] Gilman, like others in her camp, "believed that venereal disease needed to be perceived as a punishment for immoral behavior and not merely a disease like any other." Though this position was, as Elizabeth Temkin suggests, a feminist stance in that it "forced men to take responsibility for their behavior," it also operated within a discourse that had the potential to become extremely repressive.[74] "Beware of a biological sin, my dear" Dr. Bellair warns Vivian, "for it there is no forgiveness" (*Crux* 193). Like the push for reporting, the agitation for premarital examinations was increasingly successful.[75] Such policies, while often granting women needed control over

their health and sexuality, were not entirely unproblem-
atic, of course. Though it has been firmly established that
they were "distinct in orientation and objective" from the
eugenics groups flourishing at the time, these groups' support of the policies regulating marriage suggests a troubling overlap in philosophy, at least in some cases, and
some reformers were vocal advocates on both issues.[76]

Gilman was an enthusiastic follower of one such reformer: Prince Albert Morrow, a eugenicist and a leading
figure in the struggle to eradicate venereal disease, au-
thor of *Social Diseases and Marriage* (1904), and founder of
the American Society for Sanitary and Moral Prophylaxis.[77] Not only did Gilman give a favorable review to *Social Diseases and Marriage* in *The Forerunner*, but she also
cites Morrow explicitly in her preface as one of her
sources, the other being Lavinia Dock, for much of the information given in *The Crux* about venereal disease.[78] Vivian's grandmother mentions him by name, as well, in her
discussion of reform efforts (*Crux* 202–3). Unfortunately,
then, Gilman's enthusiasm for premarital examination
legislation, as well as for venereal disease reforms in general, is tainted by pro-eugenics sentiments. Though her
progressive beliefs often serve to belie these troubling
aspects of her philosophy, she did uphold "white Protestant supremacy; belonged for a time to eugenics and nationalist organizations";[79] and "embraced a biology that
reinforced racism and blatant nativism."[80] Indeed, Gary
Scharnhorst has pointed out that it is inaccurate to separate the two, for Gilman's "racism was deep-woven into
the fabric of her social thought, as inextricable from it as
a Gordian knot"; her "racial theories, her ethnocentrism
and xenophobia, . . . were . . . key to many of her" most
progressive theories for social change.[81]

Certainly, in *The Crux*, Gilman does not discuss issues
of genetics directly; but her pronouncements on venereal
disease at times veer very close to that territory. Vivian's
grandmother, Mrs. Pettigrew, reveals the slippage between racist, potentially eugenicist, sentiments and the
discourse of venereal disease when she reassures the
young woman with her optimism. To Vivian's worries that
75 percent of men are infected with the disease, her

grandmother explains, "Not everybody" is ill, "thank goodness. Our girls are mostly clean, and they save the race, I guess" (*Crux* 202). Gilman's use of the term *race* in her work is ambiguous, referring at times to *Homo sapiens* and at times to what she conceives of as Anglo-Saxon lineage; in either sense, it implicates her in eugenic theories of "improvement" through heredity.[82] Her racialized language is continued in subsequent paragraphs of *The Crux*, where it also hints at xenophobia: Mrs. Pettigrew insists that women, in refusing to marry infected men, can "rid the world of all these—'undesirable citizens' " (*Crux* 203). Elsewhere, Gilman was more explicit about her eugenic views, discussing "the social duty of restricting parentage among the unfit," for whom she advocated both birth control and sterilization.[83] Though in *The Crux* she speaks explicitly of freeing (a certain cohort of) women from the vagaries of venereal disease, then, Gilman uses the language of racism, xenophobia, and eugenics which was widespread in her time. Such is what has been called her "mixed legacy," a volatile philosophy with which Gilman scholars continue to struggle.[84] Sadly, her progressive feminism cannot be separated from her other ideals, some of which were as disturbing and retrograde as those discussed here.

Like her more unfortunate social beliefs, Gilman's choice to agitate against venereal disease in a fictional forum put her in good company. The disease had inspired a number of fictional treatments before Gilman's, most of which were cautionary tales. In an introductory discussion of an excerpt from *The Crux*, Ann J. Lane has noted that Dr. Dio Lewis's *Chastity: Or Our Secret Sins* (1874) laid some of the groundwork for Gilman, tracing the tragic effects of a man's refusal to tell his wife of his infection— effects that Gilman's heroine avoids because of Dr. Bellair's intervention.[85] An early review of *The Crux* likewise notes that Gilman's book formed part of a trend of such works, likening it to James Oppenheim's novel *Wild Oats* (1910) and Eugene Brieux's play *Damaged Goods*, which opened on Broadway in 1913.[86] In her discussion of this literary tradition, however, Elaine Showalter asserts that men and women generally wrote about venereal disease differently. "The syphilitic male became the arch-villain of feminist protest fiction, a carrier of contamina-tion and madness, and a threat to the spiritual evolution of the human race," she notes, while "[f]or the male liter-ary avant-garde, . . . syphilis was the excrescence of a sexually diseased society, one that systematically suppressed desire and so produced anxious fathers and disfigured sons."[87] Gilman's own fiction, which certainly fits Showalter's profile, treated the topic frequently: as Janet Beer explains, "The story of sexually transmitted disease is one of the most powerful reiterations in Gil-man's body of fiction."[88] Her short stories "Wild Oats and Tame Wheat" (1913) and "The Vintage" (1916) are among what Beer calls "the most naked and unadorned of awful warnings in Gilman's moral fictions."[89] The former story is a parable that critiques equally her culture's valorization and acceptance of male sexual experience, and its blind worship of female chastity and innocence. In "The Vin-tage," she traces the tragic effects of syphilis on one fam-ily through several generations; as Denise D. Knight explains, this story "simultaneously instructs the reader about the evils of sexually transmitted diseases and im-plicitly promotes monogamy and honesty in relation-ships."[90] In her short stories, as Janet Beer points out, Gilman is generally "either concerned with female health or male disease," with a socialist, progressive future or a repressive tradition bogged down by its cultural and bio-logical inheritance. "[T]he source of infection in her tales is male whilst prevention and cure is female." *The Crux*, Beer suggests, combines both concerns in spinning two of Gilman's stock story lines. It portrays an idealized, woman-centered community and thus tells the "communi-tarian story, always initiated and sustained by the female collective" (a story line that is "the analogue of health and foresight"). Yet in the plot of Morton and Vivian, it tells "the sexually transmitted disease story," which, con-versely, is "the analogue of contamination and retrogres-sion."[91] Showing the links between individual and societal well-being, Gilman uses the language of health and illness, particularly around venereal disease, to express an argument for significant social change.

One of the most concrete ways Gilman hoped *The Crux* would bring such change, then, was in its detailed treatment of venereal disease, exploring the social conditions leading to its perpetuation or eradication as well as its symptoms and consequences. The novel offers "the opportunity," as an early reviewer noted, "for spreading knowledge among the uninformed."[92] Gilman said as much herself in her previously quoted preface, which begins: "This story is, first, for young women to read; second, for young men to read; after that, for anybody who wants to"; referring readers to Lavinia Dock's and Prince Morrow's books should they doubt "its facts and figures," she assures that the novel will be read within this cautionary and fact-based context (*Crux* 81). Her most important readers, she suggests, are young women like Vivian, who will learn along with the heroine not only how to recognize the symptoms of venereal disease (and thus how to escape infected suitors), but also, through an understanding of the disease's tragic consequences for women and children, why it needs to be avoided at all costs.[93] Vivian learns that the costs sometimes seem high, for she is forced to give up the cultural imperative of marriage (though she is later rewarded for this choice by a new engagement). On a cultural level, Gilman's message could be stated thus: "Men should no longer be pitied for diseases they themselves bring upon their women. Women should no longer feel the need to play the role of man's moral agent with the almost certain promise of ending up sacrificial lambs to Victorian principles, simply because of their own ignorance."[94] Gilman's critique of her culture's traditional handling of venereal disease, therefore, is of a piece with her other attacks on the medical discourse of her time and the repressive gender ideology that underlay it. She criticizes not only the physical, psychological, and material damage such discourse does to women, but also the outdated belief system that justifies such treatment. Her novel presents itself as a practical manual of-

fering her readers an alternative approach to the disease
itself, as well as to social organization as a whole.

"Come Out to Colorado with Me—and Grow": Gilman and the West

In theory, such a tale, with its explicit purpose of social
reform leading to the emancipation of women from perni-
cious medical practices and gender roles, might take
place anywhere. Yet Gilman chooses the American West
as her setting, bringing her eastern exiles to a fictional
Colorado town. Her reasons for doing so were likely personal, cultural, and literary. They add an important di-
mension to this novel, differentiating it from much of her
best-known work, which generally (if not entirely accurately) associates her with the Northeast and New England. The West was, in fact, the ideal location for a story
about sickness, health, and social regeneration: this was
the case in terms of Gilman's own biography, as well as
for the dominant culture of the United States, which had
long associated the region with vigor, democracy, and rebirth. *The Crux* is informed by these personal and cultural
issues, as well as by American literary traditions associated with the West.

Perhaps the most pervasive and enduring conception of
the American West in Gilman's time was expressed in his-
torian Frederick Jackson Turner's "Frontier Thesis" of
1893, which articulated themes associated with the West
that had long been circulating in American culture and
that continue to hold sway in some circles today.[95] Turner
conceived of the frontier as a westwardly moving zone of
freedom, individualism, innovation, and rebirth, which,
he argued, shaped American character in fundamental
ways. In this supposedly unsettled "virgin" land, this
landscape both sublime and beautiful, he and others posited that the Adamic American hero found a world of possibility: free from the stifling traditions of the past and
established "civilization," he engaged in a struggle (often
involving violent confrontation with "nature" and the indigenous peoples with whom Turner associated it) to de-

fine himself anew. This liberatory conception of the West provided a myth through which American national identity, as well as individual models of selfhood, could be defined.[96] Despite its apparent preeminence, however, this view of the West has not stood unchallenged, nor has it stood alone. It is being increasingly recognized, for example, that this dominant myth underlay the doctrine of Manifest Destiny, justifying westward expansion, and obfuscating the conquest and exploitation of lands and peoples west of America's eastern establishment.[97] Likewise, the subject or protagonist of this myth is not only white but male, the object or antagonist female: in its dominant form, the frontier myth, as Brigitte Georgi-Findlay puts it, is "a story of male individuation, dealing with both the rejection and assertion of patriarchal values"; it "necessarily encodes the conquest of the continent as an exclusively male adventure."[98] In this "melodrama of beset manhood," women are either erased altogether, or cast as obstacles to be overcome by the male hero.[99] Though it masquerades as universal, therefore, this myth is in fact conceived from a hegemonic perspective, and represents only one of many possible stories about the West. As Melody Graulich explains, a key question asked by recent scholars has been not what constitutes the "real" West (the answer to which will always yield only a "partial story"), but rather, "Who gets to tell what Western story about whom?"[100]

The dominant story, having been told from an elite perspective, gained prominence at the expense of other stories—a fact that Gilman, like other women writers, sought to rectify. Despite their relative absence from the classic Turnerian story, women of diverse races, cultures, and ethnic groups were present on frontiers throughout the West.[101] And these women, like Gilman, have told their own tales. Attempting to unearth these stories by making women's experiences central, some historians have asked to what extent women's lives on the frontier measured up to the Turnerian ideal.[102] In studies of white pioneer women, to cite the demographic with which Gilman most closely allies her story, scholars have asserted that the West was far from the egalitarian and democratic haven of mythic fame. With little say in the decision to move West, where they faced increased workloads, vulnerability to men, and isolation from other women, some found that life in the West restricted their freedom and circumscribed their opportunities.[103] Writing in diaries, letters, autobiography, fiction, and other genres, many women authors portrayed such disappointments, imagining the West as a place of captivity, danger, and unfamiliar landscapes.[104] On the other hand, some studies have emphasized the ways in which the West offered white women an array of new freedoms, citing permeable spheres of male and female activity, opportunities for land ownership, favorable demographic ratios, and early gains in woman suffrage.[105] The West's liberatory potential for such women has been explored by an array of writers, who have appropriated, molded, or rejected altogether aspects of the male frontier myth in order to make the West their own—reconceiving of the western landscape, for example, as a garden sanctuary for domesticity, or as a fenceless space in which to develop a woman's voice free of eastern conventions.[106] Recent scholarship, assessing the implications of such inquiries, has noted white women's "double positioning" in discourses about the West: though excluded from the dominant culture because of their gender, they are nevertheless implicated in the workings of conquest and empire, even if their fantasies about the region are of a different nature than men's.[107]

Charlotte Perkins Gilman certainly partakes of this double positioning in *The Crux*. As Judith A. Allen has argued, Gilman, a correspondent of Turner's colleagues at the University of Wisconsin, "absorbed contemporary theories postulating 'the frontier' as a zone of freedom, democracy, and innovation."[108] Yet, as Ann J. Lane has rightly noted, "Gilman's West . . . is not Frederick Jackson Turner's West," with its focus on remaking "male and capitalist American culture."[109] Gilman transforms such theories for use by women, positing "the fresh, democratic, and altogether modern possibilities for women of life in the West."[110] Nevertheless, *The Crux* participates in certain aspects of the Turnerian ethos and its implications in Manifest Destiny even as it offers a feminist challenge to male-centered paradigms of the frontier and society as a whole. Indeed, the novel's feminist message is underwritten by certain Turnerian sentiments. The model community Gilman proposes in the novel relies upon the classic (and ethnocentric) view of the West as a locus of social and racial regeneration.

At the base of Gilman's vision of progressive social change in the novel is the notion, common to much of her work, that the way to reform society is to free women from economic dependence on men, to allow them to develop themselves into fully human beings rather than defining themselves according to their sexual function. In order for this to occur, she asserts, women must regain their rightful position as initiators of sexual selection.[111] She was influenced in the development of these theories by what historians have labeled Reform Darwinism, which posited that rather than being shaped by the biological process of natural selection, human beings were capable of deliberately intervening in the evolutionary process; her ideas were also informed by sociologist Lester Frank Ward, whose "gynaecocentric theory" asserted that the female was the original human, the male "a mere afterthought of nature."[112] (Significantly, Vivian Lane is an avid reader of Ward, to the disapproval of her parents and the Bainville minister [*Crux* 105].) Gilman asserted that women were intended by nature to do the choosing in courtship, women being primary and men secondary in human evolution. Patriarchy, or what she called "androcentric culture," had corrupted women's human potential and thwarted their intended role as nurturers of the human race through denying them the initiative in sex selection. Though humanity had therefore deviated to its detriment from the natural order, Gilman believed it was possible for humans to change the course of their development.[113] Gilman "became increasingly convinced," writes Allen, "that women's ennoblement and advance could only proceed if, as a sex, they restored themselves to the position of being able to 'choose' the fittest of men as partners and fathers of 'the Race.' " Where, Allen asks, could such a change be brought about? "Only in places of skewed sex ratios, undersupplied with marriageable women, oversupplied with marriageable men": in short, only in the West.[114]

Self-consciously appropriating a Turnerian schema for white New England women, Gilman makes a demographic argument justifying their journey west in an essay called "Woman's 'Manifest Destiny,'" first published in 1904. Citing the overabundance of such women in the Northeast, she asks, "Why do not the women who really believe that marriage is their mission, go forth in bands of maiden emigration to the frontiers, where lonely men grow hard and bad for lack of 'women's influence'? . . . Let the conscientious surplus of women go West, like the young man."[115] Why should women wait to be chosen like the long-suffering Mrs. St. Cloud, she asks, "instead of heroically seeking opportunity?" This is precisely what Gilman's female characters do in *The Crux*, for, as Dr. Bellair assures them, "you'll have a thousandfold better opportunities [to marry] in Colorado than you ever will" in Bainville, where the ratio of men to women was so small that the narrator dubs it "the Virgin Sacrifice of New England" (*Crux* 113, 200). And indeed, by the novel's end, each of the Bainville women, from Vivian to her grandmother Mrs. Pettigrew, is either married or betrothed. Such migration for the purpose of marriage is, according to Dr. Bellair, "a woman's duty" (*Crux* 113); in "Woman's 'Manifest Destiny,'" Gilman confirms that it is also a heroic act, because it would help to accomplish the fundamental changes in sexual and gender relations she championed as a way of improving society. She predicts, as would Dr. Bellair, that "instead of competing madly for a minority of cautious and inexperienced men, [such plucky New England women] would have woman's real prerogative of choice among competing suitors." Echoing many pioneer women writers, she bemoans the fact that "the unwomaned men suffer for lack of home and love and right living; and the frontier country suffers and waits for the refining and uplifting, the pacifying and improving, which follow an established family life." Such "civilizing," she asserts, is a civic duty: "Is the historic development of America nothing to its women? If we are in truth citizens, let us get about our duties. The upbuilding of our country,

the overcoming of evil tendencies, the fostering of all social improvements—these call for the increase of good
people, and the influence of our best civilization." With
what is in essence an appropriation of the well-worn call
"Go West, young man!," Gilman claims for New England
women the freedoms and privileges conventionally offered to men in the West, among them mobility, regeneration, heroism, adventure, and an active part in
constructing American national identity. As Allen has argued, *The Crux* makes a similar appeal through the vehicle of fiction. Gilman uses the Turnerian script to justify
women's heroic quest to reform society.

The favorable demographics in the West thus made it an
ideal setting for Gilman's novel of progressive social
change, an important aspect of which was women exercising what she saw as their natural "prerogative of choice."
Yet her references to "the overcoming of evil tendencies"
and "the increase of good people" indicate that a crucial
part of women's duty in choosing their mates well was to
improve the quality of human "stock." "The eugenic and
feminist projects interlink," argues Allen, "on Gilman's
Western frontier."[116] Gilman's West is, then, a locus for renewal and regeneration, in terms not only of gender and
social organization, but also of "the race." Certainly, her
most overt argument in *The Crux* presents the need to re-
vitalize the *human* race, which she sees as decaying because of both the waste of marriageable women in the
East and the alarming prevalence of men and women infected with venereal disease. With women's increased education about infection and consequent sexual self-
determination, along with their entry into a favorable
marriage market as exists in the West, she sees an opportunity to improve society. By "not marrying" the " 'undesirable citizens,' " Mrs. Pettigrew assures Vivian, "[o]ur
girls" will be using their power of sex selection to improve the genetic stock of Americans (*Crux* 202–3).[117] It
surely is not incidental, then, that the reinvigorated
"race" of Americans in Gilman's Edenic West is white,
and is to be saved and "improved" by "clean" New England women—the "good people" and "best civilization"
cited in "Woman's 'Manifest Destiny.' " Indeed, Gilman

makes a point of revealing that "[h]eredity" is an important influence in Vivian's character: descended from
"some Pilgrim Father or Mother" (*Crux* 121), she is an
ideal candidate for Gilman's racial revitalization in the
West. The novel asserts, as she does elsewhere, that
white, native-born, eastern women have a "duty" to their
"race" to ensure their group's continued preeminence.
From its first use, after all, the term *Manifest Destiny* was
inflected by race, invoking a sense not just of American
entitlement to expansion and conquest, but of "Anglo-
Saxon" rights to dominance.[118] When Gilman penned her
story of American—and more fundamentally, human—
revitalization in the idyllic West, therefore, she was writing within a tradition that conceived of the West in
precisely these racialized terms.[119] Certainly, then, Gilman's choice to set *The Crux* in the West was influenced by
existing cultural discourses associating the region with
racial and societal recuperation: Turner's "Frontier Thesis," as well as women's appropriations of it, provided her
ample precedent for doing so.

Equally compelling, however, are aspects of Gilman's
biography that reinforce her conception of the West as a
zone of freedom, independence, and rebirth. Her biographical experience with the West begins, indeed, in a
context of illness and recuperation.[120] Responding to the
nervous breakdown that followed the birth of her daughter, but before seeking Mitchell's rest cure, Gilman
sought relief in California. She traveled to Pasadena to
spend the winter with an old friend, leaving her husband
and daughter behind. In her autobiography, she makes a
point of discussing this curative journey in the same
chapter in which she gives her better-known description
of the rest cure. "Feeble and hopeless I set forth," she explains of her trip to Pasadena, "armed with tonics and
sedatives, to cross the continent. From the moment the
wheels began to turn, the train to move, I felt better" (*Living* 92). Immersed in the mild and healthful climate, and
removed from the obligations of marriage and motherhood, Gilman "recovered so fast," she reports, that she
"was taken for a vigorous young girl" (*Living* 94). It became clear that the pressures to fulfill her traditional

gender role at the expense of her own aspirations were the main cause of her distress when she departed California for the East, for she fell ill immediately upon her return. "I now saw the stark fact," she admits, "that I was well while away and sick while at home" (*Living* 95). Significantly, after undergoing Mitchell's rest cure and then deciding to separate from her husband, it was to California that she moved in order to resume her independent way of life and devotion to her work. It was there that she launched her career and, to use Gary Scharnhorst's phrase, "made her fame" as a writer and social reformer.[121] The West represented, then, the health, freedom, and independence that Gilman had been unable to find in the East, with its imperative of women's sacrifice of self to marriage and motherhood.

Gilman's use of the West as a curative space becomes even more significant, however, when viewed in its medical context. By the middle of the nineteenth century, the West had come to be considered a healthful retreat, particularly for the eastern elite. Of course, this phenomenon, and the accompanying westward expansion of the United States it helped to justify (it was often associated with the growing tourist industry as well as with campaigns for settlement of the region), was extremely *un*healthful for the land's indigenous populations as well as, even, for prior colonizers; yet in the dominant culture's medical and cultural discourses, the West was a place to which easterners fled to regain health and vitality. Like many other western states and territories, Colorado marketed itself as "a safe and healthy haven" for "winterbound invalids."[122] In the last half of the nineteenth century, the area's climate, altitude, landscape, and lifestyle were touted as salubrious not only for those suffering from respiratory ills such as tuberculosis, but even for "the healthy," in whom it could "awaken . . . a new sense of strength and vigor."[123] During the 1870s and 1880s, "the common estimate was that one-third of the state's population was composed of recovered invalids," a fact that undoubtedly contributed to Governor Fred Pitkin's claim that "we can almost bring a dead man to life."[124] Thus, Col-

orado provided an ideal setting for Gilman's story of
health regained.

Though both men and women participated in and bene-
fited from this health-giving construction of the West, the
region's cachet as a curative region was symbolically di-
rected at men, since the West was imagined as a masculine space free of what was considered feminized
civilization and its accompanying rules, expectations,
and obligations. Throughout the second half of the nineteenth century, pursuits such as roughriding and dude
ranches, hunting, and excursions into the wilderness
gained in popularity among the middle and upper classes
of northeastern men; participating public figures such as
Teddy Roosevelt, Frederic Remington, and Theodore
Dreiser made the phenomenon all the more visible. Such
cures were necessary, it was believed, because of an epi-
demic of neurasthenia among the elite classes in the East,
caused by professional men's excessive "brain work."[125]
The consequences of the disease for male sufferers included what was considered pathological weakness, debility, and effeminacy; the cure enabled them to immerse
themselves in the hyper-masculine West, where they
could regain their vigor and virility through embracing
recognizably "masculine" pursuits and emulating a western model of manliness.[126]

Himself a partaker of this "West Cure," Weir Mitchell
prescribed it for his male neurasthenic patients along-
side his recommendation of the rest cure for his female
patients. He advocated such gendered cures because, as
was common for his day, he believed the disease had gendered causes. Women, whom he thought had inherently
weak and excitable nervous systems, would suffer from
the slightest physical, emotional, and especially mental
strain. Very often, he imagined, their attempts to exceed
what he saw as their biologically mandated role of wife
and mother drove them to nervous weakness. Conversely,
since men were not considered pathological by nature,
they suffered temporary nervous debility as a result of
overtaxing their brains in their professional endeavors—
endeavors that were culturally valuable and necessary as
part of their class-based gender role. In their common

aim to restore women and men to what were considered proper, "healthy" roles and behaviors, then, the rest cure and the West Cure were complementary parts of one process through which normative gender identities were constructed and reinforced.

A commonly cited example of Mitchell's gendered cures is a comparison between Gilman's case, with her now infamous rest cure in 1887, and that of Philadelphia novelist Owen Wister.[127] In 1885, just two years before Gilman sought Mitchell's medical help, Wister approached Mitchell, a distant cousin and old family friend, with his painful neurasthenic symptoms. Instead of putting Wister to bed, Mitchell sent him to a cattle ranch in Wyoming to recover. Unlike Gilman's rest cure, this West Cure was quite successful. Before his trip west, Wister complained of numerous ailments associated with nervous exhaustion; after settling into his cattle roundup routine in Wyoming, he was restored to health, newly invigorated and ready to return to the East.[128] As it was meant to do, Wister's West Cure left him better equipped to pursue his professional work: indeed, it formed the basis of this work, since Wister built his writing career on his status as chronicler of a supposedly dying way of life in the West. He fictionalized his West Cure and mythologized the West's curative powers in his Western novel *The Virginian*, thus helping to popularize the already legendary status of the West as a cure for declining virility.[129] Wister's novel is, then, not only one of the foundational texts in what would become a significant genre of American literature, a genre that helped to undergird the doctrine of Manifest Destiny; it is also a paradigmatic narrative of the West Cure, portraying as it does a widespread cultural phenomenon driven by deeply embedded ideals of gender as well as of personal and national health.

Gilman's curative sojourns in the West take on added importance when read within this context. In benefiting from her trip west, she calls the West Cure's gendered elements into question, and challenges by extension dominant cultural and medical views of healthy femininity. Women, too, can find renewal and rejuvenation in escaping eastern tradition and home obligations and by immersing themselves in the healing landscape and culture of the West. Furthermore, women can use this experience to remake themselves personally and professionally, as Gilman surely did. Like Wister, she appropriated the West Cure both in her life and in her writing, arguably quite self-consciously. Certainly, she would have been aware of the West Cure as a cultural phenomenon among elite men. But she is also known to have owned and enthusiastically read Wister's *The Virginian*, to which she alludes in *The Crux* and which she mentions explicitly in her autobiography when discussing her first visit to the West (*Living* 93).[130] In both texts, she does not simply retell Wister's West Cure story; rather, she revises the narrative so that it is informed by her feminist principles and worldview. In doing so, Gilman offers an alternative to Mitchell's gendered therapeutics—a significant critique of medical discourses that would deny women the authority to determine and to express their own definitions of health. Yet she also asserts the entitlement as a woman writer to participate in a genre theretofore dominated by men and used largely for masculinist purposes: the popular Western.

The Western genre, sparked by *The Virginian* but inspired by earlier literary forms from the early nineteenth century, gained great momentum at the dawn of the twentieth century. Scholars have given many reasons for its development, from the overcrowding and dehumanizing effects of urbanization and industrialization in eastern cities, to the militarism encouraged by the Spanish-American War, to the popularity of Social Darwinism. Certainly, the Western is centrally concerned with justifying conquest and its accompanying values.[131] Jane Tompkins has added yet another hypothesis, asserting that the Western arose in response to the moral authority granted to women by the cult of domesticity and claimed by New Women reformers later in the century. Furthermore, she suggests that the genre's valorization of masculinity, male homosociality, violence and physical struggle, and public, outdoor life constitute a deliberate rejection of values espoused in the most popular literary form of the nineteenth century, the so-called domestic novel, which was written largely by women and made women's experience central to the plot. The Western, in contrast, "seeks to marginalize and suppress" women and attempts "the destruction of female authority"; its plots, she argues, replay "the plot of the domestic novels in reverse; Westerns either push women out of the picture completely, or assign them roles in which they exist only to serve the needs of men."[132] In *The Crux*, Gilman counteracts this tendency by appropriating the Western genre and molding it to her own purposes. As Deborah Evans has argued, Gilman "recogniz[es] a literary landscape from which women had been systematically excluded, and she subsequently sets about the heroic task of reclaiming it." She does so in order to "reject some of those same constricting values of the female sphere" that were so hated by her "male counterparts" writing Westerns; like them, she "wrestles against the constraining limits of eastern society, but she sees the West as a site for female heroism as well."[133] As Evans has suggested, *The Crux* can be read as Gilman's intervention into the Western genre. Indeed, it is an attempt to meld some of the most liberatory aspects of "domestic fiction"—particularly, as I have suggested, its focus on women's lives and female moral authority—with those aspects of the Western theretofore claimed as inherently masculine—such as heroism and freedom from stifling tradition.[134]

In *The Crux*, Gilman writes a woman-centered Western that is shaped by the principles of the West Cure—a generic combination that allows her to critique traditional gender roles and social organization, and to offer a new vision of individual and social health. Tracing her allusions to and revisions of *The Virginian* and Mitchell's West Cure helps to illuminate this process. Wister, for example, centers his plot on one individual, a sickly, eastern man whose escape from the obligations of the East and foray into the West are encouraged by the male-dominated medical establishment. Gilman sketches a group of eastern women who are oppressed by the same cultural obligations to tradition, propriety, and gender-based codes of behavior. Like male West Cure patients, these women have been made ill, figuratively, by such a stifling

environment, a fact that is made explicit when a woman
physician, Dr. Bellair, diagnoses and treats the problem:
the "whole town," she complains, has *arthritis deformans*
of the soul," causing women to suffer from "bed-ridden
intellects" and "arrested development" (*Crux* 109–10,
114). She offers a West Cure—that is, change, mobility, and
freedom in the West—as a prescription. "Come out to Colorado with me," she urges, "—and Grow" (*Crux* 110).
Whereas a male physician like Mitchell would have prescribed a rest cure, the aptly named Dr. Bellair urges that
these women regain their vigor by "roughing it" in the
fresh air of the West (*Crux* 219). As Deborah Evans has
noted, in this way Gilman revises the script for women
popularized earlier in the century by writers such as Harriet Beecher Stowe, in which women wait patiently and
are "left in dying communities while the men venture
West or to sea."[135] Gilman's female characters, encouraged, according to Gilman's own convention, by a woman
doctor, respond actively by going west themselves.

When the Bainville women venture west, they do indeed become revitalized. The most striking example of
such recovery is Vivian Lane, who resembles the autobiographical Gilman: Vivian, like Gilman, notes on her train
journey to Colorado that a "strange, new sense of freedom
grew in her heart, a feeling of lightness and hope and unfolding purpose" (*Crux* 125). Perhaps even more significantly, it is through Vivian that Gilman answers Wister's
Western and West Cure directly. Gary Scharnhorst has
noted the parallel between Vivian, with her "Pilgrim" ancestors (*Crux* 121), and Wister's blue-blooded school-
marm, Molly Wood.[136] Though in *The Virginian* Molly
resembles the marginalized female characters decried by
Jane Tompkins, standing in for feminized "civilization"
and domesticity, Gilman gives this character center stage,
telling her Western, as it were, from Molly's point of view.
Like Molly, Vivian identifies herself with the East and is
valued in the text for her Anglo-Saxon bloodline; both
women are vessels through which the West will be popu-
lated with the "best race" of new Americans. Yet, while in
Wister's novel it is the male West Cure that drives the
plot, in *The Crux* it is the heroine Vivian who undergoes

such a cure. Not only does she venture west to find health and personal fulfillment, but, more specifically, she also participates in a girls' camp on the urging of Dr. Bellair, a camp that has many of the hallmarks of a Mitchell West Cure. As Evans has pointed out, this scene in the novel, in which Vivian swims in a clear mountain lake, echoes a similar passage in *The Virginian* representing the male hero's transcendent melding with the natural landscape. In addition to this swim, however, she also ventures into the "wild, rough country," "an untouched wilderness" where she "cook[s] in primitive fashion" and sleeps long and deeply in the outdoors, after which it is revealed that, at last, "She was well" (*Crux* 219–20). These passages echo strikingly Mitchell's writings on the West Cure, which outline the same health-giving activities performed among men at camp.[137]

Though Vivian is the most explicit example of a female West Cure, all of the Bainville women benefit from their migration to Colorado. Dr. Bellair has succeeded in uprooting not only Vivian, but Morton Elder's aunt Orella (considered an old maid at thirty-five) and his sister, Susie, a young woman who seeks above all else to marry well. These travelers are joined at the last moment by Vivian's spirited grandmother, Mrs. Servilla Pettigrew, who comes of her own accord. Through a profusion of plant imagery and metaphors, Gilman establishes the healthy growth and change undergone by each of the women in this multigenerational group. This growth comes about not only because they have left a culture in which their contributions were not valued, but also because, in Colorado, they form the heart of a growing community in which their presence is crucial. This is a striking contrast to the typical Western and to the West Cure that inspired it. Gilman's Colorado is not, indeed, Wister's or even Turner's West.[138] These eastern migrants are surprised upon their arrival to find "modern conveniences everywhere—electric cars, electric lights, telephones, soda fountains, where they had rather expected to find tents and wigwams" (*Crux* 126). Soon enough, they have helped to build a community in Colorado and to infuse it with a valorization not of the individual, who was traditionally the focus of the Western, but of the collective.

Gilman's portrayal of this idealized community is of a piece with much of her other work, both fiction and nonfiction. It is informed by her involvement in the Socialist and Nationalist movements, which rejected class distinctions, capitalism, and other kinds of inequality, and advocated social reorganization.[139] It also partakes of some of her major theories, including socialized housekeeping, "social motherhood" incorporating professionalized child care, the "economic emancipation of women through specialization and remunerative work," and "the gynaecocentric theory of sexual differentiation" already discussed.[140] Because of this, her portrayal of the new, western community in *The Crux* could in a sense be categorized with her utopian writings, which range from short stories to novels, for Gilman's utopian imagination has been noted for being generally on a continuum with, rather than completely distinct from, her realism. As Carol Farley Kessler has explained, "In Gilman's utopianism, a discourse of possibility (or realizability) collides with a discourse of realism, completely changing the latter"; "she uses realism subversively" in melding it with utopianism, in order to sketch possibilities for real social change.[141] Kessler has also used Riane Eisler's term "pragmatopia," meaning "the . . . possible, or achievable utopia," and Elaine Hedges's phrase "visionary realism," denoting the "presentation of possibilities that currently do not exist," which "simply by naming them begins to generate belief in their realizability," to describe Gilman's utopian-realistic work.[142] Indeed, Denise D. Knight has suggested that, if we use the most general definition of utopia to designate an ideal world, then "a utopian vision characterizes nearly all of Gilman's fictional works."[143] This "emphasis on the ideal" found in so much of Gilman's work, Knight asserts, focuses largely on "the reeducation of society as to the benefits inherent in removing women from the exclusive (and exclusionary) realms of the domestic and the maternal and eliminating the roots of patriarchal oppression."[144] In these works, including *The Crux*, women are the "active agents" in establishing an idealized community, "although men are not [usually] excluded from participation." Such "communitarian living," according to Janet Beer, is "concerned with finding solutions through the collective will toward making radical changes to an existing social order which is seen neither to support women's needs nor to provide a decent future for their children."[145]

The idealized community in *The Crux* centers on a boardinghouse, called "The Cottonwoods," arranged for by Dr. Bellair and run by Orella.[146] It becomes the domestic, civilizing center of a "family of twenty-five" (*Crux* 129), thus embodying a progressive model of community commonly discussed in Gilman's work.[147] Boardinghouses and apartment hotels appear frequently in Gilman's fiction, functioning as "the setting for progressively liberated life styles"[148] and as places of refuge for women.[149] The boardinghouse, though "the very symbol of the home and domestic service," explains Ann J. Lane, "is not for the private service of a single family; it is socialized, servicing many people and offering independence to those who run it and work in it."[150] It serves, then, as a model of the socialized housekeeping Gilman advocated in *The Home: Its Work and Influence* (1903) and other works. Domestic labor, she argued, should be professionalized and done by specialists, rather than undertaken by every woman to the point that she has not the time, energy, nor opportunity to pursue her own intellectual and creative interests.[151] This is what Polly Wynn Allen calls Gilman's "architectural feminism," which included not only the concept of kitchenless houses, but also alternative models of communal living like the boardinghouse.[152]

The centrality of "The Cottonwoods" to Gilman's idealized West effects a significant revision, then, of the conventional Western. As Evans explains, Gilman "deflates the western expectation that women are unwelcome representatives" of domesticity, family, and civilization, "and instead represents them as welcome additions who win the admiration of the lonely young men" who presumably are in need of such institutions. Even Mr. Skee, the aged cowboy who is "a relic of . . . the once Wild West which had left so few surviving" (*Crux* 140–41), marries into the community in the end, as Evans notes.[153] In addition, this boardinghouse and the progressive social change it represents may be an explicit revision of Wister's West as portrayed in *The Virginian*. In that prototypical Western, the cottonwood tree symbolizes masculinist, violent frontier justice, for it is from such a tree that the Virginian, as ranch foreman, is obligated by a code of manly responsibility to lynch a dear friend of his who had turned to rustling cattle. In the aftermath of the deed, chronicled in a chapter called "The Cottonwoods," the Virginian laments the costs to friendship and emotional ties necessitated by such a masculinist ethic. Gilman's boardinghouse revises this symbol, replacing its associations with violence, individualism, and masculinity with cooperation, communal values, and femininity. Her Western, then, absorbs Wister's symbolism in order to advocate a new set of values.

Like her support of socialized housekeeping, Gilman's theory of "social motherhood" undergirds her female-based Colorado community. Just as professional cooks could free middle-class women from domestic drudgery, so professional child care providers could free them from the all-consuming duties of rearing children. If children were removed from their homes for a certain amount of time each day, their mothers would gain the opportunity to develop their own skills and interests, for which they could be paid; this would not only provide society with more dedicated, skilled female citizens; it would grant families more financial stability. Similarly, children would benefit greatly from being raised in "baby gardens" (or child care centers) by trained professionals. "Because not every woman has the talent, training, or experience to make her an effective mother, children who are raised by professional caretakers are healthier, brighter, and better adjusted, Gilman believed."[154] Gilman thus frequently portrayed such "baby gardens" or kindergartens in her work; in addition to advocating social motherhood in her 1900 treatise *Concerning Children*, she also featured socialized child care in her stories, including "A Garden of Babies" (1909), "Making a Change" (1911), and, of course, *The Crux*.[155] Part of Dr. Bellair's "prescription" to improve Vivian's health and spirits after her breakup with Morton involves arranging for Vivian to run a kindergarten, which is indeed beneficial for the children and their mothers, as well as for Vivian herself (*Crux* 215–16). Vivian's "baby garden" is yet one more aspect of the growing and thriving that occurs in Gilman's community of women transplanted in the life-giving West.

Tied inherently to Gilman's advocacy of socialized housekeeping and professionalized child care is, of course, her conviction that women should be free to pursue useful, meaningful, and remunerative work, and that they should be economically independent. Laid out in her book *Women and Economics* (1898) and its less successful sequel, *Human Work* (1904), her theories included the notion that division or specialization of labor leads to greater efficiency and freedom for all. Once again, these tenets promised fewer benefits for working-class women who would be apportioned the unskilled (though not untrained) and manual tasks: Gilman's "proposals," Dolores Hayden notes, "promised to subject women to the hierarchy and alienation of wage work under capitalism as the price for ending their physical isolation and economic dependence."[156] Yet for middle-class white women, Gilman's theories of work and economics held significant promise, as the idealized western community in *The Crux* suggests. For example, "The Cottonwoods" not only serves as a model of socialized housekeeping with the cooking and heavy household labor being performed by a servant; it also serves an important function for Orella. It is like the boardinghouses in many of Gilman's stories, which provide "investment opportunities for women seeking economic security" and financial independence.[157]

Furthermore, this is a community in which women professionals are not only welcome, but perform crucial functions. In addition to Vivian's kindergarten, Dr. Bellair, with her thriving practice, serves as a model of successful professional womanhood. It has already been established that Dr. Bellair represents many of the most positive aspects of New Womanhood in not only seeking her own education and professional fulfillment, but also enabling other women to do so. Yet as a woman physician practicing in the West, she takes on special significance.[158] Among pioneer societies, women had particular authority as healers, just as they had in earlier periods in the East, before medicine became professionalized and dominated by men.[159] Not only were male practitioners often less skilled and thus unwelcome in unregulated regions, but trained physicians in general tended to be sparse, particularly in rural areas.[160] And, in fact, women physicians "were not uncommon in the West" by the late nineteenth century.[161] Certainly, women seeking medical education and practice faced resistance and discrimination in the West as they did in the East.[162] Yet they were a significant presence: Regina Markell Morantz-Sanchez notes that "[m]any women chose to . . . pioneer [as medical professionals] in the Midwest and West," which gained them great geographical mobility. Medical education, particularly in California, "was remarkably integrated" from the late nineteenth century: "Indeed," writes Morantz-Sanchez, "the proportion of women students in California was roughly a consistent 10 percent—approximately twice the national average."[163] In Colorado, women physicians tended to be slightly more conventional than in California, embracing a maternalist rhetoric to justify female medical education and practice—an ethos in which Dr. Bellair certainly participates.[164] Thus, Dr. Bellair's status as a *western* woman physician likely contributes to her rhetorical power as a character in Gilman's idealized West, for she embodies women's pursuit of fulfilling, remunerative, and socially useful work in a progressive community that, by and large, values her contributions.[165]

The fact that Dr. Bellair and the Bainville women as a group are so welcomed in Gilman's West is, as I have said, a significant reworking of the Western genre: rather than representing impediments to freedom, innovation, and regeneration, they make such processes possible. And this is the case for both women and men. Not only do they provide a much-needed family and domestic center for Colorado's womanless men and former cowboys; not only do they provide "clean" wives for marriageable bachelors; they also succeed in reforming—in an act that

strains credulity—the book's most confirmed misogynist.
Indeed, one of the most troubling aspects of the plot for a
feminist reader is the fact that Vivian becomes betrothed
to Dr. Hale, the very physician who would have had her
marry the infected Morton because of his devotion to professional "honor." Because one of Gilman's most strident
critiques in the novel is leveled at such male physicians
and their collusion in the "medical secret," it seems entirely contradictory that Hale should win the heroine Vivian's hand. If read in the context of some of the novel's
other arguments, however, it can be seen to have a certain, if unsatisfying, logic. Gilman reveals late in the story
that the source of Hale's misogyny is the selfish and
thoughtless Mrs. St. Cloud: when she drove his brother to
suicide through her True Womanly wiles, he promised
himself that he would never propose marriage to any
woman. The wise Mrs. Pettigrew confirms to Vivian, however, that "Dr. Hale doesn't hate women, . . . but a woman
broke his heart once," leading to his solemn vow (*Crux*
230). Such is the tragic waste caused by "this particular
type of sex parasite" (*Crux* 229–30); only the new sort of
New Woman in Vivian can redeem him from his misogyny,
the novel suggests. That Hale is worth saving is established not only by Dr. Bellair's confidence that "he is one
of the best of men" (*Crux* 137), but also by his enlightened
housekeeping. He asks the progressive question, "Is there
any deficiency, mental or physical, about a man, to prevent his attempting" to keep house? (*Crux* 133). Sure
enough, he exemplifies Gilman's principles of enlightened housekeeping by both his judicious use of servants
and his profusion of "labor-saving devices," which allow
him to run his home with "intelligent efficiency" (*Crux*
135). He is, therefore, precisely the kind of man for Gilman's reformed world of egalitarian partnerships between men and women. His misogyny, though embraced
a bit too stridently, perhaps, to be convincingly cured, is
effectively jettisoned by novel's end, when the new models of womanhood and community have reformed him.

The Bainville women's establishment of this community in Colorado is, then, a curative endeavor, a feminist
West Cure that has implications beyond simply bettering

the lives of individual women. As such a story, *The Crux* participates in a widespread phenomenon in Gilman's fiction, which often "celebrates the existence of recuperative spaces, most often located in the country, run by women for women."[166] Among such stories are several set explicitly in the West, including *What Diantha Did* (1910), "Bee Wise" (1913), and "Dr. Clair's Place" (1915).[167] Like *The Crux*, for example, "Dr. Clair's Place" pictures a woman physician prescribing a kind of West Cure; in what seems a direct response to Weir Mitchell, Gilman describes "how a female physician might treat neurasthenia."[168] Complaining that "[t]he trouble with Sanatoriums . . . is that the sick folks have nothing to do but sit about and think of themselves and their 'cases' " (Mitchell commonly berated women invalids for precisely this behavior, which he inculcated through the rest cure), she sets up a sanatorium in Southern California where patients are encouraged to "keep . . . busy" with artistic, physical, and intellectual pursuits, and generally to amuse themselves.[169] Gilman's utopian or pseudo-utopian western stories, of which *The Crux* is by far the most developed, are, then, innovative appropriations of existing literary and cultural conventions associated with the frontier.

Engaging as it does with turn-of-the-century cultural debates about gender identity, medical discourse, social organization, and Manifest Destiny, *The Crux* brings together a number of the most persistent themes in Gilman's work and life, in their more and less progressive aspects. In providing a locus for the enactment of "Woman's Manifest Destiny," the novel imagines empowering possibilities for eastern white women in the West even as it participates in a discourse of conquest and elitism. Its woman-centered community modeled on Gilman's central tenets for positive social change offers refreshing new visions of life in the West and American society as a whole. And yet these same visions must be recognized for their ethnocentric, classist, and racist biases, problematic theories that also underlie Gilman's otherwise compelling argument for women's sexual and medical self-determination. The complexity of her powerful "mixed legacy" in the novel is encapsulated in the poem she uses to preface *The Crux*. Arguing for women's full knowledge about sexually transmitted disease, the poem ends with the hope that the informed woman "may build a new race of new men" (*Crux* 82), implying to those aware of Gilman's more retrograde ideas a disturbing eugenic vision of the future. Yet the poem also articulates a progressive vision that the young woman be "strong in her knowledge and free in her truth":

> Who should know but the woman?—The
>   young wife-to-be?
>   Whose whole life hangs on the choice;
> To her the ruin, the misery;
>   To her, the deciding voice.

(Crux 82)

Ultimately, it is Gilman's understanding of the interconnectedness between women's voices and their material existence that may be her most significant and lasting contribution offered in *The Crux*. For in her novel, the "crux" of the matter is indeed the fact that women must reject cultural imperatives that objectify them through their silence, ignorance, and inaction, claiming instead the knowledge and authority needed for bodily self-determination.

NOTES

1. *Topeka State Journal* (15 June 1896), vol. 7, quoted in Gary Scharnhorst, *Charlotte Perkins Gilman* (Boston: Twayne, 1985), 40.

2. Gilman uses these terms to describe herself in a letter cited by Denise D. Knight in *Charlotte Perkins Gilman: A Study of the Short Fiction* (New York: Twayne, 1997), 3. For a detailed discussion of Gilman's didacticism, see Knight's introduction, 3–6.

3. Charlotte Perkins Gilman, *The Living of Charlotte Perkins Gilman: An Autobiography* (1935; reprint, New York: Harper & Row, 1975), 308. All subsequent quotations are from this edition and are cited parenthetically in the text as *Living*, followed by the page number.

4. Charlotte Perkins Gilman, "Masculine Literature," from *The Man-Made World; Or, Our Androcentric Culture* (1911; reprint in *Charlotte Perkins Gilman: A Study of the Short Fiction*, ed. Denise D. Knight [New York: Twayne, 1997]), 117, 122.

5. Gilman's critique of this phenomenon has been widely noted. See, for example, Ann J. Lane, introduction to Gilman's *Herland* (1915; reprint, New York: Pantheon, 1979), xi; and Knight, *Charlotte Perkins Gilman*, 79.

6. Floyd Dell, "Books and Writers," *Progressive Woman* 5 (February 1912): 10.

7. Because so many sketches of Gilman's biography are now available, I have limited my discussion here to a brief overview; throughout this introduction additional information about her life will be included when relevant. For a useful biographical summary of her life as it relates to her work and philosophy, see Catherine J. Golden, "Charlotte Perkins Gilman (1860-1935)," in *Nineteenth-Century American Women Writers: A Bio-Bibliographical Critical Sourcebook*, ed. Denise D. Knight (Westport, CT: Greenwood Press, 1997), 160–67.

8. Though Gilman was often dependent upon monetary gifts from others, the autobiographical self she constructs in *The Living of Charlotte Perkins Gilman* (1935) is generally economically independent. Joanne Karpinski explores the effects and implications of this discrepancy between the "real" and "theoretical" Gilman in "The Economic Conundrum of the Lifewriting of Charlotte Perkins Gilman," in *The Mixed Legacy of Charlotte Perkins Gilman*, ed. Catherine J. Golden and Joanna Schneider Zangrando (Newark: University of Delaware Press, 2000), 35–46.

9. For an example of her endorsement of such self-identification, see her novel *Moving the Mountain*, ed. Minna Doskow (1911; reprint, Cranbury, NJ: Associated University Presses, 1999), 81. As her biographer Ann J. Lane puts it, "She is known today as a feminist. She saw herself as a humanist. She was both." See Lane, *To Herland and Beyond: The Life and Work of Charlotte Perkins Gilman* (New York: Pantheon Books, 1990), 230.

10. Lane, introduction to *The Living of Charlotte Perkins Gilman: An Autobiography* (1935; reprint, Madison: University of Wisconsin Press, 1990), xvii.

11. Though *The Crux* is mentioned briefly in biographies of Gilman as well as in a few overviews of her work, it has been analyzed in some detail only by Judith A. Allen, in "Reconfiguring Vice: Charlotte Perkins Gilman, Prostitution, and Frontier Sexual Contracts," in *Charlotte Perkins Gilman: Optimist Reformer*, ed. Jill Rudd and Val Gough (Iowa City: University of Iowa Press, 1999), 173–99; Janet Beer, in *Kate Chopin, Edith Wharton, and Charlotte Perkins Gilman: Studies in Short Fiction* (New York: St. Martin's Press, 1997), 179, 182; Ann J. Lane, in "The Fictional World of Charlotte Perkins Gilman," her introduction to *The Charlotte Perkins Gilman Reader*, ed. Ann J. Lane (New York: Pantheon Books, 1980), xxiii–xxiv; and Anne E. Tanski, in "The Sins of the Innocent: Breaking the Barriers of Role Conflict," in *A Very Different Story: Studies in the Fiction of Charlotte Perkins Gilman*, ed. Val Gough and Jill Rudd (Liverpool: Liverpool University Press, 1998), 68–80. With the exception of part of a chapter in Aleta Cane, "Charlotte Per-

kins Gilman's *Forerunner:* Text and Context" (Ph.D. diss., Northeastern University, 1996), 107–14, 128–38, to date there have been no major studies of the novel, in large part because it is so difficult to obtain. Those brief studies that do exist are often based largely on the chapter excerpted by Lane in *The Charlotte Perkins Gilman Reader*, 116–22. The novel was also excerpted very briefly in *Women of America: A History*, ed. Carol Ruth Berkin and Mary Beth Norton (Boston: Houghton Mifflin, 1979), 176. While *The Forerunner* was reprinted by Greenwood Press in 1968, making the magazine (and hence the novel) available to libraries, this edition, like Gilman's single-volume edition of *The Crux*, is now out of print.

12. Gilman, *The Forerunner* 7, no. 2 (1916): 56.

13. Gilman, "As to Purpose," *The Forerunner* 1, no. 1 (1909): 32.

14. For a detailed discussion of the *Woman's Journal* as possible inspiration for *The Forerunner*, see Cane, "Charlotte Perkins Gilman's *Forerunner*," 71–76.

15. Ibid., ii.

16. Lane, "The Fictional World," xl.

17. See Carol Farley Kessler, *Charlotte Perkins Gilman: Her Progress Toward Utopia with Selected Writings* (Syracuse, NY: Syracuse University Press, 1995), 40.

18. Throughout *The Crux*, Gilman presents for her readers' serious perusal only those models of womanhood that were circulating in her own realm of experience, that of the white, middle-class, native-born woman who identifies herself with the East.

19. Lane, "The Fictional World," xxiii.

20. Barbara Welter has defined "True Womanhood" as a cultlike phenomenon in the nineteenth-century United States in which women were idealized in precisely these terms. See Welter, "The Cult of True Womanhood: 1820–1860," *American Quarterly* 18 (1966): 151–74. "True Womanhood" represents, however, less women's actual behavior in the world than an ideology, a set of terms that were used on a discursive level to regulate and to mask behaviors thought to exceed women's proper "place." Equally important, the ideology was bound by factors such as class, race, region, and religion: "True Woman" encoded a very narrow demographic of white, middle-class, Protestant, native-born, largely northeastern women, and it was only one of many models of gender identity for women circulating during this time. See, for example, Frances B. Cogan, *All-American Girl: The Ideal of Real Womanhood in Mid-Nineteenth-Century America* (Athens: University of Georgia Press, 1989). Some of the most influential sources exploring the uses and limits of the discourse of True Womanhood are Hazel V. Carby, *Reconstructing Womanhood: The Emergence of the Afro-American Woman Novelist* (New York: Oxford University Press, 1987); Linda Kerber, "Separate Spheres, Female Worlds, Woman's Place: The Rhetoric of Women's History," *Journal of American History* 75 (1988): 9–39; and Laura McCall, " 'The Reign of Brute Force Is Now Over': A Content Analysis of *Godey's Lady's Book*, 1830–1860," *Journal of the Early Republic* 9 (1989): 217–36.

21. Charlotte Perkins Gilman, *The Crux*, 104, 105. All subsequent quotations are from the present edition and are cited parenthetically in the text as *Crux*, followed by the page number.

22. Gilman, *Women and Economics: A Study of the Economic Relation Between Men and Women as a Factor in Social Evolution*, ed. Carl N. Degler (1898; reprint, New York: Harper & Row, 1966), 38.

23. Cane, "Charlotte Perkins Gilman's *Forerunner*," 137.

24. Coming of age in the second half of the nineteenth century and the early part of the twentieth, so-called New Women married later than had been the custom (if at all) and sought college educations and professional training. They rejected traditional female roles, claiming prerogatives theretofore reserved for men, including fulfilling careers and economic independence. Many New Women also rejected the imperative of heterosexuality, pursuing instead lifelong relationships with other women. Later generations of New Women overtly claimed sexual liberation and rejected motherhood. Not surprisingly, New Women generally had access to all of these opportunities because, like True Women, they were in a privileged position with respect to class, race, region, and religion. New Womanhood was necessarily more problematic for women not of the dominant group; in some cases, this was the result of their being denied such opportunities on the basis of racial prejudice or economic inequality. But they also often approached the phenomenon from a different philosophical position: if a woman is unfairly denied the virtues associated with True Womanhood, she may not be as eager to reject them. One of the foundational sources exploring the phenomenon of New Womanhood is Carroll Smith-Rosenberg, *Disorderly Conduct: Visions of Gender in Victorian America* (New York: Knopf, 1985), 245–96; see also Martha Banta, *Imaging American Women: Idea and Ideals in Cultural History* (New York: Columbia University Press, 1987), esp. 45–91. For a discussion of Gilman's aversion to later generations of New Women, see Sandra M. Gilbert and Susan Gubar, " 'Fecundate! Discriminate!' Charlotte Perkins Gilman and the Theologizing of Maternity," in Rudd and Gough, *Optimist Reformer*, 200–218.

25. Gilman discusses her love of "common sense" shoes and her dislike of fashion in *Living* 65–66, ideas expressed as well in her commitment to dress reform. She also explores the significance of pockets and comfortable shoes in her story "If I Were a Man" (1914), in which a woman who wakes up one morning in her husband's body and clothing discovers the power, freedom, and convenience these supposedly masculine accoutrements allow.

26. Frederick Wegener discusses at length the ways in which Gilman associated women physicians with New Womanhood and her own ideals for reform (56). See Wegener, " 'What a Comfort a Woman Doctor Is!' Medical Women in the Life and Writing of Charlotte Perkins Gilman," in Rudd and Gough, *Optimist Reformer*, 45–73.

27. On the development of professionalism in the United States, see, for example, Burton J. Bledstein, *The Culture of Professionalism:*

The Middle Class and the Development of Higher Education in America (New York: Norton, 1976); and Joan Jacobs Brumberg and Nancy Tomes, "Women in the Professions: A Research Agenda for American Historians," *Reviews in American History* 10, no. 2 (1982): 275–96.

28. Susan Coultrap-McQuin, *Doing Literary Business: American Women Writers in the Nineteenth Century* (Chapel Hill: University of North Carolina Press, 1990), 198.

29. Regina Markell Morantz-Sanchez has characterized Drs. Elizabeth Blackwell and Mary Putnam Jacobi (who is known to have treated Gilman) as "representative types" in this split of opinions. For a detailed discussion of such competing constructions of women physicians, see Morantz-Sanchez, *Sympathy and Science: Women Physicians in American Medicine* (New York: Oxford University Press, 1985), 184; as well as her "Feminism, Professionalism, and Germs: The Thought of Mary Putnam Jacobi and Elizabeth Blackwell," *American Quarterly* 34, no. 5 (1982): 459–78. For excellent reviews of the literature on the debate over women physicians, see Regina Markell Morantz, "The 'Connecting Link': The Case for the Woman Doctor in 19th-Century America," in *Sickness and Health in America: Readings in the History of Medicine and Public Health,* ed. Judith Waltzer Leavitt and Ronald L. Numbers (Madison: University of Wisconsin Press, 1978), 117–28; and Martha L. Hildreth, "Delicacy and Propriety: The Acceptance of the Woman Physician in Victorian America," *Halcyon* 9 (1987): 149–65.

30. See, for example, S. Weir Mitchell's argument against women physicians in *Fat and Blood: An Essay on the Treatment of Certain Forms of Neurasthenia and Hysteria,* 4th ed. (Philadelphia: Lippincott, 1877), 55–56. For a discussion of women physicians' uses of domestic discourse, see Morantz-Sanchez, *Sympathy and Science;* and Seth Koven and Sonya Michel, "Womanly Duties: Maternalist Politics and the Origins of Welfare States in France, Germany, Great Britain, and the United States, 1880–1920," *American Historical Review* 95, no. 4 (1990): 1076–108.

31. For example, in 1860, only 0.2 percent of physicians nationally (about 200 individuals) were women; by 1900, the number had risen to 5.6 percent (7,387). See Mary Roth Walsh, *"Doctors Wanted: No Women Need Apply": Sexual Barriers in the Medical Profession, 1835–1975* (New Haven: Yale University Press, 1977), 186.

32. In the early twentieth century the medical profession closed ranks and underwent a series of "reforms" (one of the most effective being the Flexner Report of 1910, an investigation into medical schools commissioned by the American Medical Association), which had the effect of closing the profession to nonwhites, Jews, women of all races and creeds, and the lower classes. In Boston, which led the nation in the number of women physicians, the figures slipped from 18.2 percent in 1900 to 8.7 percent by 1930. See Regina Morantz-Sanchez, "So Honored, So Loved? The Women's Medical Movement in Decline," in *"Send Us a Lady Physician": Women Doctors in America, 1835–1920,* ed. Ruth J. Abram (New York: Norton, 1985), 233; Paul Starr,

The Social Transformation of American Medicine: The Rise of a Sovereign Profession and the Making of a Vast Industry (New York: Basic Books, 1982), 124; and Walsh, *"Doctors Wanted,"* 185–86.

33. Wegener, "What a Comfort a Woman Doctor Is!," 50.

34. Barbara Bardes and Suzanne Gossett discuss these conventions in *Declarations of Independence: Women and Political Power in 19th Century American Fiction* (New Brunswick, NJ: Rutgers University Press, 1990), 130–31. The conventions were variously developed, invoked, and critiqued by American writers. Some of the best known examples can be found in Harriet Beecher Stowe's *My Wife and I* (1871), Mark Twain and Charles Dudley Warner's *The Gilded Age* (1873), William Dean Howells's *Doctor Breen's Practice* (1881), Elizabeth Stuart Phelps's *Doctor Zay* (1882), Sarah Orne Jewett's *A Country Doctor* (1884), and Henry James's *The Bostonians* (1886). For recent discussions of the "lady doctor" novel, see Lillian R. Furst, "Halfway Up the Hill: Doctresses in Late Nineteenth-Century American Fiction," in *Women Healers and Physicians: Climbing a Long Hill*, ed. Lillian R. Furst (Lexington: University Press of Kentucky, 1997), 221–38; Wegener, "What a Comfort a Woman Doctor Is!," 59–60, and his " 'A Line of Her Own': Henry James's 'Sturdy Little Doctress' and the Medical Woman as Literary Type in Gilded-Age America," *Texas Studies in Literature and Language* 39, no. 2 (1997): 139–80.

35. Gilman defends women physicians against charges of mannishness in *Women and Economics*, 167.

36. Aleta Cane also notes that while Dr. Bellair "acts to mentor and protect the other women there is no appropriate happy ending for her because she is not the role model that Gilman holds up to the *Forerunner*'s audience" ("Charlotte Perkins Gilman's *Forerunner*," 131).

37. Lane, "The Fictional World," xv. Frederick Wegener discusses the profusion of woman doctor-mentor figures in Gilman's work. See his "What a Comfort a Woman Doctor Is!," 60–67. He confirms that "women doctors throughout Gilman's fiction . . . become implicated indirectly or tacitly in another woman's gesture toward self-determination." "In Vivian and Dr. Bellair," he argues, "Gilman offers her most complex account of such a relationship" (64, 61).

38. Wegener notes that Gilman's women physicians are often associated with kindergartens. ("What a Comfort a Woman Doctor Is!," 65).

39. Gilman espoused what she called "right motherhood"—that is, motherhood practiced and understood as a sacred duty to society and the human race—in much of her work, most notably her essay "The New Motherhood" in *The Forerunner* 1, no. 14 (1910): 17–18; and *Women and Economics*. Sandra Gilbert and Susan Gubar analyze the ways her maternalism seemingly contradicts other aspects of her feminism (Gilbert and Gubar, " 'Fecundate! Discriminate!' ").

40. Elaine Showalter, *Sexual Anarchy: Gender and Culture at the Fin de Siècle* (New York: Penguin, 1990), 45. Showalter's term *higher race* is well chosen, for like some other progressive reformers of her day, Gilman's ideals of community and maternity were severely tainted by their basis in eugenics, to be discussed in more depth below.

41. Aleta Cane has argued that Vivian resembles what Frances Cogan calls the "All-American Girl," an ideal of womanhood valuing "intelligence, physical fitness and health, self-sufficiency, economic self-reliance, and careful marriage" though not explicitly feminist (Cogan, *All-American Girl*, 4). See Cane, "Charlotte Perkins Gilman's *Forerunner*," 130.

42. Stetson copied this and other letters from Gilman into his diary, published in *Endure: The Diaries of Charles Walter Stetson*, ed. Mary Armfield Hill (Philadelphia: Temple University Press, 1985), 63.

43. Ibid., 279.

44. Gilman, diary entry, 31 Dec. 1883; italics are Gilman's. *The Diaries of Charlotte Perkins Gilman*, ed. Denise D. Knight, 2 vols. (Charlottesville: University Press of Virginia, 1994), 1: 246.

45. Stetson, *Endure*, 279.

46. Mitchell treated Edith Wharton and Alice James with apparent success, while his treatment of Jane Addams, Winifred Howells (daughter of William Dean Howells), and, indirectly, Virginia Woolf (whose own doctor used Mitchell's cure) inspired criticism. Some of the most enduring studies in the extensive feminist analysis of the rest cure are Ellen L. Bassuk, "The Rest Cure: Repetition or Resolution of Victorian Women's Conflicts?," in *The Female Body in Western Culture*, ed. Susan Rubin Suleiman (Cambridge: Harvard University Press, 1986), 139–51; Suzanne Poirier, "The Weir Mitchell Rest Cure: Doctor and Patients," *Women's Studies* 10 (1983): 15–40; and Ann Douglas Wood, " 'The Fashionable Diseases': Women's Complaints and Their Treatment in Nineteenth-Century America," *Journal of Interdisciplinary History* 4 (1973): 25–52.

47. Mitchell had previously treated both Gilman's great-aunt, Catharine Beecher, and her cousin, Georgiana Beecher, daughter of Harriet Beecher Stowe.

48. There are dozens of articles analyzing Gilman's critique of the treatment in "The Yellow Wall-Paper." For excellent reviews of this scholarship, see Catherine Golden, "One Hundred Years of Reading 'The Yellow Wallpaper,' " in *The Captive Imagination: A Casebook on The Yellow Wallpaper*, ed. Catherine Golden (New York: The Feminist Press, 1992), 1–23; and Elaine R. Hedges, " 'Out at Last'? 'The Yellow Wallpaper' after Two Decades of Feminist Criticism," in Golden, *The Captive Imagination*, 319–33.

49. Gilman, "Why I Wrote 'The Yellow Wallpaper'?," *The Forerunner* 4, no. 10 (1913): 271.

50. Mark Thomas Connelly discusses these statistical debates at length on pp. 197–99 of "Prostitution, Venereal Disease, and American Medicine," in *Women and Health in America: Historical Readings*, ed. Judith Waltzer Leavitt (Madison: University of Wisconsin Press, 1984), 196–221.

51. The history of venereal disease in the United States is explored in depth by Connelly as well as by Allan M. Brandt in *No Magic Bullet: A Social History of Venereal Disease in the United States Since 1880* (New York: Oxford University Press, 1985).

52. Elizabeth Temkin, "Turn-of-the-Century Nursing Perspectives on Venereal Disease," *Image: Journal of Nursing Scholarship* 26, no. 3 (fall 1994): 208.

53. For a discussion of women's clubs' support of both prostitutes and "innocent wives" in their agitation against the disease, see Ruth Rosen, *The Lost Sisterhood: Prostitution in America, 1900–1918* (Baltimore: Johns Hopkins University Press, 1982), 53–54. Gilman's participation in the efforts of such clubs is discussed in Beer, *Studies in Short Fiction*, 177.

54. Temkin, "Nursing Perspectives on Venereal Disease," 210.

55. Though "Gilman represented individual prostitutes with some sympathy" in her work, writes Judith A. Allen, she "saw prostitutes as a group, a sexual-political entity, as the enemies of women's advancement" ("Reconfiguring Vice," 175). In her extended analysis of Gilman's views on prostitution, however, Allen elucidates Gilman's contention that the true root of the problem was women's economic dependence on men, which forced them to enter into the twin sexual contracts of prostitution and marriage, denying them what she saw as their natural prerogative of mate selection.

56. Connelly, "Prostitution, Venereal Disease," 199.

57. See Nancy F. Cott, "Passionlessness: An Interpretation of Victorian Sexual Ideology, 1790–1850," in Leavitt, *Women and Health in America*, 57–69; Carl Degler, "What Ought to Be and What Was: Women's Sexuality in the Nineteenth Century," in Leavitt, *Women and Health in America*, 40–56; and Showalter, *Sexual Anarchy*, 196.

58. Brandt, *No Magic Bullet*, 28.

59. Temkin, "Nursing Perspectives on Venereal Disease," 209.

60. Connelly, "Prostitution, Venereal Disease," 199. Significantly, Connelly notes that there were no women physicians included in this symposium. See p. 213 n.29.

61. Gilman, "Comment and Review," *The Forerunner* 1, no. 13 (1910): 22.

62. Gilman, "In Its Sociological Aspects," *Transactions of the American Society for Sanitary and Moral Prophylaxis* 3 (1910): 143.

63. See, for example, Ben Barker-Benfield, "The Spermatic Economy: A Nineteenth-Century View of Sexuality," *Feminist Studies* 1 (1972): 54; and Bryan Strong, "Ideas of the Early Sex Education Movement in America, 1890–1920," *History of Education Quarterly* 12 (summer 1972): 144–45. For a review of historical arguments in favor of male sexual continence, see Connelly, "Prostitution, Venereal Disease," 216 n.56.

64. See Carl Degler, *At Odds: Women and the Family in America from the Revolution to the Present* (New York: Oxford University Press, 1980), 294–95.

65. Dock, *Hygiene and Morality* (1910; reprinted in *A Lavinia Dock Reader*, ed. Janet Wilson James [New York: Garland Publishing, 1985]), 143.

66. Connelly, "Prostitution, Venereal Disease," 202.

67. By the beginning of the twentieth century, the link between venereal disease and such ailments as infant blindness and birth deformities was well known.

68. Temkin, "Nursing Perspectives on Venereal Disease," 208.

69. See, for example, George P. Dale, M.D., "Moral Prophylaxis," *American Journal of Nursing* 11 (1911): 782–88. For discussions of these ethical debates about confidentiality, see Temkin, "Nursing Perspectives on Venereal Disease," 207–8, and Connelly, "Prostitution, Venereal Disease," 202–4.

70. Gilman, "The American Social Hygiene Association," *The Forerunner* 7, no. 10 (1916): 258.

71. Lane, "The Fictional World," xxiv.

72. Although reporting of communicable diseases was already required in numerous states by the turn of the century, venereal disease was not included in this legislation. This would change in the early decades of the twentieth century as it gained the support of more and more physicians—this despite the continued appeals of some to confidentiality. Connelly reports that "by 1922 all forty-eight states had enacted some kind of legislation requiring the reporting of venereal disease" ("Prostitution, Venereal Disease," 202).

73. Like many states, however, Ohio did not then require that names and addresses of the infected parties be released. Gilman echoed many reformers in opposing such policy: "Suppose theft or murder was frequently followed by a disease which was presumptive evidence of guilt. Should we try to shield thieves and murderers as we do fornicators and adulterers?" See Gilman, "Comment and Review," *The Forerunner* 6, no. 4 (1915): 111.

74. Temkin, "Nursing Perspectives on Venereal Disease," 210.

75. By the time *The Crux* was published, Michigan, Utah, and Washington had established the regulation in some form, and by 1921, various kinds of statutes making freedom from venereal disease a prerequisite for marriage had been passed in twenty states. See Connelly, "Prostitution, Venereal Disease," 203. For extended discussion of this issue, see Ibid., 217–18 n.64.

76. Ibid., 203. Eugenicists argued that selective breeding could effect hereditary improvement in the human race. Mark H. Haller explains the differences between the eugenics and anti–venereal disease campaigns in *Eugenics: Hereditarian Attitudes in American Thought* (New Brunswick, NJ: Rutgers University Press, 1963), 142.

77. Morrow expressed anxiety at the falling birthrate among native-born Americans, in contrast to birthrates among recently arrived immigrant populations, and this anxiety infused his medical arguments. "The function of eugenics is to produce a race healthy, well-formed, and vigorous by keeping the springs of heredity pure and undefiled," he wrote. "The effect of venereal diseases is to produce a race of inferior beings." Though he was aware that venereal disease is not transmitted genetically, he still considered it "directly antagonistic to the eugenic ideal" because of its destructive effects on "the

race." See Morrow, "Eugenics and Venereal Diseases," *Proceedings of the Child Conference for Research and Welfare* 2 (1910): 192; and his *Eugenics and Racial Poisons* (New York, 1912), 11. See also Morrow's book *Social Diseases and Marriage, Social Prophylaxis* (New York and Philadelphia: Lea Brothers and Co., 1904).

78. Gilman reviewed Morrow's book in "Comment and Review," *The Forerunner* 2, no. 1 (1911): 26–27.

79. Susan S. Lanser, "Feminist Criticism, 'The Yellow Wallpaper,' and the Politics of Color in America," *Feminist Studies* 15, no. 3 (fall 1989): 429.

80. Scharnhorst, *Charlotte Perkins Gilman*, 65. Gilman's racist and stereotypical views of immigrants, nonwhites, and the disabled in *The Crux* are, unfortunately, thus in keeping with many of her ideas and much of her work. Scholars have increasingly acknowledged Gilman's disturbing ideas about race, class, eugenics, immigration, and other issues. See, for example, Gail Bederman, *Manliness and Civilization: A Cultural History of Gender and Race in the United States, 1880–1917* (Chicago: University of Chicago Press, 1995), 121–69; Lisa Ganobcsik-Williams, "The Intellectualism of Charlotte Perkins Gilman: Evolutionary Perspectives on Race, Ethnicity, Class," in Rudd and Gough, *Optimist Reformer*, 16–41; Gilbert and Gubar, " 'Fecundate! Discriminate' ", esp. 214–15; Golden and Zangrando's introduction to *The Mixed Legacy*, 11–22; Denise D. Knight, "Charlotte Perkins Gilman and the Shadow of Racism," *American Literary Realism* 32, no. 2 (2000): 159–69; Lanser, "Feminist Criticism"; and Scharnhorst, "Historicizing Gilman: A Bibliographer's View," in Golden and Zangrando, *The Mixed Legacy*, 65–73.

81. Scharnhorst, "Historicizing Gilman," 67.

82. Allen discusses this ambiguity in more depth; see her "Reconfiguring Vice," 197 n.18.

83. Gilman, "The 'Nervous Breakdown' of Women," *The Forerunner* 7, no. 8 (1916): 205. See also Scharnhorst, *Charlotte Perkins Gilman*, 65, 128 n.29.

84. Golden and Zangrando argue that this legacy includes Gilman's "uncompromising critique of what she viewed as an unjust, inequitable society and her vision for a truly humane, egalitarian world," as well as the "repugnant racial theories, xenophobia, and ethnocentrism" espoused in her poetry, fiction, theory, and private writing. See their introduction to *The Mixed Legacy*, 12.

85. Lane, "The Fictional World," xxiv.

86. Dell, "Books and Writers," 10.

87. Showalter, *Sexual Anarchy*, 198, 199.

88. Beer, *Studies in Short Fiction*, 176.

89. Ibid., 180.

90. Knight, *Charlotte Perkins Gilman*, 75. Gilman's "The Unnatural Mother" (1895) presents the obverse of "Wild Oats and Tame Wheat," in that the heroine is dubbed an "unnatural" woman in part because her father *has* taught her about venereal disease. While "Cleaning Up Elita" (1916) addresses the disease's association with prostitution as a

town attempts to eliminate the practice, "Bee Wise" (1913) presents a new community established in the West (California, specifically) which carefully selects its men based on their ability to prove they are free of all disease, including venereal disease. Janet Beer has suggested that Gilman chose to set this story in California because, in the same year the story was published, that state had enacted legislation mandating that men obtain a health certificate before marriage (*Studies in Short Fiction*, 176). For additional discussion of this issue, see Rosen, *The Lost Sisterhood*, 54. In a similar vein, "The Cottagette" (1910) broaches this topic indirectly in its positive portrayal of a man who evidently is not infected.

91. Beer, *Studies in Short Fiction*, 180, 177–78.

92. Dell, "Books and Writers," 10.

93. In this way, Gilman's novel recalls the so-called seduction novels popular in the late eighteenth and early nineteenth centuries, which functioned in part as cautionary tales for young women readers. As Cathy Davidson has argued, such novels "fulfilled the social function of testing some of the possibilities for romance and courtship— testing better conducted in the world of fiction than in the world of fact"; in doing so, these texts also implied that "the woman must take greater control of her life and must make shrewd judgments of the men who come into her life." See Davidson, *Revolution and the Word: The Rise of the Novel in America* (New York: Oxford University Press, 1986), 113.

94. Tanski, "Sins of the Innocent," 76.

95. Frederick Jackson Turner, "The Significance of the Frontier in American History" (1893; reprint, Ann Arbor, MI: University Microfilms Inc., 1966).

96. Some of the most influential studies of this conception of the American West include Henry Nash Smith, *Virgin Land: The American West as Symbol and Myth* (1950; reprint, New York: Vintage Books, 1957); Richard Slotkin, *The Fatal Environment: The Myth of the Frontier in the Age of Industrialization, 1800–1890* (New York: Atheneum, 1985); and Slotkin, *Regeneration Through Violence: The Mythology of the American Frontier, 1600–1860* (Middletown, CT: Wesleyan University Press, 1973).

97. Many practitioners of the "New Western History," influenced by fields such as ethnic, postcolonial, and, to a lesser extent, women's studies, have explored these problems. See, for example, Patricia Nelson Limerick, *The Legacy of Conquest: The Unbroken Past of the American West* (New York: Norton, 1987); Patricia Nelson Limerick, Clyde A. Milner II, and Charles E. Rankin, eds., *Trails: Toward a New Western History* (Lawrence: University Press of Kansas, 1991); Clyde A. Milner, ed., *A New Significance: Re-Envisioning the History of the American West* (New York: Oxford University Press, 1996); Forrest G. Robinson, ed., *The New Western History: The Territory Ahead* (Tucson: University of Arizona Press, 1997); and Richard White, *"It's Your Own Misfortune and None of My Own": A New History of the American West* (Norman: University of Oklahoma Press, 1993).

98. Brigitte Georgi-Findlay, *The Frontiers of Women's Writing: Women's Narratives and the Rhetoric of Westward Expansion* (Tucson: University of Arizona Press, 1996), 7.

99. Nina Baym, "Melodramas of Beset Manhood: How Theories of American Fiction Exclude Women Authors," *American Quarterly* 33 (1981): 123–39. See also Melody Graulich, " 'O Beautiful for Spacious Guys': An Essay on the Legitimate Inclinations of the Sexes," in *The Frontier Experience and the American Dream*, ed. David Mogen, Paul Bryant, and Mark Busby (College Station: Texas A & M Press, 1989), 186–201; and Annette Kolodny, *The Lay of the Land: Metaphor as Experience and History in American Life and Letters* (Chapel Hill: University of North Carolina Press, 1975).

100. Melody Graulich, "Western Biodiversity: Rereading Nineteenth-Century American Women's Writing," in *Nineteenth-Century American Women Writers: A Critical Reader*, ed. Karen L. Kilcup (Malden, MA: Blackwell Publishers, 1998), 47–61; 52, 50.

101. Some recent surveys of this multicultural western women's history include Antonia Castañeda, "Women of Color and the Rewriting of Western History: The Discourse, Politics, and Decolonization of History," *Pacific Historical Review*, Special Issue: Western Women's History Revisited, 61, no. 4 (1992): 501–33; Elizabeth Jameson, "Toward a Multicultural History of Women in the Western United States," *Signs* 13, no. 4 (1988): 761–91; Elizabeth Jameson and Susan Armitage, eds., *Writing the Range: Race, Class, and Culture in the Women's West* (Norman: University of Oklahoma Press, 1997); and Elizabeth Jameson and Susan Armitage, eds., *The Women's West* (Norman: University of Oklahoma Press, 1987).

102. Framing the question in Turnerian terms has, of course, many theoretical problems: not only does it elide the experience of many (such as Native American, Hispanic, Latina, Canadian, and African American, Asian women) who viewed the westwardly moving Anglo frontier from different geographical and ideological perspectives; it also measures women's experience against a "male" model, thus limiting the possibilities for conceiving of this experience. Recently, scholars have sought new metaphors for understanding the West and American representations of it, such as contact zones, borderlands, hybridity, and biodiversity. See Graulich, "Western Biodiversity," 57–59.

103. See, for example, Julie Roy Jeffrey, *Frontier Women: "Civilizing" the West? 1840–1880* (1979; rev. ed., New York: Hill and Wang, 1998); Peggy Pascoe, "Western Women at the Cultural Crossroads," in Limerick, Milner, and Rankin, *Trails*, 40–58; and Lillian Schlissel, *Women's Diaries of the Westward Journey* (New York: Schocken Books, 1982).

104. Women's writing of this type, which was particularly prevalent among the first generation of white settlers, is explored, for example, in Christiane Fisher, *Let Them Speak for Themselves: Women in the American West, 1849–1900* (New York: Dutton, 1977), which also analyzes the younger generations' more positive view of the West; and Schlissel, *Women's Diaries*.

105. Recent examples of such work include Beverly Beeton, "How the West Was Won for Woman Suffrage," in *Rediscovering the Woman Suffrage Movement*, ed. Marjorie Spruill Wheeler (Troutdale, OR: New Sage Publications, 1995), 99–116; Katherine Harris, "Homesteading in Northeastern Colorado, 1873–1920: Sex Roles and Women's Experience," in Jameson and Armitage, *The Women's West*, 165–78; Elizabeth Jameson, "Women as Workers, Women as Civilizers: True Womanhood in the American West," in Jameson and Armitage, *The Women's West*, 145–64; and Sandra L. Myers, *Westering Women and the Frontier Experience, 1800–1915* (Albuquerque: University of New Mexico Press, 1982).

106. For studies of such women's literature, see, for example, Annette Kolodny, *The Land Before Her: Fantasy and Experience of the American Frontiers, 1630–1860* (Chapel Hill: University of North Carolina Press, 1984); and Vera Norwood and Janice Monk, eds., *The Desert Is No Lady: Southwestern Landscapes in Women's Writing and Art* (New Haven: Yale University Press, 1987). See also Kolodny, "Letting Go Our Grand Obsessions: Notes Toward a New Literary History of the American Frontiers," *American Literature* 64 (1992): 1–18.

107. Georgi-Findlay, *Frontiers of Women's Writing*, 11. See also Graulich, "Western Biodiversity," 50–51; and Carroll Smith-Rosenberg, "Subject Female: Authorizing American Identity," *American Literary History* 5 (1993): 481–511.

108. Allen, "Reconfiguring Vice," 176.

109. Lane, "The Fictional World," xxxviii.

110. Allen, "Reconfiguring Vice," 190.

111. Gilman was by no means alone in her use and appropriation of Darwin's theory of sexual selection. Though he mentions Gilman only briefly, Bert Bender explores such work by many of her contemporaries in *The Descent of Love: Darwin and the Theory of Sexual Selection in American Fiction, 1871–1926* (Philadelphia: University of Pennsylvania Press, 1996).

112. Lester F. Ward, *Pure Sociology: A Treatise on the Origin and Spontaneous Development of Society*, 2nd ed. (1903; New York: Macmillan, 1916), 314. For a detailed discussion of Gilman's relationship with Ward as well as her uses of Reform Darwinism, see Mary A. Hill, *Charlotte Perkins Gilman: The Making of a Radical Feminist 1860–1896* (Philadelphia: Temple University Press, 1980), 263–70; see also Minna Doskow, "Charlotte Perkins Gilman: The Female Face of Social Darwinism," *Weber Studies* 14, no. 3 (1997): 9–22; and Cynthia Eagle Russett, *Sexual Science: The Victorian Construction of Womanhood* (Cambridge: Harvard University Press, 1989), 151–54. Sandra Gilbert and Susan Gubar have argued that Gilman in fact misread Ward's theories because of her "aversion to female physicality and her repudiation of the erotic." See Gilbert and Gubar, "Fecundate! Discriminate!," 213.

113. See Gilman, *The Man-Made World, or Our Androcentric Culture* (1911; reprint, New York: Source Book Press, 1970); and Gilman, *Women and Economics*.

114. Allen, "Reconfiguring Vice," 178. Dr. Bellair claims that "there

are three men to one woman" in the Colorado town to which the Bainville women will migrate (*Crux* 115). According to the U.S. Census, in 1910, Massachusetts had 56,000 more women than men. In contrast, Colorado had 63,000 more men than women in the same year. See *Historical Statistics of the United States, Colonial Times to 1970, Part I*, Bicentennial Edition (Washington, DC: U.S. Bureau of the Census, 1975), 29, 25. However, Carolyn Stefanco reports that in Denver, "a focal point for suffrage activity" and "the largest urban center within the state," women slightly outnumbered men in 1900 (265). See Stefanco, "Networking on the Frontier: the Colorado Women's Suffrage Movement, 1876–1893," in Jameson and Armitage, *The Women's West*, 265–76.

115. Gilman, "Woman's 'Manifest Destiny,' " *The Forerunner* 4, no. 12 (1913): 335. This article was published previously in the *Woman's Journal* (4 June 1904): 178.

116. Allen, "Reconfiguring Vice," 190.

117. Gilbert and Gubar assert, in fact, that "the way in which Gilman conceives of woman as the First Sex [in evolution] attributes a unique genetic centrality to mothers that not only undermines the feminist movement's ideal of sex equality but even degenerates into precisely the racism that marks much Social Darwinist thinking about racial betterment" ("Fecundate! Discriminate!," 201).

118. See Reginald Horsman, *Race and Manifest Destiny: The Origins of American Racial Anglo-Saxonism* (Cambridge: Harvard University Press, 1981), 219–21.

119. It has been widely noted, for example, that Western novelist Owen Wister idealized the West as a haven for a regeneration of Anglo-Saxon America. See his "The Evolution of the Cow-Puncher," *Harper's New Monthly Magazine* 91 (1895): 602–17. Along with Horsman, G. Edward White discusses the Anglo-Saxonism in eastern ideals of the frontier in *The Eastern Establishment and the Western Experience: The West of Frederic Remington, Theodore Roosevelt, and Owen Wister* (New Haven: Yale University Press, 1968), 197.

120. The material in the following paragraphs is condensed in part from a longer piece; for more detailed discussion of the issues, see Jennifer S. Tuttle, "Rewriting the West Cure: Charlotte Perkins Gilman, Owen Wister, and the Sexual Politics of Neurasthenia," in Golden and Zangrando, *The Mixed Legacy*, 103–21.

121. Many scholars have noted that the West, particularly California, was a liberatory region for Gilman. See esp. Gary Scharnhorst, "Making Her Fame: Charlotte Perkins Gilman in California," *California History* (summer 1985): 192.

122. William Wyckoff, *Creating Colorado: The Making of a Western American Landscape 1860–1940* (New Haven: Yale University Press, 1999), 137.

123. Ibid., 138.

124. Carl Abbott, Stephen J. Leonard, and David McComb, *Colorado: A History of the Centennial State*, rev. ed. (Boulder: Colorado Associated University Press, 1982), 222.

125. See, for example, George Miller Beard, M.D., *American Nervousness: Its Causes and Consequences*, ed. Charles E. Rosenberg (1881; reprint, New York: Arno Press, 1972); and Silas Weir Mitchell, *Wear and Tear, or Hints for the Overworked*, 5th ed., ed. Gerald N. Grob (1887; reprint, New York: Arno Press, 1973).

126. For discussions of the theories and treatments for male neurasthenia, see Bederman, *Manliness and Civilization*; Michael Kimmel, *Manhood in America: A Cultural History* (New York: The Free Press, 1996); Tom Lutz, *American Nervousness, 1903: An Anecdotal History* (Ithaca: Cornell University Press, 1991); E. Anthony Rotundo, *American Manhood: Transformations in Masculinity from the Revolution to the Modern Era* (New York: Basic Books, 1993); Barbara Will, "The Nervous Origins of the American Western," *American Literature* 70, no. 2 (1998): 293–316; and Tuttle, "Rewriting the West Cure."

127. Barbara Will also compares the rest and West cures, and Gilman's and Wister's cases, in "The Nervous Origins of the American Western."

128. For a discussion of Wister's curative trip to Wyoming, see White, *The Eastern Establishment*, 89.

129. The novel's narrator, like Wister, is a sickly, northeastern, upper-class white man who travels to Wyoming for his health, which he eventually regains by learning the presumably masculine skills of roughriding and hunting. He achieves these skills largely through emulating the novel's title hero, the manly and mysterious cowboy known as "the Virginian."

130. Gilman's enjoyment of Wister's novel is noted in Scharnhorst, *Charlotte Perkins Gilman*, 98, and Scharnhorst and Denise D. Knight, "Charlotte Perkins Gilman's Library: A Reconstruction," *Resources for American Literary Study* 23, no. 2 (1997): 181–219.

131. There has been considerable disagreement about exactly what constitutes the "Western" genre, when it began, and why it arose. Some of the most useful studies of the genre are: Christine Bold, *Selling the Wild West: Popular Western Fiction, 1860–1960* (Bloomington: Indiana University Press, 1987); John G. Cawelti, *The Six-Gun Mystique* (Bowling Green, OH: Bowling Green University Popular Press, 1971); Richard W. Etulain, "The Historical Development of the Western," in *The Popular Western: Essays Toward a Definition*, ed. Richard W. Etulain and Michael T. Marsden (Bowling Green, OH: Bowling Green University Popular Press, 1974), 717–26; Michael Kowalewski, ed., *Reading the West: New Essays on the Literature of the American West* (Cambridge: Cambridge University Press, 1996); Thomas J. Lyon, "The Literary West," in *The Oxford History of the American West*, ed. Clyde A. Milner, Carol A. O'Connor, and Martha A. Sandweiss (New York: Oxford University Press, 1994), 707–16; and Lee Clark Mitchell, *Westerns: Making the Man in Fiction and Film* (Chicago: University of Chicago Press, 1996).

132. Jane Tompkins, *West of Everything: The Inner Life of Westerns* (New York: Oxford University Press, 1992), 39, 40. The Western is not monolithic, however, in its portrayal of women. For example, Nicole

Tonkovich has noted in her analysis of Pauline Hopkins's *Winona: A Tale of Negro Life in the South and Southwest* and Ned Buntline's *Deadwood Dick on Deck*, both of which feature central female characters who "cross-dress, defy the law, and infringe on territory traditionally marked as masculine" (243), that such conventions of the Western were available to female as well as male characters, to women as well as men (and to nonwhites as well as whites). See Tonkovich, "Guardian Angels and Missing Mothers: Race and Domesticity in *Winona* and *Deadwood Dick on Deck*," *Western American Literature* 32, no. 3 (1997): 240-64.

133. Deborah Evans, " 'Come out to Colorado with me—and Grow': *The Crux* and Gilman's New Western Hero(ines)" (Paper delivered at "Many Wests, Many Traditions," the Western Literature Association 32nd Annual Meeting, Albuquerque, NM, 16 October 1997; and the Second International Charlotte Perkins Gilman Conference, Skidmore College, Saratoga Springs, NY, 28 June 1997), 5.

134. Nineteenth-century women writers valorized female experience and moral authority (and simultaneously manipulated the discourses of domesticity and True Womanhood) in what has variously been called "domestic fiction," "literary domesticity," "woman's fiction," and "exploratory" and "didactic" novels. See, for example, Nina Baym, *Woman's Fiction: A Guide to Novels by and About Women in America, 1820–70* 2nd ed. (Urbana: University of Illinois Press, 1993); Susan K. Harris, *19th-Century American Women's Novels: Interpretive Strategies* (New York: Cambridge University Press, 1990); and Mary Kelley, *Private Woman, Public Stage: Literary Domesticity in Nineteenth-Century America* (New York: Oxford University Press, 1984).

135. Evans, " 'Come Out to Colorado,' " 2.

136. See Scharnhorst, *Charlotte Perkins Gilman*, 98.

137. This includes the homosociality of the West Cure, for while male bonding was an important component of Mitchell's cure, Vivian undergoes her healing experience with a group of girls and young women. For a detailed description of Mitchell's West Cure, see, for example, Mitchell, *Nurse and Patient; and, Camp Cure* (Philadelphia: Lippincott, 1877), 39–73; and Tuttle, "Rewriting the West Cure."

138. The easterners at home in Bainville are distinctly disappointed, in fact, to read nothing of " 'chaps,' 'sombreros,' or 'shooting up the town' " in Vivian's letters home; their conception of the West is, Gilman suggests, a fictionalized and unrealistic view. "To Bainville," the narrator explains, " 'Out West' was a large blank space on the map, and the blank space in the mind which matched it was but sparsely dotted with a few disconnected ideas such as 'cowboy,' 'blizzard,' 'prairie fire,' 'tornado,' 'border ruffian,' and the like" (*Crux* 130).

139. Gilman's involvement with such movements is discussed in more detail in Hill, *Charlotte Perkins Gilman*, 167–83, 283–93; and Scharnhorst, "Making Her Fame."

140. Scharnhorst, *Charlotte Perkins Gilman*, 59. Gary Scharnhorst discusses these four "intellectual threads" at length in his biography of Gilman; see Scharnhorst, Ibid., 57–83.

141. Kessler, *Charlotte Perkins Gilman*, 8.

142. Ibid., 7, 81. Ann J. Lane also has noted the interconnectedness between the utopian and the realistic in Gilman's *oeuvre*. See Lane, "The Fictional World," xxxiv.

143. Knight, *Charlotte Perkins Gilman*, 79.

144. Knight, ed., *"The Yellow Wall-Paper" and Selected Stories of Charlotte Perkins Gilman* (Newark: University of Delaware Press, 1994), 26.

145. Beer, *Studies in Short Fiction*, 175. Minna Doskow points out, in fact, that "the didactic form of utopian fiction . . . provided an ideal vehicle through which to popularize and dramatize [Gilman's] ideas of social reform." See her introduction to *Charlotte Perkins Gilman's Utopian Novels* (Cranbury, NJ: Associated University Presses, 1999), 14.

146. It has been noted that Hull House, Jane Addams's Chicago settlement house (where Gilman lived for a time in 1895), served as a model for many of her stories presenting positive domestic organization, including professionally prepared meals and professionally run child care. See Hill, *Charlotte Perkins Gilman*, 277; Kessler, *Charlotte Perkins Gilman*, 90–93; and Beer, *Studies in Short Fiction*, 187–89.

147. Ann J. Lane has noted that for Gilman, the conventional family often "embodies deadening tradition, foolish obedience, unexamined belief." People must leave the family they inherit and create one anew by going out into the world; in such endeavors, she notes, the boardinghouse "is often instrumental in Gilman's family-building" (Lane, "The Fictional World," xxxviii). This despite the fact that, in her own life, Gilman found that running a boardinghouse "drained her energies" and prevented her from being able to do the writing and thinking needed for her life's work (Lane, *To Herland and Beyond*, 178).

148. Polly Wynn Allen, *Building Domestic Liberty: Charlotte Perkins Gilman's Architectural Feminism* (Amherst: University of Massachusetts Press, 1988), 146.

149. Knight, *Charlotte Perkins Gilman*, 67. Such boardinghouses appear in a number of stories published around the time of *The Crux*, including "Her Housekeeper" (1910), "Martha's Mother" (1910), "The Jumping-Off Place" (1911), "The Boarder Bit" (1911), and "Turned" (1911).

150. Lane, "The Fictional World," xxvii.

151. Allen, *Building Domestic Liberty*, 146. It is important to note, however, that such a model is not necessarily "ideal" for all classes of women: while it was, as Dolores Hayden puts it, "an ideal business venture for the female capitalist, and offered an ideal managerial position for the professional domestic economist," the question of "who will do the drudge work," as Gary Scharnhorst suggests, cannot be overlooked. Gilman neglected, he explains, "to view the problem from the perspective of the cooks and laundresses hired under her plan" (Scharnhorst, *Charlotte Perkins Gilman*, 74; Hayden quoted in Scharnhorst, *Charlotte Perkins Gilman*, 74). See also Scharnhorst, "Historicizing Gilman," 70–71. In short, middle-class women's freedom from domestic drudgery to pursue other endeavors would be made possible

by working-class women assuming those undesirable duties, "The Cottonwoods' " cook Jeanne Jeaune being one example.

152. Allen, *Building Domestic Liberty*. Gilman insisted on distinguishing her recommendations for such living arrangements from cooperative housekeeping, which she felt was sure to fail. See Scharnhorst, *Charlotte Perkins Gilman*, 73.

153. Evans, " 'Come Out to Colorado,' " 8. With his peculiar laugh, "which looked so uproarious and made so little noise" (*Crux* 173), Mr. Skee seems also to be an allusion to one of the cowboy's best-known precursors, James Fenimore Cooper's Natty Bumppo. Also, in his initial interview with Mrs. Pettigrew on her arrival to Colorado, he bears a striking resemblance to a character Gilman would later portray in her autobiography, educating the New England woman about the process of scalping (*Crux* 140; *Living* 93).

154. Knight, *Charlotte Perkins Gilman*, 63.

155. As Gary Scharnhorst rightly points out, Gilman's proposals for professionalized child care were based in large part on obsolete Lamarckian theories arguing that parents could transmit acquired characteristics to their offspring. She used these theories to illustrate the ways that, as good tools for "breeding," "baby gardens" could contribute to social evolution in "advanced" cultures, making them superior to "savage" ones. "However commendable [Gilman's] plea for the professionalization of childcare in *Concerning Children* and elsewhere may have been, it was rooted in her ignorance of science and her assumption of Anglo-Saxon racial superiority," writes Scharnhorst in "Historicizing Gilman," 68.

156. Quoted on p. 232 of Dolores Hayden, "Charlotte Perkins Gilman and the Kitchenless House," *Radical History Review* 21 (1979): 225–47.

157. Knight, *Charlotte Perkins Gilman*, 67.

158. Certainly, her character would have been informed by Gilman's own experiences with women physicians in the West, for, as Frederick Wegener has established, Gilman's diaries of her time in the West "amount almost to a roll-call of California's early women doctors," many of them true "luminaries." See Wegener, "What a Comfort a Woman Doctor Is!," 46.

159. See, for example, Mary de Mund, *Women Physicians of Colorado* (Denver, CO: The Range Press, 1976); Harris, "Homesteading in Northeastern Colorado," 167; Charles R. King, "The Woman's Experience of Childbirth on the Western Frontier," *Journal of the West* 29, no. 1 (1990): 79–82; and Cathy Luchetti, *Women of the West* (St. George, UT: Antelope Island Press, 1982), 27. Barbara Ehrenreich and Deirdre English discuss women healers' defeat by competing male physicians in *For Her Own Good: 150 Years of the Experts' Advice to Women* (New York: Anchor Books, 1978). For a discussion of Native American women's roles as healers and physicians, see Valerie Sherer Mathes, "Native American Women in Medicine and the Military," *Journal of the West* 21, no. 2 (1982): 41–48.

160. Phyllis M. Japp reports, "A 1906 survey of American health care

showed the average distance between physicians to be about 13 miles in the West Central states, 39 miles in the Mountain states, and 22 miles in the Pacific region. The tendency of physicians to cluster in cities rather than in rural areas renders such averages relatively meaningless" (16). See Japp, "Pioneer Medicines: Doctors, Nostrums, and Folk Cures," *Journal of the West* 21, no. 3 (1982): 15–22.

161. John Duffy, "Medicine in the West: An Historical Overview," *Journal of the West* 21, no. 3 (1982): 13.

162. This is explained in de Mund, *Women Physicians of Colorado*, 52; and in Morantz-Sanchez, *Sympathy and Science*, 254.

163. Morantz-Sanchez, *Sympathy and Science*, 249.

164. See Rickey Hendricks, "Feminism and Maternalism in Early Hospitals for Children: San Francisco and Denver, 1875–1915," *Journal of the West* 32, no. 3 (1993): 61.

165. More scholarship remains to be done in order to establish the status of the woman physician in the American West. I would speculate that women may have enjoyed a higher status as physicians in the West because of the region's association with the rejection of eastern traditions and codes and its permissiveness of female freedom and unconventionality. And yet such high status likely diminished according to the degree to which a particular locale was urbanized and influenced by eastern mores and regulations.

166. Allen, *Building Domestic Liberty*, 146.

167. Gilman's earlier story, "The Giant Wistaria" (1891), however, though also set in the West, pictures a heroine who is unable to escape the social constraints she had rejected in the East. For an analysis of this story, see Gary Scharnhorst, "Charlotte Perkins Gilman's 'The Giant Wistaria': A Hieroglyph of the Female Frontier Gothic," in *Frontier Gothic: Terror and Wonder at the Frontier in American Literature*, ed. David Mogen, Scott P. Sanders, and Joanne B. Karpinski (Rutherford, NJ: Fairleigh Dickinson University Press, 1993), 156–64.

168. Scharnhorst, *Charlotte Perkins Gilman*, 97.

169. Gilman, "Dr. Clair's Place," *The Forerunner* 6, no. 6 (1915): 142. In his biography of Gilman, Gary Scharnhorst has argued that this story was inspired by Dr. Mary Putnam Jacobi's treatment of Gilman. See Scharnhorst, *Charlotte Perkins Gilman*, 97.

A Note on the Text

The text of *The Crux* has been taken directly from Gilman's 1911 single-volume edition of the novel, published by the Charlton Company. In this 1911 edition, Gilman enhanced the version of the story that had appeared serially in *The Forerunner* that same year by adding a preface, table of contents, and prefatory poem; correcting a number of typographical errors and inconsistencies; and polishing her punctuation and prose. Any of Gilman's revisions deemed potentially significant for interpretation of the novel have been described in notes appended to the text.

I have made every effort to respect Gilman's choices by preserving spelling, punctuation, italics, capitalization, and indentations to the greatest extent possible. Silent alterations have been made to enhance readability in some cases of obvious typographical or grammatical error. However, I have left Gilman's commas, semicolons, and dashes intact except for the occasional instance in which clarification was needed. In most cases of apparent inconsistency in verbiage or plot, I likewise have left Gilman's text unchanged, appending instead an explanatory endnote. Any insertions of missing words are indicated by brackets. Ellipses in the text are Gilman's. Spellings of some characters' names have been regularized for clarity. For example, in the 1911 single-volume edition, *Jimmie* appears in variant form as *Jimmy*, *Josie* appears also as *Jessie*, *Rella* appears as *'Rella;* these have been made consistent throughout. Beyond this, however, in cases where Gilman used alternative spellings for the same word (such as *peephole* and *peep-hole*, *traveler* and *traveller*), I have left them as they are. I also have preserved period spelling. When addressing apparent errors in the single-volume edition, I have used the *Forerunner* edition as a guide to Gilman's intention whenever possible; in cases where both editions seem in error, I have modified or annotated the text as explained above.

In addition to elucidating editorial issues, the explanatory notes at the back of this edition define archaic words and figures of speech, and words or phrases in languages other than English; they also explain allusions to people, events, objects, or biblical verse that might be unfamiliar to the contemporary reader.

THE CRUX

Preface

This story is, first, for young women to read; second, for young men to read; after that, for anybody who wants to. Anyone who doubts its facts and figures is referred to "Social Diseases and Marriage," by Dr. Prince Morrow, or to "Hygiene and Morality," by Miss Lavinia Dock, a trained nurse of long experience.[1]

Some will hold that the painful facts disclosed are unfit for young girls to know. Young girls are precisely the ones who must know them, in order that they may protect themselves and their children to come. The time to know of danger is before it is too late to avoid it.

If some say "Innocence is the greatest charm of young girls," the answer is, "What good does it do them?"

Who should know but the woman?—The
    young wife-to-be?
  Whose whole life hangs on the choice;
To her the ruin, the misery;
  To her, the deciding voice.

Who should know but the woman?—The
    mother-to-be?
  Guardian, Giver, and Guide;
If she may not foreknow, forejudge and
    foresee,
  What safety has childhood beside?

Who should know but the woman?—The
    girl in her youth?
  The hour of the warning is then,
That, strong in her knowledge and free in
    her truth,
  She may build a new race of new men.

1

The Back Way

Along the same old garden path,
Sweet with the same old flowers;
Under the lilacs, darkly dense,
The easy gate in the backyard fence—
Those unforgotten hours!

The "Foote girls" were bustling along Margate Street with an air of united purpose that was unusual with them. Miss Rebecca wore her black silk cloak, by which it might be seen that "a call" was toward. Miss Josie, the thin sister, and Miss Sallie, the fat one, were more hastily attired. They were persons of less impressiveness than Miss Rebecca, as was tacitly admitted by their more familiar nicknames, a concession never made by the older sister.

Even Miss Rebecca was hurrying a little, for her, but the others were swifter and more impatient.

"Do come on, Rebecca. Anybody'd think you were eighty instead of fifty!" said Miss Sallie.

"There's Mrs. Williams going in! I wonder if she's heard already. Do hurry!" urged Miss Josie.

But Miss Rebecca, being concerned about her dignity, would not allow herself to be hustled, and the three proceeded in irregular order under the high-arched elms and fence-topping syringas of the small New England town toward the austere home of Mr. Samuel Lane.[2]

It was a large, uncompromising, square, white house, planted starkly in the close-cut grass. It had no porch for summer lounging, no front gate for evening dalliance, no path-bordering beds of flowers from which to pluck a hasty offering or more redundant tribute. The fragrance which surrounded it came from the back yard, or over the

fences of neighbors; the trees which waved greenly about
it were the trees of other people. Mr. Lane had but two
trees, one on each side of the straight and narrow path,
evenly placed between house and sidewalk—evergreens.

Mrs. Lane received them amiably; the minister's new
wife, Mrs. Williams, was proving a little difficult to enter-
tain. She was from Cambridge, Mass., and emanated a restrained consciousness of that fact. Mr. Lane rose stiffly
and greeted them. He did not like the Foote girls, not having the usual American's share of the sense of humor. He
had no enjoyment of the town joke, as old as they were,
that "the three of them made a full yard;" and had
frowned down as a profane impertinent the man—a little
sore under some effect of gossip—who had amended it
with "make an 'ell, I say."[3]

Safely seated in their several rocking chairs, and sever-
ally rocking them, the Misses Foote burst forth, as was
their custom, in simultaneous, though by no means identi-
cal remarks.

"I suppose you've heard about Morton Elder?"

"What do you think Mort Elder's been doing now?"

"We've got bad news for poor Miss Elder!"

Mrs. Lane was intensely interested. Even Mr. Lane
showed signs of animation.

"I'm not surprised," he said.

"He's done it now," opined Miss Josie with conviction.
"I always said Rella Elder was spoiling that boy."

"It's too bad—after all she's done for him! He always
was a scamp!" Thus Miss Sallie.

"I've been afraid of it all along," Miss Rebecca was saying, her voice booming through the lighter tones of her
sisters. "I always said he'd never get through college."

"But who is Morton Elder, and what has he done?"
asked Mrs. Williams as soon as she could be heard.

This lady now proved a most valuable asset. She was so
new to the town, and had been so immersed in the suddenly widening range of her unsalaried duties as "minister's wife," that she had never even heard of Morton
Elder.

A new resident always fans the languishing flame of
local conversation. The whole shopworn stock takes on a

fresh lustre, topics long trampled flat in much discussion lift their heads anew, opinions one scarce dared to repeat again become almost authoritative, old stories flourish freshly, acquiring new detail and more vivid color.

Mrs. Lane, seizing her opportunity while the sisters gasped a momentary amazement at anyone's not knowing the town scapegrace, and taking advantage of her position as old friend and near neighbor of the family under discussion, swept into the field under such headway that even the Foote girls remained silent perforce; surcharged, however, and holding their breaths in readiness to burst forth at the first opening.

"He's the nephew—orphan nephew—of Miss Elder—who lives right back of us—our yards touch—we've always been friends—went to school together, Rella's never married—she teaches, you know—and her brother—he owned the home—it's all hers now, he died all of a sudden and left two children—Morton and Susie. Mort was about seven years old and Susie just a baby. He's been an awful cross—but she just idolizes him—she's spoiled him, I tell her."

Mrs. Lane had to breathe, and even the briefest pause left her stranded to wait another chance. The three social benefactors proceeded to distribute their information in a clattering torrent. They sought to inform Mrs. Williams in especial, of numberless details of the early life and education of their subject, matters which would have been treated more appreciatively if they had not been blessed with the later news; and, at the same time, each was seeking for a more dramatic emphasis to give this last supply of incident with due effect.

No regular record is possible where three persons pour forth statement and comment in a rapid, tumultuous stream, interrupted by cross currents of heated contradiction, and further varied by the exclamations and protests of three hearers, or at least, of two; for the one man present soon relapsed into disgusted silence.

Mrs. Williams, turning a perplexed face from one to the other, inwardly condemning the darkening flood of talk, yet conscious of a sinful pleasure in it, and anxious as a guest, *and* a minister's wife, to be most amiable, felt like one watching three kinetescopes at once.[4] She saw, in confused pictures of blurred and varying outline, Orella Elder, the young New England girl, only eighteen, already a "school ma'am," suddenly left with two children to bring up, and doing it, as best she could. She saw the boy, momentarily changing, in his shuttle-cock flight from mouth to mouth,[5] through pale shades of open mischief to the black and scarlet of hinted sin, the terror of the neighborhood, the darling of his aunt, clever, audacious, scandalizing the quiet town.

"Boys are apt to be mischievous, aren't they?" she suggested when it was possible.

"He's worse than mischievous," Mr. Lane assured her sourly. "There's a mean streak in that family."

"That's on his mother's side," Mrs. Lane hastened to add. "She was a queer girl—came from New York."

The Foote girls began again, with rich profusion of detail, their voices rising shrill, one above the other, and playing together at their full height like emulous fountains.

"We ought not to judge, you know;" urged Mrs. Williams. "What do you say he's really done?"

Being sifted, it appeared that this last and most terrible performance was to go to "the city" with a group of "the worst boys of college," to get undeniably drunk, to do some piece of mischief. (Here was great licence in opinion, and in contradiction.)

"*Anyway* he's to be suspended!" said Miss Rebecca with finality.

"Suspended!" Miss Josie's voice rose in scorn. "*Expelled!* They said he was expelled."

"In disgrace!" added Miss Sallie.

Vivian Lane sat in the back room at the window, studying in the lingering light of the long June evening. At least, she appeared to be studying. Her tall figure was bent over her books, but the dark eyes blazed under their delicate level brows, and her face flushed and paled with changing feelings.

She had heard—who, in the same house, could escape hearing the Misses Foote?—and had followed the torrent of description, hearsay, surmise and allegation with an interest that was painful in its intensity.

"It's a *shame!*" she whispered under her breath. "A *shame!* And nobody to stand up for him!"

She half rose to her feet as if to do it herself, but sank back irresolutely.

A fresh wave of talk rolled forth.

"It'll half kill his aunt."

"Poor Miss Elder! I don't know what she'll do!"

"I don't know what *he'll* do. He can't go back to college."

"He'll have to go to work."

"I'd like to know where—nobody'd hire him in this town."

The girl could bear it no longer. She came to the door, and there, as they paused to speak to her, her purpose ebbed again.

"My daughter, Vivian, Mrs. Williams," said her mother; and the other callers greeted her familiarly.

"You'd better finish your lessons, Vivian," Mr. Lane suggested.

"I have, father," said the girl, and took a chair by the minister's wife. She had a vague feeling that if she were there, they would not talk so about Morton Elder.

Mrs. Williams hailed the interruption gratefully. She liked the slender girl with the thoughtful eyes and pretty, rather pathetic mouth, and sought to draw her out. But her questions soon led to unfortunate results.

"You are going to college, I suppose?" she presently inquired; and Vivian owned that it was the desire of her heart.

"Nonsense!" said her father. "Stuff and nonsense, Vivian! You're not going to college."

The Foote girls now burst forth in voluble agreement with Mr. Lane. His wife was evidently of the same mind; and Mrs. Williams plainly regretted her question. But Vivian mustered courage enough to make a stand, strengthened perhaps by the depth of the feeling which had brought her into the room.

"I don't know why you're all so down on a girl's going to college. Eve Marks has gone, and Mary Spring is going— and both the Austin girls. Everybody goes now."

"I know one girl that won't," was her father's incisive comment, and her mother said quietly, "A girl's place is at home—'till she marries."

"Suppose I don't want to marry?" said Vivian.

"Don't talk nonsense," her father answered. "Marriage is a woman's duty."

"What do you want to do?" asked Miss Josie in the interests of further combat. "Do you want to be a doctor, like Jane Bellair?"

"I should like to very much indeed," said the girl with quiet intensity. "I'd like to be a doctor in a babies' hospital."

"More nonsense," said Mr. Lane. "Don't talk to me about that woman! You attend to your studies, and then to your home duties, my dear."

The talk rose anew, the three sisters contriving all to agree with Mr. Lane in his opinions about college, marriage and Dr. Bellair, yet to disagree violently among themselves.

Mrs. Williams rose to go, and in the lull that followed the liquid note of a whippoorwill met the girl's quick ear. She quietly slipped out, unnoticed.

The Lanes' home stood near the outer edge of the town, with an outlook across wide meadows and soft wooded hills. Behind, their long garden backed on that of Miss Orella Elder, with a connecting gate in the gray board fence. Mrs. Lane had grown up here. The house belonged to her mother, Mrs. Servilla Pettigrew, though that able lady was seldom in it, preferring to make herself useful among two growing sets of grandchildren.

Miss Elder was Vivian's favorite teacher. She was a careful and conscientious instructor, and the girl was a careful and conscientious scholar; so they got on admirably together; indeed, there was a real affection between them. And just as the young Laura Pettigrew had played with the younger Orella Elder, so Vivian had played with little Susie Elder, Miss Orella's orphan niece.[6] Susie regarded the older girl with worshipful affection, which was not at all unpleasant to an emotional young creature with unemotional parents, and no brothers or sisters of her own.

Moreover, Susie was Morton's sister.

The whippoorwill's cry sounded again through the soft June night. Vivian came quickly down the garden path between the bordering beds of sweet alyssum and mignonette. A dew-wet rose brushed against her hand. She broke it off, pricking her fingers, and hastily fastened it in the bosom of her white frock.

Large old lilac bushes hung over the dividing fence, a thick mass of honeysuckle climbed up by the gate and mingled with them, spreading over to a pear tree on the Lane side. In this fragrant, hidden corner was a rough seat, and from it a boy's hand reached out and seized the girl's, drawing her down beside him. She drew away from him as far as the seat allowed.

"Oh Morton!" she said. "What have you done?"

Morton was sulky.

"Now Vivian, are you down on me too? I thought I had one friend."

"You ought to tell me," she said more gently. "How can I be your friend if I don't know the facts? They are saying perfectly awful things."

"Who are?"

"Why—the Foote girls—everybody."

"Oh those old maids aren't everybody, I assure you. You see, Vivian, you live right here in this old oyster of a town—and you make mountains out of molehills like everybody else. A girl of your intelligence ought to know better."

She drew a great breath of relief. "Then you haven't—done it?"

"Done what? What's all this mysterious talk anyhow? The prisoner has a right to know what he's charged with before he commits himself."

The girl was silent, finding it difficult to begin.

"Well, out with it. What do they say I did?" He picked up a long dry twig and broke it, gradually, into tiny, half-inch bits.

"They say you—went to the city—with a lot of the worst boys in college—"

"Well? Many persons go to the city every day. That's no crime, surely. As for 'the worst boys in college,' "—he laughed scornfully—"I suppose those old ladies think if a fellow smokes a cigarette or says 'darn' he's a tough. They're mighty nice fellows, that bunch—most of 'em. Got some ginger in 'em, that's all. What else?"

"They say—you drank."

"O ho! Said I got drunk, I warrant! Well—we did have a skate on that time, I admit!" And he laughed as if this charge were but a familiar joke.

"Why Morton Elder! I think it is a—disgrace!"

"Pshaw, Vivian!—You ought to have more sense. All the fellows get gay once in a while. A college isn't a young ladies' seminary."

He reached out and got hold of her hand again, but she drew it away.

"There was something else," she said.

"What was it?" he questioned sharply. "What did they say?"

But she would not satisfy him—perhaps could not.

"I should think you'd be ashamed, to make your aunt so much trouble. They said you were suspended—or—*expelled!*"

He shrugged his big shoulders and threw away the handful of broken twigs.

"That's true enough—I might as well admit that."

"Oh, *Morton!*—I didn't believe it. *Expelled!*"

"Yes, expelled—turned down—thrown out—fired! And I'm glad of it." He leaned back against the fence and whistled very softly through his teeth.

"Sh! Sh!" she urged. "Please!"

He was quiet.

"But Morton—what are you going to do?—Won't it spoil your career?"

"No, my dear little girl, it will not!" said he. "On the contrary, it will be the making of me. I tell you, Vivian, I'm sick to death of this town of maiden ladies—and 'good family men.' I'm sick of being fussed over for ever and ever, and having wristers and mufflers knitted for me— and being told to put on my rubbers! There's no fun in this old clamshell—this kitchen-midden of a town—and I'm going to quit it."[7]

He stood up and stretched his long arms. "I'm going to quit it for good and all."

The girl sat still, her hands gripping the seat on either side.

"Where are you going?" she asked in a low voice.

"I'm going west—clear out west. I've been talking with Aunt Rella about it. Dr. Bellair'll help me to a job, she thinks. She's awful cut up, of course. I'm sorry she feels bad—but she needn't, I tell her. I shall do better there than I ever should have here. I know a fellow that left college—his father failed—and he went into business and made two thousand dollars in a year. I always wanted to take up business—you know that!"

She knew it—he had talked of it freely before they had argued and persuaded him into the college life. She knew, too, how his aunt's hopes all centered in him, and in his academic honors and future professional life. "Business," to his aunt's mind, was a necessary evil, which could at best be undertaken only after a "liberal education."

"When are you going," she asked at length.

"Right off—to-morrow."

She gave a little gasp.

"That's what I was whippoorwilling about—I knew I'd get no other chance to talk to you—I wanted to say good-by, you know."

The girl sat silent, struggling not to cry. He dropped beside her, stole an arm about her waist, and felt her tremble.

"Now, Viva, don't you go and cry! I'm sorry—I really am sorry—to make *you* feel bad."

This was too much for her, and she sobbed frankly.

"Oh, Morton! How could you! How could you!—And now you've got to go away!"

"There now—don't cry—sh!—they'll hear you."

She did hush at that.

"And don't feel so bad—I'll come back some time—to see you."

"No, you won't!" she answered with sudden fierceness. "You'll just go—and stay—and I never shall see you again!"

He drew her closer to him. "And do you care—so much—Viva?"

"Of course, I care!" she said, "Haven't we always been friends, the best of friends?"

"Yes—you and Aunt Rella have been about all I had," he admitted with a cheerful laugh. "I hope I'll make more friends out yonder. But Viva"—his hand pressed closer—"is it only—friends?"

She took fright at once and drew away from him. "You mustn't do that, Morton!"

"Do what?" A shaft of moonlight shone on his teasing face. "What am I doing?" he said.

It is difficult—it is well nigh impossible—for a girl to put a name to certain small cuddlings not in themselves terrifying, nor even unpleasant, but which she obscurely feels to be wrong.

Viva flushed and was silent—he could see the rich color flood her face.

"Come now—don't be hard on a fellow!" he urged. "I shan't see you again in ever so long. You'll forget all about me before a year's over."

She shook her head, still silent.

"Won't you speak to me—Viva?"

"I wish—" She could not find the words she wanted. "Oh, I wish you—wouldn't!"

"Wouldn't what, Girlie? Wouldn't go away? Sorry to disoblige—but I have to. There's no place for me here."

The girl felt the sad truth of that.

"Aunt Rella will get used to it after a while. I'll write to her—I'll make lots of money—and come back in a few years—astonish you all!—Meanwhile—kiss me goodby, Viva!"

She drew back shyly. She had never kissed him. She had never in her life kissed any man younger than an uncle.

"No, Morton—you mustn't—" She shrank away into the shadow.

But, there was no great distance to shrink to, and his strong arms soon drew her close again.

"Suppose you never see me again," he said. "Then you'll wish you hadn't been so stiff about it."

She thought of this dread possibility with a sudden chill

of horror, and while she hesitated, he took her face between his hands and kissed her on the mouth.

Steps were heard coming down the path.

"They're on," he said with a little laugh. "Good-by,
Viva!"

He vaulted the fence and was gone.

"What are you doing here, Vivian?" demanded her
father.

"I was saying good-by to Morton," she answered with a
sob.

"You ought to be ashamed of yourself—philandering
out here in the middle of the night with that scapegrace!
Come in the house and go to bed at once—it's ten o'clock."

Bowing to this confused but almost equally incriminat-
ing chronology, she followed him in, meekly enough as to
her outward seeming, but inwardly in a state of stormy tumult.

She had been kissed!

Her father's stiff back before her could not blot out the
radiant, melting moonlight, the rich sweetness of the
flowers, the tender, soft, June night.

"You go to bed," said he once more. "I'm ashamed of
you."

"Yes, father," she answered.

Her little room, when at last she was safely in it and had
shut the door and put a chair against it—she had no key—
seemed somehow changed.

She lit the lamp and stood looking at herself in the mirror. Her eyes were star-bright. Her cheeks flamed softly.
Her mouth looked guilty and yet glad.

She put the light out and went to the window, kneeling
there, leaning out in the fragrant stillness, trying to arrange in her mind this mixture of grief, disapproval,
shame and triumph.

When the Episcopal church clock struck eleven, she
went to bed in guilty haste, but not to sleep.

For a long time she lay there watching the changing
play of moonlight on the floor.

She felt almost as if she were married.

2

Bainville Effects

Lockstep, handcuffs, ankle-ball-and-chain,
Dull toil and dreary food and drink;
Small cell, cold cell, narrow bed and hard;
High wall, thick wall, window iron-barred;
Stone-paved, stone-pent little prison yard—
Young hearts weary of monotony and pain,
Young hearts weary of reiterant refrain:
"They say—they do—what will people think?"

At the two front windows of their rather crowded little parlor sat Miss Rebecca and Miss Josie Foote, Miss Sallie being out on a foraging expedition—marketing, as it were, among their neighbors to collect fresh food for thought.

A tall, slender girl in brown passed on the opposite walk.

"I should think Vivian Lane would get tired of wearing brown," said Miss Rebecca.

"I don't know why she should," her sister promptly protested, "it's a good enough wearing color, and becoming to her."

"She could afford to have more variety," said Miss Rebecca. "The Lanes are mean enough about some things, but I know they'd like to have her dress better. She'll never get married in the world."

"I don't know why not. She's only twenty-five—and good-looking."

"Good-looking! That's not everything. Plenty of girls marry that are not good-looking—and plenty of good-looking girls stay single."

"Plenty of homely ones, too, Rebecca," said Miss Josie, with meaning. Miss Rebecca certainly was not handsome. "Going to the library, of course!" she pursued presently. "That girl reads all the time."

94

"So does her grandmother. I see her going and coming from that library every day almost."

"Oh, well—she reads stories and things like that. Sallie goes pretty often and she notices. We use that library enough, goodness knows, but they are there every day. Vivian Lane reads the queerest things—doctors' books and works on pedagoggy."

"Godgy," said Miss Rebecca, "not goggy."[8] And as her sister ignored this correction, she continued: "they might as well have let her go to college when she was so set on it."

"College! I don't believe she'd have learned as much in any college, from what I hear of 'em, as she has in all this time at home." The Foote girls had never entertained a high opinion of extensive culture.

"I don't see any use in a girl's studying so much," said Miss Rebecca with decision.

"Nor I," agreed Miss Josie. "Men don't like learned women."

"They don't seem to always like those that aren't learned, either," remarked Miss Rebecca with a pleasant sense of retribution for that remark about "homely ones."

The tall girl in brown had seen the two faces at the windows opposite, and had held her shoulders a little straighter as she turned the corner.

"Nine years this Summer since Morton Elder went West," murmured Miss Josie, reminiscently. "I shouldn't wonder if Vivian had stayed single on his account."

"Nonsense!" her sister answered sharply. "She's not that kind. She's not popular with men, that's all. She's too intellectual."

"She ought to be in the library instead of Sue Elder," Miss Rebecca suggested. "She's far more competent. Sue's a feather-headed little thing."

"She seems to give satisfaction so far. If the trustees are pleased with her, there's no reason for you to complain that I see," said Miss Rebecca with decision.

* * * *

Vivian Lane waited at the library desk with an armful of books to take home. She had her card, her mother's and her father's—all utilized. Her grandmother kept her own card—and her own counsel.

The pretty assistant librarian, withdrawing herself with some emphasis from the unnecessary questions of a too gallant old gentleman, came to attend her.

"You *have* got a load," she said, scribbling complex figures with one end of her hammer-headed pencil, and stamping violet dates with the other. She whisked out the pale blue slips from the lid pockets, dropped them into their proper openings in the desk and inserted the cards in their stead with delicate precision.

"Can't you wait a bit and go home with me?" she asked. "I'll help you carry them."

"No, thanks. I'm not going right home."

"You're going to see your Saint—I know!" said Miss Susie, tossing her bright head. "I'm jealous, and you know it."

"Don't be a goose, Susie! You know you're my very best friend, but—she's different."

"I should think she was different!" Susie sharply agreed. "And you've been 'different' ever since she came."

"I hope so," said Vivian gravely. "Mrs. St. Cloud brings out one's very best and highest. I wish you liked her better, Susie."

"I like you," Susie answered. "You bring out my 'best and highest'—if I've got any. She don't. She's like a lovely, faint, bright—bubble! I want to prick it!"

Vivian smiled down upon her.

"You bad little mouse!" she said. "Come, give me the books."

"Leave them with me, and I'll bring them in the car." Susie looked anxious to make amends for her bit of blasphemy.

"All right, dear. Thank you. I'll be home by that time, probably."

* * * *

In the street she stopped before a little shop where papers and magazines were sold.

"I believe Father'd like the new Centurion," she said to herself, and got it for him, chatting a little with the one-armed man who kept the place.[9] She stopped again at a small florist's and bought a little bag of bulbs.

"Your mother's forgotten about those, I guess," said Mrs. Crothers, the florist's wife, "but they'll do just as well now. Lucky you thought of them before it got too late in the season. Bennie was awfully pleased with that red and blue pencil you gave him, Miss Lane."

Vivian walked on. A child ran out suddenly from a gate and seized upon her.

"Aren't you coming in to see me—ever?" she demanded.

Vivian stooped and kissed her.

"Yes, dear, but not to-night. How's that dear baby getting on?"

"She's better," said the little girl. "Mother said thank you—lots of times. Wait a minute—"

The child fumbled in Vivian's coat pocket with a mischievous upward glance, fished out a handful of peanuts, and ran up the path laughing while the tall girl smiled down upon her lovingly.

A long-legged boy was lounging along the wet sidewalk. Vivian caught up with him and he joined her with eagerness.

"Good evening, Miss Lane. Say—are you coming to the club to-morrow night?"

She smiled cordially.

"Of course I am, Johnny. I wouldn't disappoint my boys for anything—nor myself, either."

They walked on together chatting until, at the minister's house, she bade him a cheery "good-night."

Mrs. St. Cloud was at the window pensively watching the western sky. She saw the girl coming and let her in with a tender, radiant smile—a lovely being in a most unlovely room.

There was a chill refinement above subdued confusion in that Cambridge-Bainville parlor, where the higher culture of the second Mrs. Williams, superimposed upon the lower culture of the first, as that upon the varying tastes of a combined ancestry, made the place somehow suggestive of excavations at Abydos.[10]

It was much the kind of parlor Vivian had been accustomed to from childhood, but Mrs. St. Cloud was of a type

quite new to her. Clothed in soft, clinging fabrics, always
with a misty, veiled effect to them, wearing pale amber,
large, dull stones of uncertain shapes, and slender chains
that glittered here and there among her scarfs and laces,
sinking gracefully among deep cushions, even able to sink
gracefully into a common Bainville chair—this beautiful
woman had captured the girl's imagination from the first.

Clearly known, she was a sister of Mrs. Williams, visiting indefinitely. Vaguely—and very frequently—hinted,
her husband had "left her," and "she did not believe in
divorce." Against her background of dumb patience, he
shone darkly forth as A Brute of unknown cruelties. Nothing against him would she ever say, and every young masculine heart yearned to make life brighter to the Ideal
Woman, so strangely neglected; also some older ones. Her
Young Men's Bible Class was the pride of Mr. Williams'
heart and joy of such young men as the town possessed;
most of Bainville's boys had gone.

"A wonderful uplifting influence," Mr. Williams called
her, and refused to say anything, even when directly approached, as to "the facts" of her trouble. "It is an old
story," he would say. "She bears up wonderfully. She sac-
rifices her life rather than her principles."

To Vivian, sitting now on a hassock at the lady's feet and
looking up at her with adoring eyes, she was indeed a star,
a saint, a cloud of mystery.

She reached out a soft hand, white, slender, delicately
kept, wearing one thin gold ring, and stroked the girl's
smooth hair. Vivian seized the hand and kissed it, blushing as she did so.

"You foolish child! Don't waste your young affection on
an old lady like me."

"Old! You! You don't look as old as I do this minute!"
said the girl with hushed intensity.

"Life wears on you, I'm afraid, my dear. . . . Do you ever
hear from him?"

To no one else, not even to Susie, could Vivian speak of
what now seemed the tragedy of her lost youth.

"No," said she. "Never now. He did write once or
twice—at first."

"He writes to his aunt, of course?"

"Yes," said Vivian. "But not often. And he never—says anything."

"I understand. Poor child! You must be true, and wait." And the lady turned the thin ring on her finger. Vivian watched her in a passion of admiring tenderness.

"Oh, you understand!" she exclaimed. "You understand!"

"I understand, my dear," said Mrs. St. Cloud.

When Vivian reached her own gate she leaned her arms upon it and looked first one way and then the other, down the long, still street. The country was in sight at both ends—the low, monotonous, wooded hills that shut them in. It was all familiar, wearingly familiar. She had known it continuously for such part of her lifetime as was sensitive to landscape effects, and had at times a mad wish for an earthquake to change the outlines a little.

The infrequent trolley car passed just then and Sue Elder joined her, to take the short cut home through the Lanes' yard.

"Here you are," she said cheerfully, "and here are the books."

Vivian thanked her.

"Oh, say—come in after supper, can't you? Aunt Rella's had another letter from Mort."

Vivian's sombre eyes lit up a little.

"How's he getting on? In the same business he was last year?" she asked with an elaborately cheerful air. Morton had seemed to change occupations oftener than he wrote letters.

"Yes, I believe so. I guess he's well. He never says much, you know. I don't think it's good for him out there—good for any boy." And Susie looked quite the older sister.

"What are they to do? They can't stay here."

"No, I suppose not—but we have to."

"Dr. Bellair didn't," remarked Vivian. "I like her—tremendously, don't you?" In truth, Dr. Bellair was already a close second to Mrs. St. Cloud in the girl's hero-worshipping heart.

"Oh, yes; she's splendid! Aunt Rella is so glad to have her with us. They have great times recalling their school days together. Aunty used to like her then, though she is five years older—but you'd never dream it. And I think she's real handsome."

"She's not beautiful," said Vivian, with decision, "but she's a lot better. Sue Elder, I wish—"

"Wish what?" asked her friend.

Sue put the books on the gate-post, and the two girls, arm in arm, walked slowly up and down.

Susie was a round, palely rosy little person, with a delicate face and soft, light hair waving fluffily about her small head. Vivian's hair was twice the length, but so straight and fine that its mass had no effect. She wore it in smooth plaits wound like a wreath from brow to nape.

After an understanding silence and a walk past three gates and back again, Vivian answered her.

"I wish I were in your shoes," she said.

"What do you mean—having the Doctor in the house?"

"No—I'd like that too; but I mean work to do—your position."

"Oh, the library! You needn't; it's horrid. I wish I were in your shoes, and had a father and mother to take care of me. I can tell you, it's no fun—having to be there just on time or get fined, and having to poke away all day with those phooty old ladies and tiresome children."

"But you're independent."

"Oh, yes, I'm independent. I have to be. Aunt Rella *could* take care of me, I suppose, but of course I wouldn't let her. And I dare say library work is better than school-teaching."

"What'll we be doing when we're forty, I wonder?" said Vivian, after another turn.

"Forty! Why I expect to be a grandma by that time," said Sue. She was but twenty-one, and forty looked a long way off to her.

"A grandma! And knit?" suggested Vivian.

"Oh, yes—baby jackets—and blankets—and socks—and little shawls. I love to knit," said Sue, cheerfully.

"But suppose you don't marry?" pursued her friend.

"Oh, but I shall marry—you see if I don't. Marriage"— here she carefully went inside the gate and latched it— "marriage is—a woman's duty!" And she ran up the path laughing.

Vivian laughed too, rather grimly, and slowly walked towards her own door.

The little sitting-room was hot, very hot; but Mr. Lane sat with his carpet-slippered feet on its narrow hearth with a shawl around him.

"Shut the door, Vivian!" he exclaimed irritably. "I'll never get over this cold if such draughts are let in on me."

"Why, it's not cold out, Father—and it's very close in here."

Mrs. Lane looked up from her darning. "You think it's close because you've come in from outdoors. Sit down—and don't fret your father; I'm real worried about him."

Mr. Lane coughed hollowly. He had become a little dry old man with gray, glassy eyes, and had been having colds in this fashion ever since Vivian could remember.

"Dr. Bellair says that the out-door air is the best medicine for a cold," remarked Vivian, as she took off her things.

"Dr. Bellair has not been consulted in this case," her father returned wheezingly. "I'm quite satisfied with my family physician. He's a man, at any rate."

"Save me from these women doctors!" exclaimed his wife.

Vivian set her lips patiently. She had long since learned how widely she differed from both father and mother, and preferred silence to dispute.

Mr. Lane was a plain, ordinary person, who spent most of a moderately useful life in the shoe business, from which he had of late withdrawn. Both he and his wife "had property" to a certain extent; and now lived peacefully on their income with neither fear nor hope, ambition nor responsibility to trouble them. The one thing they were yet anxious about was to see Vivian married, but this wish seemed to be no nearer to fulfillment for the passing years.

"I don't know what the women are thinking of, these days," went on the old gentleman, putting another shovelful of coal on the fire with a careful hand. "Doctors and lawyers and even ministers, some of 'em! The Lord certainly set down a woman's duty pretty plain—she was to cleave unto her husband!"

"Some women have no husbands to cleave to, Father."

"They'd have husbands fast enough if they'd behave themselves," he answered. "No man's going to want to marry one of these self-sufficient independent, professional women, of course."

"I do hope, Viva," said her mother, "that you're not letting that Dr. Bellair put foolish ideas into your head."

"I want to do something to support myself—sometime, Mother. I can't live on my parents forever."

"You be patient, child. There's money enough for you to live on. It's a woman's place to wait," put in Mr. Lane.

"How long?" inquired Vivian. "I'm twenty-five. No man has asked me to marry him yet. Some of the women in this town have waited thirty—forty—fifty—sixty years. No one has asked them."

"I was married at sixteen," suddenly remarked Vivian's grandmother. "And my mother wasn't but fifteen. Huh!" A sudden little derisive noise she made; such as used to be written "humph!"

For the past five years, Mrs. Pettigrew had made her home with the Lanes. Mrs. Lane herself was but a feeble replica of her energetic parent. There was but seventeen years difference in their ages, and comparative idleness with some ill-health on the part of the daughter, had made the difference appear less.

Mrs. Pettigrew had but a poor opinion of the present generation. In her active youth she had reared a large family on a small income; in her active middle-age, she had trotted about from daughter's house to son's house, helping with the grandchildren. And now she still trotted about in all weathers, visiting among the neighbors and vibrating as regularly as a pendulum between her daughter's house and the public library.

The books she brought home were mainly novels, and if she perused anything else in the severe quiet of the reading-room, she did not talk about it. Indeed, it was a striking characteristic of Mrs. Pettigrew that she talked very little, though she listened to all that went on with a bright and beady eye, as of a highly intelligent parrot. And now, having dropped her single remark into the conversation, she shut her lips tight as was her habit, and drew another ball of worsted from the black bag that always hung at her elbow.[11]

She was making one of those perennial knitted garments, which, in her young days, were called "Cardigan jackets," later "Jerseys," and now by the offensive name of "sweater." These she constructed in great numbers, and their probable expense was a source of discussion in the town. "How do you find friends enough to give them to?" they asked her, and she would smile enigmatically and reply, "Good presents make good friends."

"If a woman minds her P's and Q's she can get a husband easy enough," insisted the invalid. "Just shove that lamp nearer, Vivian, will you."

Vivian moved the lamp. Her mother moved her chair to follow it and dropped her darning egg, which the girl handed to her.[12]

"Supper's ready," announced a hard-featured middle-aged woman, opening the dining-room door.

At this moment the gate clicked, and a firm step was heard coming up the path.

"Gracious, that's the minister!" cried Mrs. Lane. "He said he'd be in this afternoon if he got time. I thought likely 'twould be to supper."

She received him cordially, and insisted on his staying, slipping out presently to open a jar of quinces.[13]

The Reverend Otis Williams was by no means loathe to take occasional meals with his parishioners. It was noted that, in making pastoral calls, he began with the poorer members of his flock, and frequently arrived about meal-time at the houses of those whose cooking he approved.

"It is always a treat to take supper here," he said. "Not feeling well, Mr. Lane? I'm sorry to hear it. Ah! Mrs. Pettigrew! Is that jacket for me, by any chance? A little sombre, isn't it? Good evening, Vivian. You are looking well—as you always do."

Vivian did not like him. He had married her mother, he had christened her, she had "sat under" him for long, dull, uninterrupted years; yet still she didn't like him.

"A chilly evening, Mr. Lane," he pursued.

"That's what I say," his host agreed. "Vivian says it isn't; I say it is."

"Disagreement in the family! This won't do, Vivian," said the minister jocosely. "Duty to parents, you know! Duty to parents!"

"Does duty to parents alter the temperature?" the girl asked, in a voice of quiet sweetness, yet with a rebellious spark in her soft eyes.

"Huh!" said her grandmother—and dropped her gray ball. Vivian picked it up and the old lady surreptitiously patted her.

"Pardon me," said the reverend gentleman to Mrs. Pettigrew, "did you speak?"

"No," said the old lady, "Seldom do."

"Silence is golden, Mrs. Pettigrew. Silence is golden. Speech is silver, but silence is golden. It is a rare gift."

Mrs. Pettigrew set her lips so tightly that they quite disappeared, leaving only a thin dented line in her smoothly pale face. She was called by the neighbors "wonderfully well preserved," a phrase she herself despised. Some visitor, new to the town, had the hardihood to use it to her face once. "Huh!" was the response. "I'm just sixty. Henry Haskins and George Baker and Stephen Doolittle are all older'n I am—and still doing business, doing it better'n any of the young folks as far as I can see. You don't compare them to canned pears, do you?"

Mr. Williams knew her value in church work, and took no umbrage at her somewhat inimical expression; particularly as just then Mrs. Lane appeared and asked them to walk out to supper.

Vivian sat among them, restrained and courteous, but inwardly at war with her surroundings. Here was her mother, busy, responsible, serving creamed codfish and hot biscuit; her father, eating wheezily, and finding fault with the biscuit, also with the codfish; her grandmother, bright-eyed, thin-lipped and silent. Vivian got on well with her grandmother, though neither of them talked much.

"My mother used to say that the perfect supper was cake, preserves, hot bread, and a 'relish,' " said Mr. Williams genially. "You have the perfect supper, Mrs. Lane."

"I'm glad if you enjoy it, I'm sure," said that lady. "I'm fond of a bit of salt myself."

"And what are you reading now, Vivian," he asked paternally.

"Ward," she answered, modestly and briefly.

"Ward? Dr. Ward of the *Centurion?*"

Vivian smiled her gentlest.

"Oh, no," she replied; "Lester F. Ward, the Sociologist."[14]

"Poor stuff, I think!" said her father. "Girls have no business to read such things."

"I wish you'd speak to Vivian about it, Mr. Williams. She's got beyond me," protested her mother.

"Huh!" said Mrs. Pettigrew. "I'd like some more of that quince, Laura."

"My dear young lady, you are not reading books of which your parents disapprove, I hope?" urged the minister.

"Shouldn't I—ever?" asked the girl, in her soft, disarming manner. "I'm surely old enough!"

"The duty of a daughter is not measured by years," he replied sonorously. "Does parental duty cease? Are you not yet a child in your father's house?"

"Is a daughter always a child if she lives at home?" inquired the girl, as one seeking instruction.

He set down his cup and wiped his lips, flushing somewhat.

"The duty of a daughter begins at the age when she can understand the distinction between right and wrong," he said, "and continues as long as she is blessed with parents."

"And what is it?" she asked, large-eyed, attentive.

"What is it?" he repeated, looking at her in some surprise. "It is submission, obedience—obedience."

"I see. So Mother ought to obey Grandmother," she pursued meditatively, and Mrs. Pettigrew nearly choked in her tea.

Vivian was boiling with rebellion. To sit there and be lectured at the table, to have her father complain of her, her mother invite pastoral interference, the minister preach like that. She slapped her grandmother's shoulder, readjusted the little knit shawl on the straight back— and refrained from further speech.

When Mrs. Pettigrew could talk, she demanded suddenly of the minister, "Have you read Campbell's New
Theology?" and from that on they were all occupied in listening to Mr. Williams' strong, clear and extensive views
on the subject—which lasted into the parlor again.[15]

Vivian sat for awhile in the chair nearest the window,
where some thin thread of air might possibly leak in, and
watched the minister with a curious expression. All her
life he had been held up to her as a person to honor, as a
man of irreproachable character, great learning and wisdom. Of late she found a sense of surprise that she did not
honor him at all. He seemed to her suddenly like a relic
of past ages, a piece of an old parchment—or papyrus. In
the light of the studies she had been pursuing in the well-
stored town library, the teachings of this worthy old gentleman appeared a jumble of age-old traditions, superimposed one upon another.

"He's a palimpsest," she said to herself, "and a poor palimpsest at that."[16]

"She sat with her shapely hands quiet in her lap while
her grandmother's shining needles twinkled in the dark
wool, and her mother's slim crochet hook ran along the
widening spaces of some thin, white, fuzzy thing. The rich
powers of her young womanhood longed for occupation,
but she could never hypnotize herself with "fancy-work."
Her work must be worth while. She felt the crushing
cramp and loneliness of a young mind, really stronger
than those about her, yet held in dumb subjection. She
could not solace herself by loving them; her father would
have none of it, and her mother had small use for what she
called "sentiment." All her life Vivian had longed for
more loving, both to give and take; but no one ever imagined it of her, she was so quiet and repressed in manner.
The local opinion was that if a woman had a head, she
could not have a heart; and as to having a body—it was in-
delicate to consider such a thing.

"I mean to have six children," Vivian had planned
when she was younger. "And they shall never be hungry
for more loving." She meant to make up to her vaguely
imagined future family for all that her own youth missed.

Even Grandma, though far more sympathetic in temperament, was not given to demonstration, and Vivian solaced her big, tender heart by cuddling all the babies she could reach, and petting cats and dogs when no children were to be found.

Presently she arose and bade a courteous goodnight to the still prolix parson.

"I'm going over to Sue's," she said, and went out.

* * * *

There was a moon again—a low, large moon, hazily brilliant. The air was sweet with the odors of scarce-gone Summer, of coming Autumn.

The girl stood still, half-way down the path, and looked steadily into that silver radiance. Moonlight always filled her heart with a vague excitement, a feeling that something ought to happen—soon.

This flat, narrow life, so long, so endlessly long—would nothing ever end it? Nine years since Morton went away! Nine years since the strange, invading thrill of her first kiss! Back of that was only childhood; these years really constituted Life; and Life, in the girl's eyes, was a dreary treadmill.

She was externally quiet, and by conscience dutiful; so dutiful, so quiet, so without powers of expression, that the ache of an unsatisfied heart, the stir of young ambitions, were wholly unsuspected by those about her. A studious, earnest, thoughtful girl—but study alone does not supply life's needs, nor does such friendship as her life afforded.

Susie was "a dear"—Susie was Morton's sister, and she was very fond of her. But that bright-haired child did not understand—could not understand—all that she needed.

Then came Mrs. St. Cloud into her life, stirring the depths of romance, of the buried past, and of the unborn future. From her she learned to face a life of utter renunciation, to be true, true to her ideals, true to her principles, true to the past, to be patient; and to wait.

So strengthened, she had turned a deaf ear to such possible voice of admiration as might have come from the scant membership of the Young Men's Bible Class, leaving them the more devoted to Scripture study. There was no thin ring to turn upon her finger; but, for lack of better token, she had saved the rose she wore upon her breast that night, keeping it hidden among her precious things.

And then, into the gray, flat current of her daily life, sharply across the trend of Mrs. St. Cloud's soft influence, had come a new force—Dr. Bellair.

Vivian liked her, yet felt afraid, a slight, shivering hesitancy as before a too cold bath, a subtle sense that this breezy woman, strong, cheerful, full of new ideas, if not ideals, and radiating actual power, power used and enjoyed, might in some way change the movement of her life.

Change she desired, she longed for, but dreaded the unknown.

Slowly she followed the long garden path, paused lingeringly by that rough garden seat, went through and closed the gate.

3

The Outbreak

There comes a time
After white months of ice—
Slow months of ice—long months of ice—
There comes a time when the still floods below
Rise, lift, and overflow—
Fast, far they go.

Miss Orella sat in her low armless rocker, lifting perplexed, patient eyes to look up at Dr. Bellair.

Dr. Bellair stood squarely before her, stood easily, on broad-soled, low-heeled shoes, and looked down at Miss Orella; her eyes were earnest, compelling, full of hope and cheer.

"You are as pretty as a girl, Orella," she observed irrelevantly.

Miss Orella blushed. She was not used to compliments, even from a woman, and did not know how to take them.

"How you talk!" she murmured shyly.

"I mean to talk," continued the doctor, "until you listen to reason."

Reason in this case, to Dr. Bellair's mind, lay in her advice to Miss Elder to come West with her—to live.

"I don't see how I can. It's—it's such a Complete Change."

Miss Orella spoke as if Change were equivalent to Sin, or at least to Danger.

"Do you good. As a physician, I can prescribe nothing better. You need a complete change if anybody ever did."

"Why, Jane! I am quite well."

"I didn't say you were sick. But you are in an advanced stage of *arthritis deformans* of the soul.[17] The whole town's got it!"

109

The doctor tramped up and down the little room, freeing her mind.

"I never saw such bed-ridden intellects in my life! I suppose it was so when I was a child—and I was too young to notice it. But surely it's worse now. The world goes faster and faster every day, the people who keep still get farther behind! I'm fond of you, Rella. You've got an intellect, and a conscience, and a will—a will like iron. But you spend most of your strength in keeping yourself down. Now, do wake up and use it to break loose! You don't have to stay here. Come out to Colorado with me—and Grow."

Miss Elder moved uneasily in her chair. She laid her small embroidery hoop on the table, and straightened out the loose threads of silk, the doctor watching her impatiently.

"I'm too old," she said at length.

Jane Bellair laughed aloud, shortly.

"Old!" she cried. "You're five years younger than I am. You're only thirty-six! Old! Why, child, your life's before you—to make."

"You don't realize, Jane. You struck out for yourself so young—and you've grown up out there—it seems to be so different—there."

"It is. People aren't afraid to move. What have you got here you so hate to leave, Rella?"

"Why, it's—Home."

"Yes. It's home—now. Are you happy in it?"

"I'm—contented."

"Don't you deceive yourself, Rella. You are not contented—not by a long chalk. You are doing your duty as you see it; and you've kept yourself down so long you've almost lost the power of motion. I'm trying to galvanize you awake—and I mean to do it."

"You might as well sit down while you're doing it, anyway," Miss Elder suggested meekly.

Dr. Bellair sat down, selecting a formidable fiddle-backed chair, the unflinching determination of its widely-placed feet being repeated by her own square toes. She placed herself in front of her friend and leaned forward, elbows on knees, her strong, intelligent hands clasped loosely.

"What have you got to look forward to, Rella?"

"I want to see Susie happily married—"

"I said *you*—not Susie."

"Oh—me? Why, I hope some day Morton will come back—"

"I said *you*—not Morton."

"Why I—you know I have friends, Jane—and neighbors. And some day, perhaps—I mean to go abroad."

"Are you scolding Aunt Rella again, Dr. Bellair? I won't stand it." Pretty Susie stood in the door smiling.

"Come and help me then," the doctor said, "and it won't sound so much like scolding."

"I want Mort's letter—to show to Viva," the girl answered, and slipped out with it.

She sat with Vivian on the stiff little sofa in the back room; the arms of the two girls were around one another, and they read the letter together. More than six months had passed since his last one.

It was not much of a letter. Vivian took it in her own hands and went through it again, carefully. The "Remember me to Viva—unless she's married," at the end did not seem at all satisfying. Still it might mean more than appeared—far more. Men were reticent and proud, she had read. It was perfectly possible that he might be concealing deep emotion under the open friendliness. He was in no condition to speak freely, to come back and claim her. He did not wish her to feel bound to him. She had discussed it with Mrs. St. Cloud, shrinkingly, tenderly, led on by tactful, delicate questions, by the longing of her longing heart for expression and sympathy.

"A man who cannot marry must [not] speak of marriage—it is not honorable," her friend had told her.

"Couldn't he—write to me—as a friend?"

And the low-voiced lady had explained with a little sigh that men thought little of friendship with women. "I have tried, all my life, to be a true and helpful friend to men, to such men as seemed worthy, and they so often—misunderstood."

The girl, sympathetic and admiring, thought hotly of how other people misunderstood this noble, lovely soul;

how they even hinted that she "tried to attract men," a deadly charge in Bainville.

"No," Mrs. St. Cloud had told her, "he might love you better than all the world—yet not write to you—till he was ready to say 'come.' And, of course, he wouldn't say anything in his letters to his aunt."

So Vivian sat there, silent, weaving frail dreams out of "remember me to Viva—unless she's married." That last clause might mean much.

Dr. Bellair's voice sounded clear and insistent in the next room.

"She's trying to persuade Aunt Rella to go West!" said Susie. "Wouldn't it be funny if she did!"

In Susie's eyes her aunt's age was as the age of mountains, and also her fixity. Since she could remember, Aunt Rella, always palely pretty and neat, like the delicate, faintly-colored Spring flowers of New England, had presided over the small white house, the small green garden and the large black and white school-room. In her vacation she sewed, keeping that quiet wardrobe of hers in exquisite order—and also making Susie's pretty dresses. To think of Aunt Orella actually "breaking up housekeeping," giving up her school, leaving Bainville, was like a vision of trees walking.

To Dr. Jane Bellair, forty-one, vigorous, successful, full of new plans and purposes, Miss Elder's life appeared as an arrested girlhood, stagnating unnecessarily in this quiet town, while all the world was open to her.

"I couldn't think of leaving Susie!" protested Miss Orella.

"Bring her along," said the doctor. "Best thing in the world for her!"

She rose and came to the door. The two girls made a pretty picture. Vivian's oval face, with its smooth Madonna curves under the encircling wreath of soft, dark plaits, and the long grace of her figure, delicately built, yet strong, beside the pink, plump little Susie, roguish and pretty, with the look that made everyone want to take care of her.

"Come in here, girls," said the doctor. "I want you to help me. You're young enough to be movable, I hope."

They cheerfully joined the controversy, but Miss Orella found small support in them.

"Why don't you do it, Auntie!" Susie thought it an excellent joke. "I suppose you could teach school in Denver as well as here. And you could Vote! Oh, Auntie—to think of your Voting!"[18]

Miss Elder, too modestly feminine, too inherently conservative even to be an outspoken "Anti," fairly blushed at the idea.

"She's hesitating on your account," Dr. Bellair explained to the girl. "Wants to see you safely married! I tell her you'll have a thousandfold better opportunities in Colorado than you ever will here."[19]

Vivian was grieved. She had heard enough of this getting married, and had expected Dr. Bellair to hold a different position.

"Surely, that's not the only thing to do," she protested.

"No, but it's a very important thing to do—and to do right. It's a woman's duty."

Vivian groaned in spirit. That again!

The doctor watched her understandingly.

"If women only did their duty in that line there wouldn't be so much unhappiness in the world," she said. "All you New England girls sit here and cut one another's throats. You can't possibly marry, your boys go West, you overcrowd the labor market, lower wages, steadily drive the weakest sisters down till they—drop."

They heard the back door latch lift and close again, a quick, decided step—and Mrs. Pettigrew joined them.

Miss Elder greeted her cordially, and the old lady seated herself in the halo of the big lamp, as one well accustomed to the chair.

"Go right on," she said—and knitted briskly.

"Do take my side, Mrs. Pettigrew," Miss Orella implored her. "Jane Bellair is trying to pull me up by the roots and transplant me to Colorado."

"And she says I shall have a better chance to marry out there—and ought to do it!" said Susie, very solemnly. "And Vivian objects to being shown the path of duty."

Vivian smiled. Her quiet, rather sad face lit with sudden sparkling beauty when she smiled.

"Grandma knows I hate that—point of view," she said. "I think men and women ought to be friends, and not always be thinking about—that."

"I have some real good friends—boys, I mean" Susie agreed, looking so serious in her platonic boast that even Vivian was a little amused, and Dr. Bellair laughed outright.

"You won't have a 'friend' in that sense till you're fifty, Miss Susan—if you ever do. There can be, there are, real friendships between men and women, but most of that talk is—talk, sometimes worse.

"I knew a woman once, ever so long ago," the doctor continued musingly, clasping her hands behind her head, "a long way from here—in a college town—who talked about 'friends.' She was married. She was a 'good' woman—perfectly 'good' woman. Her husband was not a very good man, I've heard, and strangely impatient of her virtues. She had a string of boys—college boys—always at her heels. Quite too young and too charming she was for this friendship game. She said that such a friendship was 'an ennobling influence' for the boys. She called them her 'acolytes.' Lots of them were fairly mad about her—one young chap was so desperate over it that he shot himself."

There was a pained silence.

"I don't see what this has to do with going to Colorado," said Mrs. Pettigrew, looking from one to the other with a keen, observing eye. "What's your plan, Dr. Bellair?"

"Why, I'm trying to persuade my old friend here to leave this place, change her occupation, come out to Colorado with me, and grow up. She's a case of arrested development."[20]

"She wants me to keep boarders!" Miss Elder plaintively protested to Mrs. Pettigrew.

That lady was not impressed.

"It's quite a different matter out there, Mrs. Pettigrew," the doctor explained. " 'Keeping boarders' in this country goes to the tune of 'Come Ye Disconsolate!' It's a doubtful refuge for women who are widows or would be better off if they were. Where I live it's a sure thing if well managed—it's a good business."

Mrs. Pettigrew wore an unconvinced aspect.

"What do you call 'a good business?' " she asked.

"The house I have in mind cleared a thousand a year when it was in right hands. That's not bad, over and above one's board and lodging. That house is in the market now. I've just had a letter from a friend about it. Orella could go out with me, and step right into Mrs. Annerly's shoes—she's just giving up."

"What'd she give up for?" Mrs. Pettigrew inquired suspiciously.

"Oh—she got married; they all do. There are three men to one woman in that town, you see."

"I didn't know there was such a place in the world—unless it was a man-of-war," remarked Susie, looking much interested.

Dr. Bellair went on more quietly.

"It's not even a risk, Mrs. Pettigrew. Rella has a cousin who would gladly run this house for her. She's admitted that much. So there's no loss here, and she's got her home to come back to. I can write to Dick Hale to nail the proposition at once. She can go when I go, in about a fortnight, and I'll guarantee the first year definitely."

"I wouldn't think of letting you do that, Jane! And if it's as good as you say, there's no need. But a fortnight! To leave home—in a fortnight!"

"What are the difficulties?" the old lady inquired. "There are always some difficulties."

"You are right, there," agreed the doctor. "The difficulties in this place are servants. But just now there's a special chance in that line. Dick says the best cook in town is going begging. I'll read you his letter."

She produced it, promptly, from the breast pocket of her neat coat. Dr. Bellair wore rather short, tailored skirts of first-class material; natty, starched blouses—silk ones for "dress," and perfectly fitting light coats. Their color and texture might vary with the season, but their pockets, never.[21]

" 'My dear Jane' (This is my best friend out there—a doctor, too. We were in the same class, both college and medical school. We fight—he's a misogynist of the worst type—but we're good friends all the same.) 'Why don't you come back? My boys are lonesome without you, and I am overworked—you left so many mishandled invalids for me to struggle with. Your boarding house is going to the dogs. Mrs. Annerly got worse and worse, failed completely and has cleared out, with a species of husband, I believe. The owner has put in a sort of caretaker, and the roomers get board outside—it's better than what they were having. Moreover, the best cook in town is hunting a job. Wire me and I'll nail her. You know the place pays well. Now, why don't you give up your unnatural attempt to be a doctor and assume woman's proper sphere? Come back and keep house!'

"He's a great tease, but he tells the truth. The house is there, crying to be kept. The boarders are there—unfed. Now, Orella Elder, why don't you wake up and seize the opportunity?"

Miss Orella was thinking.

"Where's that last letter of Morton's?"

Susie looked for it. Vivian handed it to her, and Miss Elder read it once more.

"There's plenty of homeless boys out there besides yours, Orella," the doctor assured her. "Come on—and bring both these girls with you. It's a chance for any girl, Miss Lane."

But her friend did not hear her. She found what she was looking for in the letter and read it aloud. "I'm on the road again now, likely to be doing Colorado most of the year if things go right. It's a fine country."

Susie hopped up with a little cry.

"Just the thing, Aunt Rella! Let's go out and surprise Mort. He thinks we are just built into the ground here. Won't it be fun, Viva?"

Vivian had risen from her seat and stood at the window, gazing out with unseeing eyes at the shadowy little front yard. Morton might be there. She might see him. But—was it womanly to go there—for that? There were other reasons, surely. She had longed for freedom, for a chance to grow, to do something in life—something great and beautiful! Perhaps this was the opening of the gate, the opportunity of a lifetime.

"You folks are so strong on duty," the doctor was saying, "Why can't you see a real duty in this? I tell you, the place is full of men that need mothering, and sistering—good honest sweethearting and marrying, too. Come on, Rella. Do bigger work than you've ever done yet—and, as I said, bring both these nice girls with you. What do you say, Miss Lane?"

Vivian turned to her, her fine face flushed with hope, yet with a small Greek fret on the broad forehead.[22]

"I'd like to, very much, Dr. Bellair—on some accounts. But—" She could not quite voice her dim objections, her obscure withdrawals; and so fell back on the excuse of childhood—"I'm sure Mother wouldn't let me."

Dr. Bellair smiled broadly.

"Aren't you over twenty-one?" she asked.

"I'm twenty-five," the girl replied, with proud acceptance of a life long done—as one who owned to ninety-seven.

"And self-supporting?" pursued the doctor.

Vivian flushed.

"No—not yet," she answered; "but I mean to be."

"Exactly! Now's your chance. Break away now, my dear, and come West. You can get work—start a kindergarten, or something. I know you love children."

The girl's heart rose within her in a great throb of hope.

"Oh—if I *could!*" she exclaimed, and even as she said it, rose half-conscious memories of the low, sweet tones of Mrs. St. Cloud. "It is a woman's place to wait—and to endure."

She heard a step on the walk outside—looked out.

"Why, here is Mrs. St. Cloud!" she cried.

"Guess I'll clear out," said the doctor, as Susie ran to the door. She was shy, socially.

"Nonsense, Jane," said her hostess, whispering. "Mrs. St. Cloud is no stranger. She's Mrs. Williams' sister—been here for years."

She came in at the word, her head and shoulders wreathed in a pearl gray shining veil, her soft long robe held up.

"I saw your light, Miss Elder, and thought I'd stop in for a moment. Good evening, Mrs. Pettigrew—and Miss Susie. Ah! Vivian!"

"This is my friend, Dr. Bellair—Mrs. St. Cloud," Miss

Elder was saying. But Dr. Bellair bowed a little stiffly, not coming forward.

"I've met Mrs. St. Cloud before, I think—when she was 'Mrs. James.' "

The lady's face grew sad.

"Ah, you knew my first husband! I lost him—many years ago—typhoid fever."

"I think I heard," said the doctor. And then, feeling that some expression of sympathy was called for, she added, "Too bad."

Not all Miss Elder's gentle hospitality, Mrs. Pettigrew's bright-eyed interest, Susie's efforts at polite attention, and Vivian's visible sympathy could compensate Mrs. St. Cloud for one inimical presence.

"You must have been a mere girl in those days," she said sweetly. "What a lovely little town it was—under the big trees."

"It certainly was," the doctor answered dryly.

"There is such a fine atmosphere in a college town, I think," pursued the lady. "Especially in a co-educational town—don't you think so?"

Vivian was a little surprised. She had had an idea that her admired friend did not approve of co-education. She must have been mistaken.

"Such a world of old memories as you call up, Dr. Bellair," their visitor pursued. "Those quiet, fruitful days! You remember Dr. Black's lectures? Of course you do, better than I. What a fine man he was! And the beautiful music club we had one Winter—and my little private dancing class—do you remember that? Such nice boys, Miss Elder! I used to call them my acolytes."

Susie gave a little gulp, and coughed to cover it.

"I guess you'll have to excuse me, ladies," said Dr. Bellair. "Good-night." And she walked upstairs.

Vivian's face flushed and paled and flushed again. A cold pain was trying to enter her heart, and she was trying to keep it out. Her grandmother glanced sharply from one face to the other.

"Glad to've met you, Mrs. St. Cloud," she said, bobbing up with decision. "Good-night, Rella—and Susie. Come on, child. It's a wonder your mother hasn't sent after us."

For once Vivian was glad to go.

"That's a good scheme of Jane Bellair's, don't you think so?" asked the old lady as they shut the gate behind them.

"I—why yes—I don't see why not."

Vivian was still dizzy with the blow to her heart's idol. All the soft, still dream-world she had so labored to keep pure and beautiful seemed to shake and waver swimmingly. She could not return to it. The flat white face of her home loomed before her, square, hard, hideously unsympathetic—

"Grandma," said she, stopping that lady suddenly and laying a pleading hand on her arm, "Grandma, I believe I'll go."

Mrs. Pettigrew nodded decisively.

"I thought you would," she said.

"Do you blame me, Grandma?"

"Not a mite, child. Not a mite. But I'd sleep on it, if I were you."

And Vivian slept on it—so far as she slept at all.

4

Transplanted

Sometimes a plant in its own habitat
  Is overcrowded, starved, oppressed and daunted;
A palely feeble thing; yet rises quickly,
  Growing in height and vigor, blooming thickly,
    When far transplanted.

The days between Vivian's decision and her departure were harder than she had foreseen. It took some courage to make the choice. Had she been alone, independent, quite free to change, the move would have been difficult enough; but to make her plan and hold to it in the face of a disapproving town, and the definite opposition of her parents, was a heavy undertaking.

By habit she would have turned to Mrs. St. Cloud for advice; but between her and that lady now rose the vague image of a young boy, dead,—she could never feel the same to her again.

Dr. Bellair proved a tower of strength. "My dear girl," she would say to her, patiently, but with repressed intensity, "do remember that you are *not* a child! You are twenty-five years old. You are a grown woman, and have as much right to decide for yourself as a grown man. This isn't wicked—it is a wise move; a practical one. Do you want to grow up like the rest of the useless single women in this social cemetery?"

Her mother took it very hard. "I don't see how you can think of leaving us. We're getting old now—and here's Grandma to take care of—"

"Huh!" said that lady, with such marked emphasis that Mrs. Lane hastily changed the phrase to "I mean to be *with*—you do like to have Vivian with you, you can't deny that, Mother."

"But Mama," said the girl, "you are not old; you are only forty-three. I am sorry to leave you—I am really; but it isn't forever! I can come back. And you don't really need me. Sarah runs the house exactly as you like; you don't depend on me for a thing, and never did. As to Grandma!"— and she looked affectionately at the old lady—"she don't need me nor anybody else. She's independent if ever anybody was. She won't miss me a mite—will you Grandma?" Mrs. Pettigrew looked at her for a moment, the corners of her mouth tucked in tightly. "No," she said, "I shan't miss you a mite!"

Vivian was a little grieved at the prompt acquiescence. She felt nearer to her grandmother in many ways than to either parent. "Well, I'll miss you!" said she, going to her and kissing her smooth pale cheek, "I'll miss you awfully!"

Mr. Lane expressed his disapproval most thoroughly, and more than once; then retired into gloomy silence, alternated with violent dissuasion; but since a woman of twenty-five is certainly free to choose her way of life, and there was no real objection to this change, except that it *was* a change, and therefore dreaded, his opposition, though unpleasant, was not prohibitive. Vivian's independent fortune of $87.50, the savings of many years, made the step possible, even without his assistance.

There were two weeks of exceeding disagreeableness in the household, but Vivian kept her temper and her determination under a rain of tears, a hail of criticism, and heavy wind of argument and exhortation. All her friends and neighbors, and many who were neither, joined in the effort to dissuade her; but she stood firm as the martyrs of old.

Heredity plays strange tricks with us. Somewhere under the girl's dumb gentleness and patience lay a store of quiet strength from some Pilgrim Father or Mother. Never before had she set her will against her parents; conscience had always told her to submit. Now conscience told her to rebel, and she did. She made her personal arrangements, said goodbye to her friends, declined to discuss with anyone, was sweet and quiet and kind at home, and finally appeared at the appointed hour on the platform of the little station.

Numbers of curious neighbors were there to see them off, all who knew them and could spare the time seemed to be on hand. Vivian's mother came, but her father did not.

At the last moment, just as the train drew in, Grandma appeared, serene and brisk, descending, with an impressive amount of hand baggage, from "the hack."[23]

"Goodbye, Laura," she said. "I think these girls need a chaperon. I'm going too."

So blasting was the astonishment caused by this proclamation, and so short a time remained to express it, that they presently found themselves gliding off in the big Pullman, all staring at one another in silent amazement.[24]

"I hate discussion," said Mrs. Pettigrew.

* * * *

None of these ladies was used to traveling, save Dr. Bellair, who had made the cross continent trip often enough to think nothing of it.

The unaccustomed travelers found much excitement in the journey. As women, embarking on a new, and, in the eyes of their friends, highly doubtful enterprise, they had emotion to spare; and to be confronted at the outset by a totally unexpected grandmother was too much for immediate comprehension.

She looked from one to the other, sparkling, triumphant.

"I made up my mind, same as you did, hearing Jane Bellair talk," she explained. "Sounded like good sense. I always wanted to travel, always, and never had the opportunity. This was a real good chance." Her mouth shut, tightened, widened, drew into a crinkly delighted smile.

They sat still staring at her.

"You needn't look at me like that! I guess it's a free country! I bought my ticket—sent for it same as you did. And I didn't have to ask *anybody*—I'm no daughter. My duty, as far as I know it, is *done!* This is a pleasure trip!"

She was triumph incarnate.

"And you never said a word!" This from Vivian.

"Not a word. Saved lots of trouble. Take care of me indeed! Laura needn't think I'm dependent on her *yet!*"

Vivian's heart rather yearned over her mother, thus doubly bereft.

"The truth is," her grandmother went on, "Samuel wants to go to Florida the worst way; I heard 'em talking about it! He wasn't willing to go alone—not he! Wants somebody to hear him cough, *I* say! And Laura couldn't go—'Mother was so dependent'—*Huh!*"

Vivian began to smile. She knew this had been talked over, and given up on that account. She herself could have been easily disposed of, but Mrs. Lane chose to think her mother a lifelong charge.

"Act as if I was ninety!" the old lady burst forth again. "I'll show 'em!"

"I think you're dead right, Mrs. Pettigrew," said Dr. Bellair. "Sixty isn't anything. You ought to have twenty years of enjoyable life yet, before they call you 'old'—maybe more."

Mrs. Pettigrew cocked an eye at her. "My grandmother lived to be a hundred and four," said she, "and kept on working up to the last year. I don't know about enjoyin' life, but she was useful for pretty near a solid century. After she broke her hip the last time she sat still and sewed and knitted. After her eyes gave out she took to hooking rugs."

"I hope it will be forty years, Mrs. Pettigrew," said Sue, "and I'm real glad you're coming. It'll make it more like home."

Miss Elder was a little slow in accommodating herself to this new accession. She liked Mrs. Pettigrew very much—but—a grandmother thus airily at large seemed to unsettle the foundations of things. She was polite, even cordial, but evidently found it difficult to accept the facts.

"Besides," said Mrs. Pettigrew, "you may not get all those boarders at once and I'll be one to count on. I stopped at the bank this morning and had 'em arrange for my account out in Carston. They were some surprised, but there was no time to ask questions!" She relapsed into silence and gazed with keen interest at the whirling landscape.

Throughout the journey she proved the best of travelers; was never car-sick, slept well in the joggling berth, enjoyed the food, and continually astonished them by producing from her handbag the most diverse and unlooked for conveniences. An old-fashioned traveller had forgotten her watchkey—Grandma produced an automatic one warranted to fit anything. "Takes up mighty little room—and I thought maybe it would come in handy," she said.

She had a small bottle of liquid court-plaster, and plenty of the solid kind. She had a delectable lotion for the hands, a real treasure on the dusty journey; also a tiny corkscrew, a strong pair of "pinchers," sewing materials, playing cards, string, safety-pins, elastic bands, lime drops, stamped envelopes, smelling salts, troches, needles and thread.[25]

"Did you bring a trunk, Grandma?" asked Vivian.

"Two," said Grandma, "excess baggage. All paid for and checked."

"How did you ever learn to arrange things so well?" Sue asked admiringly.

"Read about it," the old lady answered. "There's no end of directions nowadays. I've been studying up."

She was so gleeful and triumphant, so variously useful, so steadily gay and stimulating, that they all grew to value her presence long before they reached Carston; but they had no conception of the ultimate effect of a resident grandmother in that new and bustling town.

To Vivian the journey was a daily and nightly revelation. She had read much but traveled very little, never at night. The spreading beauty of the land was to her a new stimulus; she watched by the hour the endless panorama fly past her window, its countless shades of green, the brown and red soil, the fleeting dashes of color where wild flowers gathered thickly. She was repeatedly impressed by seeing suddenly beside her the name of some town which had only existed in her mind as "capital city" associated with "principal exports" and "bounded on the north."

At night, sleeping little, she would raise her curtain and look out, sideways, at the stars. Big shadowy trees ran by, steep cuttings rose like a wall of darkness, and the hilly curves of open country rose and fell against the sky line like a shaken carpet.

She faced the long, bright vista of the car and studied people's faces—such different people from any she had seen before. A heavy young man with small, light eyes sat near by, and cast frequent glances at both the girls, going by their seat at intervals. Vivian considered this distinctly rude, and Sue did not like his looks, so he got nothing for his pains, yet even this added color to the day.

The strange, new sense of freedom grew in her heart, a feeling of lightness and hope and unfolding purpose.

There was continued discussion as to what the girls should do.

"We can be waitresses for Auntie till we get something else," Sue practically insisted. "The doctor says it will be hard to get good service and I'm sure the boarders would like us."

"You can both find work if you want it. What do you want to do, Vivian?" asked Dr. Bellair, not for the first time.

Vivian was still uncertain.

"I love children best," she said. "I could teach—but I haven't a certificate. I'd *love* a kindergarten; I've studied that—at home."

"Shouldn't wonder if you could get up a kindergarten right off," the doctor assured her. "Meantime, as this kitten says, you could help Miss Elder out and turn an honest penny while you're waiting."

"Wouldn't it—interfere with my teaching later?" the girl inquired.

"Not a bit, not a bit. We're not so foolish out here. We'll fix you up all right in no time."

It was morning when they arrived at last and came out of the cindery, noisy, crowded cars into the wide, clean, brilliant stillness of the high plateau. They drew deep breaths; the doctor squared her shoulders with a glad, homecoming smile. Vivian lifted her head and faced the new surroundings as an unknown world. Grandma gazed all ways, still cheerful, and their baggage accrued about them as a rampart.

A big bearded man, carelessly dressed, whirled up in

a dusty runabout, and stepped out smiling. He seized Dr. Bellair by both hands, and shook them warmly.

"Thought I'd catch you, Johnny," he said. "Glad to see you back. If you've got the landlady, I've got the cook!"

"Here we are," said she. "Miss Orella Elder—Dr. Hale; Mrs. Pettigrew, Miss Susie Elder, Miss Lane—Dr. Richard Hale."

He bowed deeply to Mrs. Pettigrew, shook hands with Miss Orella, and addressed himself to her, giving only a cold nod to the two girls, and quite turning away from them.

Susie, in quiet aside to Vivian, made unfavorable comment.

"This is your Western chivalry, is it?" she said. "Even Bainville does better than that."

"I don't know why we should mind," Vivian answered. "It's Dr. Bellair's friend; he don't care anything about us."

But she was rather of Sue's opinion.

The big man took Dr. Bellair in his car, and they followed in a station carriage, eagerly observing their new surroundings, and surprised, as most Easterners are, by the broad beauty of the streets and the modern conveniences everywhere—electric cars, electric lights, telephones, soda fountains, where they had rather expected to find tents and wigwams.

The house, when they were all safely within it, turned out to be "just like a real house," as Sue said; and proved even more attractive than the doctor had described it. It was a big, rambling thing, at home they would have called it a hotel, with its neat little sign, "The Cottonwoods," and Vivian finally concluded that it looked like a seaside boarding house, built for the purpose.

A broad piazza ran all across the front, the door opening into a big square hall, a sort of general sitting-room; on either side were four good rooms, opening on a transverse passage. The long dining-room and kitchen were in the rear of the hall.

Dr. Bellair had two, her office fronting on the side street, with a bedroom behind it. They gave Mrs. Pettigrew the front corner room on that side and kept the one opening from the hall as their own parlor. In the opposite wing was Miss Elder's room next [to] the hall, and the girls in the outer back corner, while the two front ones on that side were kept for the most impressive and high-priced boarders.

Mrs. Pettigrew regarded her apartments with suspicion as being too "easy."

"I don't mind stairs," she said. "Dr. Bellair has to be next to her office—but why do I have to be next to Dr. Bellair?"

It was represented to her that she would be nearer to everything that went on and she agreed without more words.

Dr. Hale exhibited the house as if he owned it.

"The agent's out of town," he said, "and we don't need him anyway. He said he'd do anything you wanted, in reason."

Dr. Bellair watched with keen interest the effect of her somewhat daring prescription, as Miss Orella stepped from room to room examining everything with a careful eye, with an expression of growing generalship. Sue fluttered about delightedly, discovering advantages everywhere and making occasional disrespectful remarks to Vivian about Dr. Hale's clothes.

"Looks as if he never saw a clothes brush!" she said. "A finger out on his glove, a button off his coat. No need to tell us there's no woman in his house!"

"You can decide about your cook when you've tried her," he said to Miss Elder. "I engaged her for a week—on trial. She's in the kitchen now, and will have your dinner ready presently. I think you'll like her, if—"

"Good boy!" said Dr. Bellair. "Sometimes you show as much sense as a woman—almost."

"What's the 'if'?" asked Miss Orella, looking worried.

"Question of character," he answered. "She's about forty-five, with a boy of sixteen or so. He's not over bright, but a willing worker. She's a good woman—from one standpoint. She won't leave that boy nor give him up to strangers; but she has a past!"

"What is her present?" Dr. Bellair asked, "that's the main thing."

Dr. Hale clapped her approvingly on the shoulder, but looked doubtingly toward Miss Orella.

"And what's her future if somebody don't help her?" Vivian urged.

"Can she cook?" asked Grandma.

"Is she a safe person to have in the house?" inquired Dr. Bellair meaningly.

"She can cook," he replied. "She's French, or of French parentage. She used to keep a little—place of entertainment. The food was excellent. She's been a patient of mine—off and on—for five years—and I should call her perfectly safe."

Miss Orella still looked worried. "I'd like to help her and the boy, but would it—look well? I don't want to be mean about it, but this is a very serious venture with us, Dr. Hale, and I have these girls with me."

"With you and Dr. Bellair and Mrs. Pettigrew the young ladies will be quite safe, Miss Elder. As to the woman's present character, she has suffered two changes of heart, she's become a religious devotee—and a man-hater! And from a business point of view, I assure you that if Jeanne Jeaune is in your kitchen you'll never have a room empty."

"Johnny Jones! Queer name for a woman!" said Grandma. They repeated it to her carefully, but she only changed to "Jennie June," and adhered to one or the other, thereafter. "What's the boy's name?" she asked further.

"Theophile," Dr. Hale replied.

"Huh!" said she.

"Why don't she keep an eating-house still?" asked Dr. Bellair rather suspiciously.

"That's what I like best about her," he answered. "She is trying to break altogether with her past. She wants to give up 'public life'—and private life won't have her."

They decided to try the experiment, and found it worked well.

There were two bedrooms over the kitchen where "Mrs. Jones," as Grandma generally called her, and her boy, could be quite comfortable and by themselves; and although of a somewhat sour and unsociable aspect, and fiercely watchful lest anyone offend her son, this questionable character proved an unquestionable advantage. With the boy's help, she cooked for the houseful, which grew to be a family of twenty-five. He also wiped dishes, helped in the laundry work, cleaned and scrubbed and carried coal; and Miss Elder, seeing his steady usefulness, insisted on paying wages for him too. This unlooked for praise and gain won the mother's heart, and as she grew more at home with them, and he less timid, she encouraged him to do the heavier cleaning in the rest of the house.

"Huh!" said Grandma. "I wish more sane and moral persons would work like that!"

Vivian watched with amazement the swift filling of the house.

There was no trouble at all about boarders, except in discriminating among them. "Make them pay in advance, Rella," Dr. Bellair advised, "it doesn't cost them any more, and it is a great convenience. 'References exchanged,' of course. There are a good many here that I know—you can always count on Mr. Dykeman and Fordham Grier, and John Unwin."

Before a month was over the place was full to its limits with what Sue called "assorted boarders," the work ran smoothly and the business end of Miss Elder's venture seemed quite safe. They had the twenty Dr. Bellair prophesied, and except for her, Mrs. Pettigrew, Miss Peeder, a teacher of dancing and music; Mrs. Jocelyn, who was interested in mining, and Sarah Hart, who described herself as a "journalist," all were men.

Fifteen men to eight women. Miss Elder sat at the head of her table, looked down it and across the other one, and marvelled continuously. Never in her New England life had she been with so many men—except in church—and they were more scattered. This houseful of heavy feet and broad shoulders, these deep voices and loud laughs, the atmosphere of interchanging jests and tobacco smoke, was new to her. She hated the tobacco smoke, but that could not be helped. They did not smoke in her parlor, but the house was full of it none the less, in which constant presence she began to reverse the Irishman's well known judgment of whiskey, allowing that while tobacco was bad, some tobacco was much worse than others.

5

Contrasts

Old England thinks our country
  Is a wilderness at best—
And small New England thinks the same
  Of the large free-minded West.

Some people know the good old way
  Is the only way to do,
And find there must be something wrong
  In anything that's new.

To Vivian the new life offered a stimulus, a sense of stir and promise even beyond her expectations. She wrote dutiful letters to her mother, trying to describe the difference between this mountain town and Bainville, but found the New England viewpoint an insurmountable obstacle.

To Bainville "Out West" was a large blank space on the map, and the blank space in the mind which matched it was but sparsely dotted with a few disconnected ideas such as "cowboy," "blizzard," "prairie fire," "tornado," "border ruffian," and the like.

The girl's painstaking description of the spreading, vigorous young town, with its fine, modern buildings, its banks and stores and theatres, its country club and parks, its pleasant social life, made small impression on the Bainville mind. But the fact that Miss Elder's venture was successful from the first did impress old acquaintances, and Mrs. Lane read aloud to selected visitors her daughter's accounts of their new and agreeable friends. Nothing was said of "chaps," "sombreros," or "shooting up the town," however, and therein a distinct sense of loss was felt.

Much of what was passing in Vivian's mind she could not make clear to her mother had she wished to. The daily presence and very friendly advances of so many men, mostly young and all polite (with the exception of Dr. Hale, whose indifference was almost rude by contrast), gave a new life and color to the days.

She could not help giving some thought to this varied assortment, and the carefully preserved image of Morton, already nine years dim, waxed dimmer. But she had a vague consciousness of being untrue to her ideals, or to Mrs. St. Cloud's ideals, now somewhat discredited, and did not readily give herself up to the cheerful attractiveness of the position.

Susie found no such difficulty. Her ideals were simple, and while quite within the bounds of decorum, left her plenty of room for amusement. So popular did she become, so constantly in demand for rides and walks and oft-recurring dances, that Vivian felt called upon to give elder sisterly advice.

But Miss Susan scouted her admonitions.

"Why shouldn't I have a good time?" she said. "Think how we grew up! Half a dozen boys to twenty girls, and when there was anything to go to—the lordly way they'd pick and choose! And after all our efforts and machinations most of us had to dance with each other. And the quarrels we had! Here they stand around three deep asking for dances—and *they* have to dance with each other, and *they* do the quarreling. I've heard 'em." And Sue giggled delightedly.

"There's no reason we shouldn't enjoy ourselves, Susie, of course, but aren't you—rather hard on them?"

"Oh, nonsense!" Sue protested. "Dr. Bellair said I should get married out here! She says the same old thing—that it's 'a woman's duty,' and I propose to do it. That is—they'll propose, and I won't do it! Not till I make up my mind. Now see how you like this!"

She had taken a fine large block of "legal cap" and set down their fifteen men thereon, with casual comment.[26]

1. Mr. Unwin—Too old, big, quiet.
2. Mr. Elmer Skee—Big, too old, funny.

   3. Jimmie Saunders—Middle-sized, amusing, nice.
   4. P. R. Gibbs—Too little, too thin, too cocky.
   5. George Waterson—Middling, pretty nice.
   6. J. J. Cuthbert—Big, horrid.
   7. Fordham Greer—Big, pleasant.
   8. W. S. Horton—Nothing much.
   9. A. L. Dykeman—Interesting, too old.
10. Professor Toomey—Little, horrid.
11. Arthur Fitzwilliam—Ridiculous, too young.
12. Howard Winchester—Too nice, distrust him.
13. Lawson W. Briggs—Nothing much.
14. Edward S. Jenks—Fair to middling.
15. Mr. A. Smith—Minus.

She held it up in triumph. "I got 'em all out of the book—quite correct. Now, which'll you have."

"Susie Elder! You little goose! Do you imagine that all these fifteen men are going to propose to you?"

"I'm sure I hope so!" said the cheerful damsel. "We've only been settled a fortnight and one of 'em has already!"

Vivian was impressed at once. "Which?—You don't mean it!"

Sue pointed to the one marked "minus."

"It was only 'A. Smith.' I never should be willing to belong to 'A. Smith,' it's too indefinite—unless it was a last resort. Several more are—well, extremely friendly! Now don't look so severe. You needn't worry about me. I'm not quite so foolish as I talk, you know."

She was not. Her words were light and saucy, but she was as demure and decorous a little New Englander as need be desired; and she could not help it if the hearts of the unattached young men of whom the town was full, warmed towards her.

Dr. Bellair astonished them at lunch one day in their first week.

"Dick Hale wants us all to come over to tea this afternoon," she said, as if it was the most natural thing in the world.

"Tea? Where?" asked Mrs. Pettigrew sharply.

"At his house. He has 'a home of his own,' you know. And he particularly wants you, Mrs. Pettigrew—and Miss Elder—the girls, of course."

"I'm sure I don't care to go," Vivian remarked with serene indifference, but Susie did.

"Oh, come on, Vivian! It'll be so funny! A man's home!— and we may never get another chance. He's such a bear!"

Dr. Hale's big house was only across the road from theirs, standing in a large lot with bushes and trees about it.

"He's been here nine years," Dr. Bellair told them.[27] "That's an old inhabitant for us. He boarded in that house for a while; then it was for sale and he bought it. He built that little office of his at the corner—says he doesn't like to live where he works, or work where he lives. He took his meals over here for a while—and then set up for himself."

"I should think he'd be lonely," Miss Elder suggested.

"Oh, he has his boys, you know—always three or four young fellows about him. It's a mighty good thing for them, too."

Dr. Hale's home proved a genuine surprise. They had regarded it as a big, neglected-looking place, and found on entering the gate that the inside view of that rampant shrubbery was extremely pleasant. Though not close cut and swept of leaves and twigs, it still was beautiful; and the tennis court and tether-ball ring showed the ground well used.

Grandma looked about her with a keen interrogative eye, and was much impressed, as, indeed, were they all. She voiced their feelings justly when, the true inwardness of this pleasant home bursting fully upon them, she exclaimed:

"Well, of all things! A man keeping house!"

"Why not?" asked Dr. Hale with his dry smile. "Is there any deficiency, mental or physical, about a man, to prevent his attempting this abstruse art?"

She looked at him sharply. "I don't know about deficiency, but there seems to be somethin' about 'em that keeps 'em out of the business. I guess it's because women are so cheap."

"No doubt you are right, Mrs. Pettigrew. And here women are scarce and high. Hence my poor efforts."

His poor efforts had bought or built a roomy pleasant

house, and furnished it with a solid comfort and calm attractiveness that was most satisfying. Two Chinamen did the work; cooking, cleaning, washing, waiting on table, with silent efficiency. "They are as steady as eight-day clocks," said Dr. Hale. "I pay them good wages and they are worth it.

"Sun here had to go home once—to be married, also, to see his honored parents, I believe, and to leave a grand-'Sun' to attend to the ancestors; but he brought in another Chink first and trained him so well that I hardly noticed the difference. Came back in a year or so, and resumed his place without a jar."[28]

Miss Elder watched with fascinated eyes these soft-footed servants with clean, white garments and shiny coils of long, braided hair.

"I may have to come to it," she admitted, "but—dear me, it doesn't seem natural to have a man doing housework!"

Dr. Hale smiled again. "You don't want men to escape from dependence, I see. Perhaps, if more men knew how comfortably they could live without women, the world would be happier." There was a faint wire-edge to his tone, in spite of the courteous expression, but Miss Elder did not notice it and if Mrs. Pettigrew did, she made no comment.

They noted the varied excellences of his housekeeping with high approval.

"You certainly know how, Dr. Hale," said Miss Orella; "I particularly admire these beds—with the sheets buttoned down, German fashion, isn't it? What made you do that?"

"I've slept so much in hotels," he answered; "and found the sheets always inadequate to cover the blankets—and the marks of other men's whiskers! I don't like blankets in my neck. Besides it saves washing."

Mrs. Pettigrew nodded vehemently. "You have sense," she said.

The labor-saving devices were a real surprise to them. A "chute" for soiled clothing shot from the bathroom on each floor to the laundry in the basement; a dumbwaiter of construction large and strong enough to carry trunks, went from cellar to roof; the fireplaces dropped their ashes down mysterious inner holes; and for the big one in the living-room a special "lift" raised a box of wood up to the floor level, hidden by one of the "settles."[29]

"Saves work—saves dirt—saves expense," said Dr. Hale.

Miss Elder and her niece secretly thought the rooms rather bare, but Dr. Bellair was highly in favor of that very feature.

"You see Dick don't believe in jimcracks and dirt-catchers, and he likes sunlight.[30] Books all under glass—no curtains to wash and darn and fuss with—none of those fancy pincushions and embroidered thingummies—I quite envy him."

"Why don't you have one yourself, Johnny?" he asked her.

"Because I don't like housekeeping," she said, "and you do. Masculine instinct, I suppose!"

"Huh!" said Mrs. Pettigrew with her sudden one-syllable chuckle.

The girls followed from room to room, scarce noticing these comments, or the eager politeness of the four pleasant-faced young fellows who formed the doctor's present family.[31] She could not but note the intelligent efficiency of the place, but felt more deeply the underlying spirit, the big-brotherly kindness which prompted his hospitable care of these nice boys. It was delightful to hear them praise him.

"O, he's simply great," whispered Archie Burns, a ruddy-cheeked young Scotchman. "He pretends there's nothing to it—that he wants company—that we pay for all we get—and that sort of thing, you know; but this is no boarding house, I can tell you!" And then he flushed till his very hair grew redder—remembering that the guests came from one.

"Of course not!" Vivian cordially agreed with him. "You must have lovely times here. I don't wonder you appreciate it!" and she smiled so sweetly that he felt at ease again.

Beneath all this cheery good will and the gay chatter of the group her quick sense caught an impression of something hidden and repressed. She felt the large and quiet beauty of the rooms; the smooth comfort, the rational, pleasant life; but still more she felt a deep keynote of loneliness.

The pictures told her most. She noted one after another with inward comment.

"There's 'Persepolis,' " she said to herself—"loneliness incarnate; and that other lion-and-ruin thing,—loneliness and decay. Gerome's 'Lion in the Desert,' too, the same thing. Then Daniel—more lions, more loneliness, but power. 'Circe and the Companions of Ulysses'—cruel, but loneliness and power again—of a sort. There's that 'Island of Death' too—a beautiful thing—but O dear!—And young Burne-Jones' 'Vampire' was in one of the bedrooms—that one he shut the door of!"[32]

While they ate and drank in the long, low-ceiled wide-windowed room below, she sought the bookcases and looked them over curiously. Yes—there was Marcus Aurelius, Epictetus, Plato, Emerson and Carlisle—the great German philosophers, the French, the English—all showing signs of use.[33]

Dr. Hale observed her inspection. It seemed to vaguely annoy him, as if someone were asking too presuming questions.

"Interested in philosophy, Miss Lane?" he asked, drily, coming toward her.

"Yes—so far as I understand it," she answered.

"And how far does that go?"

She felt the inference, and raised her soft eyes to his rather reproachfully.

"Not far, I am afraid. But I do know that these books teach one how to bear trouble."

He met her gaze steadily, but something seemed to shut, deep in his eyes. They looked as unassailable as a steel safe. He straightened his big shoulders with a defiant shrug, and returned to sit by Mrs. Pettigrew, to whom he made himself most agreeable.

The four young men did the honors of the tea table, with devotion to all; and some especially intended for the younger ladies. Miss Elder cried out in delight at the tea.

"Where did you get it, Dr. Hale? Can it be had here?"

"I'm afraid not. That is a particular brand. Sun brought me a chest of it when he came from his visit."

When they went home each lady was given a present, Chinese fashion—lychee nuts for Sue, lily-bulbs for Vivian, a large fan for Mrs. Pettigrew, and a package of the wonderful tea for Miss Orella.

"That's a splendid thing for him to do," she said, as they walked back. "Such a safe place for those boys!"

"It's lovely of him," Sue agreed. "I don't care if he is a woman-hater."

Vivian said nothing, but admitted, on being questioned, that "he was very interesting."

Mrs. Pettigrew was delighted with their visit. "I like this country," she declared. "Things are different. A man couldn't do that in Bainville—he'd be talked out of town."

That night she sought Dr. Bellair and questioned her.

"Tell me about that man," she demanded. "How old is he?"

"Not as old as he looks by ten years," said the doctor. "No, I can't tell you why his hair's gray."

"What woman upset him?" asked the old lady.

Dr. Bellair regarded her thoughtfully. "He has made me no confidences, Mrs. Pettigrew, but I think you are right. It must have been a severe shock—for he is very bitter against women. It is a shame, too, for he is one of the best of men. He prefers men patients—and gets them. The women he will treat if he must, but he is kindest to the 'fallen' ones, and inclined to sneer at the rest. And yet he's the straightest man I ever knew. I'm thankful to have him come here so much. He needs it."

Mrs. Pettigrew marched off, nodding sagely. She felt a large and growing interest in her new surroundings, more especially in the numerous boys, but was somewhat amazed at her popularity among them. These young men were mainly exiles from home; the older ones, though more settled perhaps, had been even longer away from their early surroundings; and a real live Grandma, as Jimmie Saunders said, was an "attraction."

"If you were mine," he told her laughingly, "I'd get a pianist and some sort of little side show, and exhibit you all up and down the mountains!—for good money. Why some of the boys never had a Grandma, and those that did haven't seen one since they were kids!"

"Very complimentary, I'm sure—but impracticable," said the old lady.

The young men came to her with confidences, they asked her advice, they kept her amused with tales of their adventures; some true, some greatly diversified; and she listened with a shrewd little smile and a wag of the head—so they never were quite sure whether they were "fooling" Grandma or not.

To her, as a general confidant, came Miss Peeder with a tale of woe. The little hall that she rented for her dancing classes had burned down on a windy Sunday, and there was no other suitable and within her means.

"There's Sloan's; but it's over a barroom—it's really not possible. And Baker's is too expensive. The church rooms they won't let for dancing—I don't know what I *am* to do, Mrs. Pettigrew!"

"Why don't you ask Orella Elder to rent you her dining-room—it's big enough. They could move the tables—"

Miss Peeder's eyes opened in hopeful surprise. "Oh, if she *would! Do you* think she would? It would be ideal."

Miss Elder being called upon, was quite fluttered by the proposition, and consulted Dr. Bellair.

"Why not?" said that lady. "Dancing is first rate exercise—good for us all. Might as well have the girls dance here under your eye as going out all the time—and it's some addition to the income. They'll pay extra for refreshments, too. I'd do it."

With considerable trepidation Miss Orella consented, and their first "class night" was awaited by her in a state of suppressed excitement.

To have music and dancing—"with refreshments"—twice a week—in her own house—this seemed to her like a career of furious dissipation.

Vivian, though with a subtle sense of withdrawal from a too general intimacy, was inwardly rather pleased; and Susie bubbled over with delight.

"Oh what fun!" she cried. "I never had enough dancing! I don't believe anybody has!"

"We don't belong to the Class, you know," Vivian reminded her.

"Oh yes! Miss Peeder says we must *all* come—that she

would feel *very* badly if we didn't; and the boarders have all joined—to a man!"

Everyone seemed pleased except Mrs. Jeaune. Dancing she considered immoral; music, almost as much so—and Miss Elder trembled lest she lose her. But the offer of extra payments for herself and son on these two nights each week proved sufficient to quell her scruples.

Theophile doubled up the tables, set chairs around the walls, waxed the floor, and was then sent to bed and locked in by his anxious mother.

She labored, during the earlier hours of the evening, in the preparation of sandwiches and coffee, cake and lemonade—which viands were later shoved through the slide by the austere cook, and distributed as from a counter by Miss Peeder's assistant. Mrs. Jeaune would come no nearer, but peered darkly upon them through the peephole in the swinging door.

It was a very large room, due to the time when many "mealers" had been accommodated. There were windows on each side, windows possessing the unusual merit of opening from the top; wide double doors made the big front hall a sort of anteroom, and the stairs and piazza furnished opportunities for occasional couples who felt the wish for retirement. In the right-angled passages, long hat-racks on either side were hung with "Derbies," "Kossuths" and "Stetsons," and the ladies took off their wraps, and added finishing touches to their toilettes in Miss Elder's room.

The house was full of stir and bustle, of pretty dresses, of giggles and whispers, and the subdued exchange of comments among the gentlemen. The men predominated, so that there was no lack of partners for any of the ladies.

Miss Orella accepted her new position with a half-terrified enjoyment. Not in many years had she found herself so in demand. Her always neat and appropriate costume had blossomed suddenly for the occasion; her hair, arranged by the affectionate and admiring Susie, seemed softer and more voluminous. Her eyes grew brilliant, and the delicate color in her face warmed and deepened.

Miss Peeder had installed a pianola to cover emergencies, but on this opening evening she had both piano and violin—good, lively, sole-stirring music. Everyone was on the floor, save a few gentlemen who evidently wished they were.

Sue danced with the gaiety and lightness of a kitten among wind-blown leaves, Vivian with gliding grace, smooth and harmonious, Miss Orella with skill and evident enjoyment, though still conscientious in every accurate step.

Presently Mrs. Pettigrew appeared, sedately glorious in black silk, jet-beaded, and with much fine old lace. She bore in front of her a small wicker rocking chair, and headed for a corner near the door. Her burden was promptly taken from her by one of the latest comers, a tall person with a most devoted manner.

"Allow *me*, ma'am," he said, and placed the little chair at the point she indicated. "No lady ought to rustle for rockin' chairs with so many gentlemen present."

He was a man of somewhat advanced age, but his hair was still more black than white and had a curly, wiggish effect save as its indigenous character was proven by three small bare patches of a conspicuous nature.

He bowed so low before her that she could not help observing these distinctions, and then answered her startled look before she had time to question him.

"Yes'm," he explained, passing his hand over head; "scalped three several times and left for dead. But I'm here yet. Mr. Elmer Skee, at your service."

"I thought when an Indian scalped you there wasn't enough hair left to make Greeley whiskers," said Grandma, rising to the occasion.

"Oh, no, ma'am, they ain't so efficacious as all that—not in these parts. I don't know what the ancient Mohawks may have done, but the Apaches only want a patch—smaller to carry and just as good to show off. They're collectors, you know—like a phil-e-a-to-lol-o-gist!"

"Skee, did you say?" pursued the old lady, regarding him with interest and convinced that there was something wrong with the name of that species of collector.

"Yes'm. Skee—Elmer Skee. No'm, *not* pronounced 'she.' Do I look like it?"

Mr. Skee was an interesting relic of that stormy past of

the once Wild West which has left so few surviving. He had crossed the plains as a child, he told her, in the days of the prairie schooner, had then and there lost his parents and his first bit of scalp, was picked up alive by a party of "movers," and had grown up in a playground of sixteen states and territories.[34]

Grandma gazed upon him fascinated. "I judge you might be interesting to talk with," she said, after he had given her this brief sketch of his youth.

"Thank you, ma'am," said Mr. Skee. "May I have the pleasure of this dance?"

"I haven't danced in thirty years," said she, dubitating.

"The more reason for doing it now," he calmly insisted.

"Why not?" said Mrs. Pettigrew, and they forthwith executed a species of march, the gentleman pacing with the elaborate grace of a circus horse, and Grandma stepping at his side with great decorum.

Later on, warming to the occasion, Mr. Skee frisked and high-stepped with the youngest and gayest, and found the supper so wholly to his liking that he promptly applied for a room, and as soon as one was vacant it was given to him.

Vivian danced to her heart's content and enjoyed the friendly merriment about her; but when Fordham Greer took her out on the long piazza to rest and breathe a little, she saw the dark bulk of the house across the street and the office with its half-lit window, and could not avoid thinking of the lonely man there.

He had not come to the dance, no one expected that, of course; but all his boys had come and were having the best of times.

"It's his own fault, of course; but it's a shame," she thought.

The music sounded gaily from within, and young Greer urged for another dance.

She stood there for a moment, hesitating, her hand on his arm, when a tall figure came briskly up the street from the station, turned in at their gate, came up the steps—

The girl gave a little cry, and shrank back for an instant, then eagerly came forward and gave her hand to him.

It was Morton.

6

New Friends and Old

'Twould be too bad to be true, my dear,
　And wonders never cease;
'Twould be too bad to be true, my dear,
　If all one's swans were geese![35]

Vivian's startled cry of welcome was heard by Susie, perched on the stairs with several eager youths gathered as close as might be about her, and several pairs of hands helped her swift descent to greet her brother.

Miss Orella, dropping Mr. Dykeman's arm, came flying from the ball-room.

"Oh, Morton! Morton! When did you come? Why didn't you let us know? Oh, my *dear* boy!"

She haled him into their special parlor, took his hat away from him, pulled out the most comfortable chair.

"Have you had supper? And to think that we haven't a room for you! But there's to be one vacant—next week. I'll see that there is. You shall have my room, dear boy. Oh, I am so glad to see you!"

Susie gave him a sisterly hug, while he kissed her, somewhat gingerly, on the cheek, and then she perched herself on the arm of a chair and gazed upon him with affectionate interest. Vivian gazed also, busily engaged in fitting present facts to past memories.

Surely he had not looked just like that! The Morton of her girlhood's dream had a clear complexion, a bright eye, a brave and gallant look—the voice only had not changed.

But here was Morton in present fact, something taller, it seemed, and a good deal heavier, well dressed in a rather vivid way, and making merry over his aunt's devotion.

142

"Well, if it doesn't seem like old times to have Aunt Rella running 'round like a hen with her head cut off, to wait on me." The simile was not unjust, though certainly ungracious, but his aunt was far too happy to resent it.

"You sit right still!" she said. "I'll go and bring you some supper. You must be hungry."

"Now do sit down and hear to reason, Auntie!" he said, reaching out a detaining hand and pulling her into a seat beside him. "I'm not hungry a little bit; had a good feed on the diner. Never mind about the room—I don't know how long I can stay—and I left my grip at the Allen House anyway. How well you're looking, Auntie! I declare I'd hardly have known you! And here's little Susie—a regular belle! And Vivian—don't suppose I dare call you Vivian now, Miss Lane?"

Vivian gave a little embarrassed laugh. If he had used her first name she would never have noticed it. Now that he asked her, she hardly knew what answer to make, but presently said:

"Why, of course, I always call you Morton."

"Well, I'll come when you call me," he cheerfully replied, leaning forward, elbows on knees, and looking around the pretty room.

"How well you're fixed here. Guess it was a wise move, Aunt Rella. But I'd never have dreamed you'd do it. Your Dr. Bellair must have been a powerful promoter to get you all out here. I wouldn't have thought anybody in Bainville could move—but me. Why, there's Grandma, as I live!" and he made a low bow.

Mrs. Pettigrew, hearing of his arrival from the various would-be partners of the two girls, had come to the door and stood there regarding him with a non-committal expression. At this address she frowned perceptibly.

"My name is Mrs. Pettigrew, young man. I've known you since you were a scallawag in short pants, but I'm no Grandma of yours."

"A thousand pardons! Please excuse me, Mrs. Pettigrew," he said with exaggerated politeness. "Won't you be seated?" And he set a chair for her with a flourish.

"Thanks, no," she said. "I'll go back," and went back forthwith, attended by Mr. Skee.

"One of these happy family reunions, ma'am?" he asked with approving interest. "If there's one thing I do admire, it's a happy surprise."

" 'Tis some of a surprise," Mrs. Pettigrew admitted, and became rather glum, in spite of Mr. Skee's undeniably entertaining conversation.

"Some sort of a fandango going on?" Morton asked after a few rather stiff moments. "Don't let me interrupt! On with the dance! Let joy be unconfined! And if she must"—he looked at Vivian, and went on somewhat lamely—"dance, why not dance with me? May I have the pleasure, Miss Lane?"

"Oh, no," cried Miss Orella, "we'd much rather be with you!"

"But I'd rather dance than talk, any time," said he, and crooked his elbow to Vivian with an impressive bow.

Somewhat uncertain in her own mind, and unwilling to again disappoint Fordham Greer, who had already lost one dance and was visibly waiting for her in the hall, the girl hesitated; but Susie said, "Go on, give him part of one. I'll tell Mr. Greer." So Vivian took Morton's proffered arm and returned to the floor.

She had never danced with him in the old days; no special memory was here to contrast with the present; yet something seemed vaguely wrong. He danced well, but more actively than she admired, and during the rest of the evening devoted himself to the various ladies with an air of long usage.

She was glad when the dancing was over and he had finally departed for his hotel, glad when Susie had at last ceased chattering and dropped reluctantly to sleep.

For a long time she lay awake trying to straighten out things in her mind and account to herself for the sense of vague confusion which oppressed her.

Morton had come back! That was the prominent thing, of which she repeatedly assured herself. How often had she looked forward to that moment, and felt in anticipation a vivid joy. She had thought of it in a hundred ways, always with pleasure, but never in this particular way— among so many strangers.

It must be that which confused her, she thought, for she was extremely sensitive to the attitude of those about her. She felt an unspoken criticism of Morton on the part of her new friends in the house, and resented it; yet in her own mind a faint comparison would obtrude itself between his manners and those of Jimmie Saunders or Mr. Greer, for instance. The young Scotchman she had seen regarding Morton with an undisguised dislike, and this she inwardly resented, even while herself disliking his bearing to his aunt—and to her grandmother.

It was all contradictory and unsatisfying, and she fell asleep saying over to herself, "He has come back! He has come back!" and trying to feel happy.

Aunt Orella was happy at any rate. She would not rest until her beloved nephew was installed in the house, practically turning out Mr. Gibbs in order to accommodate him. Morton protested, talked of business and of having to go away at any time; and Mr. Gibbs, who still "mealed" with them, secretly wished he would.

But Morton did not go away. It was a long time since he had been petted and waited on, and he enjoyed it hugely, treating his aunt with a serio-comic affection that was sometimes funny, sometimes disagreeable.

At least Susie found it so. Her first surprise over, she fell back on a fund of sound common sense, strengthened by present experience, and found a good deal to criticise in her returned brother. She was so young when he left, and he had teased her so unmercifully in those days, that her early memories of him were rather mixed in sentiment, and now he appeared, not as the unquestioned idol of a manless family in a well-nigh manless town, but as one among many; and of those many several were easily his superiors.

He was her brother, and she loved him, of course; but there were so many wanting to be "brothers" if not more, and they were so much more polite! Morton petted, patronized and teased her, and she took it all in good part, as after the manner of brothers, but his demeanor with other people was not to her mind.

His adoring aunt, finding no fault whatever with this well-loved nephew, lavished upon him the affection of her unused motherhood, and he seemed to find it a patent joke, open to everyone, that she should be so fond.

To this and, indeed, to his general walk and conversation, Mrs. Pettigrew took great exception.

"Fine boy—Rella's nephew!" she said to Dr. Bellair late one night when, seeing a light over her neighbor's transom, she dropped in for a little chat.[36] Conversation seemed easier for her here than in the atmosphere of Bainville.

"Fine boy—eh? Nice complexion!"

Dr. Bellair was reading a heavy-weight book by a heavier-weight specialist. She laid it down, took off her eye-glasses, and rubbed them.

"Better not kiss him," she said.

"I thought as much!" said Grandma. "I *thought* as much! Huh!"

"Nice world, isn't it?" the doctor suggested genially.

"Nothing the matter with the world, that I know of," her visitor answered.

"Nice people, then—how's that?"

"Nothing the matter with the people but foolishness— plain foolishness. Good land! Shall we *never* learn anything!"

"Not till it's too late apparently," the doctor gloomily agreed, turning slowly in her swivel chair. "That boy never was taught anything to protect him. What did Rella know? Or for that matter, what do any boys' fathers and mothers know? Nothing, you'd think. If they do, they won't teach it to their children."

"Time they did!" said the old lady decidedly. "High time they did! It's never too late to learn. I've learned a lot out of you and your books, Jane Bellair. Interesting reading! I don't suppose you could give an absolute opinion now, could you?"

"No," said Dr. Bellair gravely, "no, I couldn't; not yet, anyway."

"Well, we've got to keep our eyes open," Mrs. Pettigrew concluded. "When I think of that girl of mine—"

"Yes—or any girl," the doctor added.

"You look out for any girl—that's your business; I'll look out for mine—if I can."

Mrs. Pettigrew's were not the only eyes to scrutinize

Morton Elder. Through the peep-hole in the swing door to the kitchen, Jeanne Jeaune watched him darkly with one hand on her lean chest.

She kept her watch on whatever went on in that dining-room, and on the two elderly waitresses whom she had helped Miss Elder to secure when the house filled up. They were rather painfully unattractive, but seemed likely to stay where no young and pretty damsel could be counted on for a year. Morton joked with perseverance about their looks, and those who were most devoted to Susie seemed to admire his wit, while Vivian's special admirers found it pointless in the extreme.

"Your waitresses are the limit, Auntie," he said, "but the cook is all to the good. Is she a plain cook or a handsome one?"

"Handsome is as handsome does, young man," Mrs. Pettigrew pointedly replied. "Mrs. Jones is a first-class cook and her looks are neither here nor there."

"You fill me with curiosity," he replied. "I must go out and make her acquaintance. I always get solid with the cook; it's worth while."

The face at the peep-hole darkened and turned away with a bitter and determined look, and Master Theophile was hastened at his work till his dim intelligence wondered, and then blessed with an unexpected cookie.

Vivian, Morton watched and followed assiduously. She was much changed from what he remembered—the young, frightened, slender girl he had kissed under the lilac bushes, a kiss long since forgotten among many.

Perhaps the very number of his subsequent acquaintances during a varied and not markedly successful career in the newer states made this type of New England womanhood more marked. Girls he had known of various sorts, women old and young had been kind to him, for Morton had the rough good looks and fluent manner which easily find their way to the good will of many female hearts; but this gentle refinement of manner and delicate beauty had a novel charm for him.

Sitting by his aunt at meals he studied Vivian opposite, he watched her in their few quiet evenings together, under the soft lamplight on Miss Elder's beloved "center table;" and studied her continually in the stimulating presence of many equally devoted men.

All that was best in him was stirred by her quiet grace, her reserved friendliness; and the spur of rivalry was by no means wanting. Both the girls had their full share of masculine attention in that busy houseful, each having her own particular devotees, and the position of comforter to the others.

Morton became openly devoted to Vivian, and followed her about, seeking every occasion to be alone with her, a thing difficult to accomplish.

"I don't ever get a chance to see anything of you," he said. "Come on, take a walk with me—won't you?"

"You can see me all day, practically," she answered. "It seems to me that I never saw a man with so little to do."

"Now that's too bad, Vivian! Just because a fellow's out of a job for a while! It isn't the first time, either; in my business you work like—like anything, part of the time, and then get laid off. I work hard enough when I'm at it."

"Do you like it—that kind of work?" the girl asked.

They were sitting in the family parlor, but the big hall was as usual well occupied, and some one or more of the boarders always eager to come in. Miss Elder at this moment had departed for special conference with her cook, and Susie was at the theatre with Jimmie Saunders. Fordham Greer had asked Vivian, as had Morton also, but she declined both on the ground that she didn't like that kind of play. Mrs. Pettigrew, being joked too persistently about her fondness for "long whist," had retired to her room— but then, her room was divided from the parlor only by a thin partition and a door with a most inefficacious latch.[37]

"Come over here by the fire," said Morton, "and I'll tell you all about it."

He seated himself on a sofa, comfortably adjacent to the fireplace, but Vivian preferred a low rocker.

"I suppose you mean travelling—and selling goods?" he pursued. "Yes, I like it. There's lots of change—and you meet people. I'd hate to be shut up in an office."

"But do you—get anywhere with it? Is there any outlook for you? Anything worth doing?"

"There's a good bit of money to be made, if you mean that; that is, if a fellow's a good salesman. I'm no slouch myself, when I feel in the mood. But it's easy come, easy go, you see. And it's uncertain. There are times like this, with nothing doing."

"I didn't mean money, altogether," said the girl meditatively, "but the work itself; I don't see any future for you."

Morton was pleased with her interest. Reaching between his knees he seized the edge of the small sofa and dragged it a little nearer, quite unconscious that the act was distasteful to her.

Though twenty-five years old, Vivian was extremely young in many ways, and her introspection had spent itself in tending the inner shrine of his early image. That ikon was now jarringly displaced by this insistent presence, and she could not satisfy herself yet as to whether the change pleased her or displeased her. Again and again his manner antagonized her, but his visible devotion carried an undeniable appeal, and his voice stirred the deep well of emotion in her heart.

"Look here, Vivian," he said, "you've no idea how it goes through me to have you speak like that! You see I've been knocking around here for all this time, and I haven't had a soul to take an interest. A fellow needs the society of good women—like you."

It is an old appeal, and always reaches the mark. To any woman it is a compliment, and to a young girl, doubly alluring. As she looked at him, the very things she most disliked, his too free manner, his coarsened complexion, a certain look about the eyes, suddenly assumed a new interest as proofs of his loneliness and lack of right companionship. What Mrs. St. Cloud had told her of the ennobling influence of a true woman, flashed upon her mind.

"You see, I had no mother," he said simply—"and Aunt Rella spoiled me—." He looked now like the boy she used to know.

"Of course I ought to have behaved better," he admitted. "I was ungrateful—I can see it now. But it did seem to me I couldn't stand that town a day longer!"

She could sympathize with this feeling and showed it.

"Then when a fellow knocks around as I have so long, he gets to where he doesn't care a hang for anything. Seeing you again makes a lot of difference, Vivian. I think, perhaps—I could take a new start."

"Oh do! Do!" she said eagerly. "You're young enough, Morton. You can do anything if you'll make up your mind to it."

"And you'll help me?"

"Of course I'll help you—if I can," said she.

A feeling of sincere remorse for wasted opportunities rose in the young man's mind; also, in the presence of this pure-eyed girl, a sense of shame for his previous habits. He walked to the window, his hands in his pockets, and looked out blankly for a moment.

"A fellow does a lot of things he shouldn't," he began, clearing his throat; she met him more than half way with the overflowing generosity of youth and ignorance:

"Never mind what you've done, Morton—you're going to do differently now! Susie'll be so proud of you—and Aunt Orella!"

"And you?" He turned upon her suddenly.

"Oh—I? Of course! I shall be very proud of my old friend."

She met his eyes bravely, with a lovely look of hope and courage, and again his heart smote him.

"I hope you will," he said and straightened his broad shoulders manfully.

"Morton Elder!" cried his aunt, bustling in with deep concern in her voice, "What's this I hear about your having a sore throat?"

"Nothing, I hope," said he cheerfully.

"Now, Morton"—Vivian showed new solicitude—"you know you have got a sore throat; Susie told me."

"Well, I wish she'd hold her tongue," he protested. "It's nothing at all—be all right in a jiffy. No, I won't take any of your fixings, Auntie."

"I want Dr. Bellair to look at it anyhow," said his aunt, anxiously. "She'll know if it's diphtheritic or anything. She's coming in."

"She can just go out again," he said with real annoyance. "If there's anything I've no use for it's a woman doctor!"

"Oh hush, hush!" cried Vivian, too late.

"Don't apologize," said Dr. Bellair from her doorway. "I'm not in the least offended. Indeed, I had rather surmised that that was your attitude; I didn't come in to prescribe, but to find Mrs. Pettigrew."

"Want me?" inquired the old lady from her doorway. "Who's got a sore throat?"

"Morton has," Vivian explained, "and he won't let Aunt Rella—why where is she?"

Miss Elder had gone out as suddenly as she had entered.

"Camphor's good for sore throat," Mrs. Pettigrew volunteered. "Three or four drops on a piece of sugar. Is it the swelled kind, or the kind that smarts?"

"Oh—Halifax!" exclaimed Morton, disgustedly. "It isn't *any* kind. I haven't a sore throat."

"Camphor's good for cold sores; you have one of them anyhow," the old lady persisted, producing a little bottle and urging it upon Morton. "Just keep it wet with camphor as often as you think of it, and it'll go away."

Vivian looked on, interested and sympathetic, but Morton put his hand to his lip and backed away.

"If you ladies don't stop trying to doctor me, I'll clear out to-morrow, so there!"

This appalling threat was fortunately unheard by his aunt, who popped in again at this moment, dragging Dr. Hale with her. Dr. Bellair smiled quietly to herself.

"I wouldn't tell him what I wanted him for, or he wouldn't have come, I'm sure—doctors are so funny," said Miss Elder, breathlessly, "but here he is. Now, Dr. Hale, here's a foolish boy who won't listen to reason, and I'm real worried about him. I want you to look at his throat."

Dr. Hale glanced briefly at Morton's angry face.

"The patient seems to be of age, Miss Elder; and, if you'll excuse me, does not seem to have authorized this call."

"My affectionate family are bound to have me an invalid," Morton explained. "I'm in imminent danger of hot

baths, cold presses, mustard plasters, aconite, bella-
donna and quinine—and if I can once reach my hat—"

He sidled to the door and fled in mock terror.

"Thank you for your good intentions, Miss Elder," Dr.
Hale remarked drily. "You can bring water to the horse,
but you can't make him drink it, you see."

"Now that that young man has gone we might have a
game of whist," Mrs. Pettigrew suggested, looking not ill-
pleased.

"For which you do not need me in the least," and Dr.
Hale was about to leave, but Dr. Bellair stopped him.

"Don't be an everlasting Winter woodchuck, Dick! Sit
down and play; do be good. I've got to see old Mrs. Graham
yet; she refuses to go to sleep without it—knowing I'm so
near. Bye bye."

Mrs. Pettigrew insisted on playing with Miss Elder, so
Vivian had the questionable pleasure of Dr. Hale as a
partner. He was an expert, used to frequent and scientific
play, and by no means patient with the girl's mistakes.

He made no protest at a lost trick, but explained briefly
between hands what she should have remembered and
how the cards lay, till she grew quite discouraged.

Her game was but mediocre, played only to oblige; and
she never could see why people cared so much about a
mere pastime. Pride came to her rescue at last; the more
he criticised, the more determined she grew to profit by
all this advice; but her mind would wander now and then
to Morton, to his young life so largely wasted, it appeared,
and to what hope might lie before him. Could she be the
help and stimulus he seemed to think? How much did he
mean by asking her to help him?

"Why waste a thirteenth trump on your partner's thirteenth card?" Dr. Hale was asking.

She flushed a deep rose color and lifted appealing eyes
to him.

"Do forgive me; my mind was elsewhere."

"Will you not invite it to return?" he suggested drily.

He excused himself after a few games, and the girl at
last was glad to have him go. She wanted to be alone with
her thoughts.

Mrs. Pettigrew, sitting unaccountably late at her front window, watched the light burn steadily in the small office at the opposite corner. Presently she saw a familiar figure slip in there, and, after a considerable stay, come out quietly, cross the street, and let himself in at their door.

"Huh!" said Mrs. Pettigrew.

7

Side Lights

High shines the golden shield in front,
  To those who are not blind;
    And clear and bright
    In all men's sight,
  The silver shield behind.

In breadth and sheen each face is seen;
  How tall it is, how wide;
    But its thinness shows
    To only those
  Who stand on either side.

Theophile wept aloud in the dining-room, nursing one hand in the other, like a hurt monkey.

Most of the diners had departed, but Professor Toomey and Mr. Cuthbert still lingered about Miss Susie's corner, to the evident displeasure of Mr. Saunders, who lingered also.

Miss Susie smiled upon them all; and Mr. Saunders speculated endlessly as to whether this was due to her general friendliness of disposition, to an interest in pleasing her aunt's boarders, to personal preference, or, as he sometimes imagined, to a desire to tease him.

Morton was talking earnestly with Vivian at the other end of the table, from which the two angular waitresses had some time since removed the last plate. One of them opened the swing door a crack and thrust her head in.

"He's burnt his hand," she said, "and his Ma's out. We don't dare go near him." Both of these damsels professed great terror of the poor boy, though he was invariably good natured, and as timid as a rabbit.

"Do get the doctor!" cried Susie, nervously; she never felt at ease with Theophile.

"Dr. Bellair, I fear, is not in her office," Professor Toomey announced. "We might summon Dr. Hale."

"Nonsense!" said Mr. Cuthbert, rising heavily. "He's a great baby, that's all. Here! Quit that howling and show me your hand!"

He advanced upon Theophile, who fled toward Vivian. Morton rose in her defence. "Get out!" he said, "Go back to the kitchen. There's nothing the matter with you."

"Wait till you get burned, and see if you think it's nothing," Jimmie Saunders remarked with some acidity. He did not like Mr. Elder. "Come here youngster, let me see it."

But the boy was afraid of all of them, and cowered in a corner, still bawling. "Stop your noise," Mr. Cuthbert shouted, "Get out of this, or I'll put you out."

Vivian rose to her feet. "You will do nothing of the kind. If you, all of you, will go away, I can quiet Theophile, myself."

Susie went promptly. She had every confidence in her friend's management. Mr. Cuthbert was sulky, but followed Susie; and Mr. Saunders, after some hesitation, followed Susie, too.

Morton lingered, distrustful.

"Please go, Morton. I know how to manage him. Just leave us alone," Vivian urged.

"You'd better let me put him out, and keep him out, till the old woman comes back," Morton insisted.

"You mean kindly, I don't doubt, but you're making me very angry," said the girl, flushing; and he reluctantly left the room. Professor Toomey had departed long since, to fulfill his suggestion of calling Dr. Hale, but when that gentleman appeared, he found that Vivian had quieted the boy, stayed him with flagons and comforted him with apples, as it were, and bound up his hand in wet cooking soda.[38]

"It's not a very bad burn," she told the doctor, "but it hurt, and he was frightened. He is afraid of everybody but his mother, and the men were cross to him."

"I see," said Dr. Hale, watching Theophile as he munched his apple, keeping carefully behind Vivian and very near her. "He does not seem much afraid of you, I notice, and he's used to me. The soda is all right. Where did you learn first aid to the injured, and how to handle—persons of limited understanding?"

"The former I studied. The latter comes by nature, I think," replied the girl, annoyed.

He laughed, rather suddenly. "It's a good quality, often needed in this world."

"What's all this rumpus?" demanded Grandma, appearing at the door. "Waking me up out of my nap!" Grandma's smooth, fine, still dark hair, which she wore in "water waves," was somewhat disarranged, and she held a little shawl about her.

"Only the household baby, playing with fire," Dr. Hale answered. "Miss Lane resolved herself into a Red Cross society, and attended to the wounded. However, I think I'll have a look at it now I'm here."

Then was Vivian surprised, and compelled to admiration, to see with what wise gentleness the big man won the confidence of the frightened boy, examined the hurt hand, and bound it up again.

"You'll do, all right, won't you Theophile," he said, and offered him a shining nickel and a lozenge, "Which will you have, old man?"

After some cautious hesitation, the boy chose the lozenge, and hastily applied it where it would do the most good.

"Where's Mrs. Jones all this time?" suddenly demanded Grandma, who had gone back to her room and fetched forth three fat, pink gumdrops for the further consolation of the afflicted.

"She had to go out to buy clothes for him, she hardly ever leaves him you know," Vivian explained. "And the girls out there are so afraid that they won't take any care of him."

This was true enough, but Vivian did not know that "Mrs. Jones" had returned and, peering through her favorite peephole, had seen her send out the others, and attend to the boy's burn with her own hand. Jeanne Jeaune was not a sentimental person, and judged from her son's easy consolation that he was little hurt, but she watched the girl's prompt tenderness with tears in her eyes.

"She regards him as any other boy;" thought the mother. "His infirmity, she does not recall it." Dr. Hale had long since won her approval, and when Theophile at last ran out, eager to share his gumdrops, he found her busy as usual in the kitchen.

She was a silent woman, professionally civil to the waitresses, but never cordial. The place pleased her, she was saving money, and she knew that there must be *some* waitresses—these were probably no worse than others. For her unfortunate son she expected little, and strove to keep him near her so far as possible; but Vivian's real kindness touched her deeply.

She kept a sharp eye on whatever went on in the dining-room, and what with the frequent dances and the little groups which used to hang about the table after meals, or fill a corner of the big room for quiet chats, she had good opportunities.

Morton's visible devotion she watched with deep disapproval; though she was not at all certain that her "young lady" was favorably disposed toward him. She could see and judge the feelings of the men, these many men who ate and drank and laughed and paid court to both the girls. Dr. Hale's brusque coldness she accepted, as from a higher order of being. Susie's gay coquetries were transparent to her; but Vivian she could not read so well.

The girl's deep conscientiousness, her courtesy and patience with all, and the gentle way in which she evaded the attentions so persistently offered, were new to Jeanne's experience. When Morton hung about and tried always to talk with Vivian exclusively, she saw her listen with kind attention, but somehow without any of that answering gleam which made Susie's blue eyes so irresistible.

"She has the lovers, but she has *no* beauty—to compare with my young lady!" Jeanne commented inwardly.

If the sad-eyed Jeanne had been of Scotch extraction instead of French, she might have quoted the explanation of the homely widow of three husbands when questioned by the good-looking spinster, who closed her inquiry by saying aggrievedly, "And y'er na sae bonny."

"It's na the bonny that does it," explained the triple widow, "It's the come hither i' the een."[39]

Susie's eyes sparkled with the "come hither," but those who came failed to make any marked progress. She was somewhat more cautious after the sudden approach and overthrow of Mr. A. Smith; yet more than one young gentleman boarder found business called him elsewhere, with marked suddenness; his place eagerly taken by another. The Cottonwoods had a waiting list, now.

Vivian made friends first, lovers afterward. Then if the love proved vain, the friendship had a way of lingering. Hers was one of those involved and over-conscientious characters, keenly sensitive to the thought of duty and to others' pain. She could not play with hearts that might be hurt in the handling, nor could she find in herself a quick and simple response to the appeals made to her; there were so many things to be considered.

Morton studied her with more intensity than he had ever before devoted to another human being; his admiration and respect grew with acquaintance, and all that was best in him rose in response to her wise, sweet womanliness. He had the background of their childhood's common experiences and her early sentiment—how much he did not know, to aid him. Then there was the unknown country of his years of changeful travel, many tales that he could tell her, many more which he found he could not.

He pressed his advantage, cautiously, finding the fullest response when he used the appeal to her uplifting influence. When they talked in the dining-room the sombre eye at the peephole watched with growing disapproval. The kitchen was largely left to her and her son by her fellow workers, on account of their nervous dislike for Theophile, and she utilized her opportunities.

Vivian had provided the boy with some big bright picture blocks, and he spent happy hours in matching them on the white scoured table, while his mother sewed, and watched. He had forgotten his burn by now, and she sewed contentedly for there was no one talking to her young lady but Dr. Hale, who lingered unaccountably.

To be sure, Vivian had brought him a plate of cakes from the pantry, and he seemed to find the little brown things efficiently seductive, or perhaps it was Grandma who held him, sitting bolt upright in her usual place, at the head of one table, and asking a series of firm but friendly questions. This she found the only way of inducing Dr. Hale to talk at all.

Yes, he was going away—Yes, he would be gone some time—A matter of weeks, perhaps—He could not say—His boys were all well—He did not wonder that they saw a good deal of them—It was a good place for them to come.

"You might come oftener yourself," said Grandma, "and play real whist with me. These young people play *Bridge!*" She used the word with angry scorn, as symbol of all degeneracy; and also despised pinochle, refusing to learn it, though any one could induce her to play bezique. Some of the more venturous and argumentative, strove to persuade her that the games were really the same.

"You needn't tell me," Mrs. Pettigrew would say, "I don't want to play any of your foreign games."

"But, Madam, bezique is not an English word," Professor Toomey had insisted, on one occasion; to which she had promptly responded, "Neither is 'bouquet!'"

Dr. Hale shook his head with a smile. He had a very nice smile, even Vivian admitted that. All the hard lines of his face curved and melted, and the light came into those deep-set eyes and shone warmly.

"I should enjoy playing whist with you very often, Mrs. Pettigrew; but a doctor has no time to call his own. And a good game of whist must not be interrupted by telephones."

"There's Miss Orella!" said Grandma, as the front door was heard to open. "She's getting to be quite a gadder."[40]

"It does her good, I don't doubt," the doctor gravely remarked, rising to go. Miss Orella met him in the hall, and bade him good-bye with regret. "We do not see much of you, doctor; I hope you'll be back soon."

"Why it's only a little trip; you good people act as if I were going to Alaska," he said. "It makes me feel as if I had a family!"

"Pity you haven't," remarked Grandma with her usual definiteness. Dykeman stood holding Miss Orella's wrap, with his dry smile. "Good-bye, Hale," he said. "I'll chaperon your orphan asylum for you. So long."

"Come out into the dining-room," said Miss Orella, after Dr. Hale had departed. "I know you must be hungry," and Mr. Dykeman did not deny it. In his quiet middle-aged way, he enjoyed this enlarged family circle as much as the younger fellows, and he and Mr. Unwin seemed to vie with one another to convince Miss Orella that life still held charms for her. Mr. Skee also hovered about her to a considerable extent, but most of his devotion was bestowed upon damsels of extreme youth.

"Here's one that's hungry, anyhow," remarked Dr. Bellair, coming out of her office at the moment, with her usual clean and clear-starched appearance. "I've been at it for eighteen hours, with only bites to eat. Yes, all over; both doing well."

It was a source of deep self-congratulation to Dr. Bellair to watch her friend grow young again in the new atmosphere. To Susie it appeared somewhat preposterous, as her aunt seemed to her mind a permanently elderly person; while to Mrs. Pettigrew it looked only natural. "Rella's only a young thing anyway," was her comment. But Jane Bellair marked and approved the added grace of each new gown, the blossoming of lace and ribbon, the appearance of long-hoarded bits of family jewelry, things held "too showy to wear" in Bainville, but somehow quite appropriate here.

Vivian and Grandma made Miss Orella sit down at her own table head, and bustled about in the pantry, bringing cheese and crackers, cake and fruit; but the doctor poked her head through the swing door and demanded meat.

"I don't want a refection, I want food," she said, and Jeanne cheerfully brought her a plate of cold beef. She was much attached to Dr. Bellair, for reasons many and good.

"What I like about this place," said Mrs. Pettigrew, surveying the scene from the head of her table, "is that there's always something going on."

"What I like about it," remarked Dr. Bellair, between well-Fletcherized mouthfuls, "is that people have a chance to grow and are growing."[41]

"What I like," Mr. Dykeman looked about him, and paused in the middle of a sentence, as was his wont; "is being beautifully taken care of and made comfortable—any man likes that."

Miss Orella beamed upon him. Emboldened, he went on: "And what I like most is the new, delightful"—he was gazing admiringly at her, and she looked so embarrassed that he concluded with a wide margin of safety—"friends I'm making."

Miss Orella's rosy flush, which had risen under his steady gaze, ebbed again to her usual soft pink. Even her coldest critics, in the most caustic Bainvillian circles, could never deny that she had "a good complexion." New England, like old England, loves roses on the cheeks, and our dry Western winds play havoc with them. But Miss Orella's bloomed brighter than at home.

"It is pleasant," she said softly; "all this coming and going—and the nice people—who stay." She looked at no one in particular, yet Mr. Dykeman seemed pleased.

"There's another coming, I guess," remarked Grandma, as a carriage was heard to stop outside, the gate slammed, and trunk-burdened steps pounded heavily across the piazza. The bell rang sharply, Mr. Dykeman opened the door, and the trunk came in first—a huge one, dumped promptly on the hall floor.

Behind the trunk and the man beneath it entered a lady; slim, elegant, graceful, in a rich silk dust coat and soft floating veils.

"My dear Miss Elder!" she said, coming forward; "and Vivian! Dear Vivian! I thought you could put me up, somewhere, and told him to come right here. O—and please—I haven't a bit of change left in my purse—will you pay the man?"

"Well, if it isn't Mrs. St. Cloud," said Grandma, without any note of welcome in her voice.

Mr. Dykeman paid the man; looked at the trunk, and paid him some more. The man departed swearing softly at nothing in particular, and Mr. Dykeman departed also to his own room.

Miss Orella's hospitable soul was much exercised. Refuse shelter to an old acquaintance, a guest, however unexpected, she could not; yet she had no vacant room. Vivian, flushed and excited, moved anew by her old attraction, eagerly helped the visitor take off her wraps, Mrs. Pettigrew standing the while, with her arms folded, in the doorway of her room, her thin lips drawn to a hard line, as one intending to repel boarders at any risk of life or limb. Dr. Bellair had returned to her apartments at the first sound of the visitor's voice.

She, gracious and calm in the midst of confusion, sat in a wreath of down-dropped silken wrappings, and held Vivian's hand.

"You dear child!" she said, "how well you look! What a charming place this is. The doctors sent me West for my health; I'm on my way to California. But when I found the train stopped here—I didn't know that it did till I saw the name—I had them take my trunk right off, and here I am! It is such a pleasure to see you all."

"Huh!" said Mrs. Pettigrew, and disappeared completely, closing the door behind her.

"Anything will do, Miss Elder," the visitor went on. "I shall find a hall bedroom palatial after a sleeping car; or a garret—anything! It's only for a few days, you know."

Vivian was restraining herself from hospitable offers by remembering that her room was also Susie's, and Miss Orella well knew that to give up hers meant sleeping on a hard, short sofa in that all-too-public parlor. She was hastily planning in her mind to take Susie in with her and persuade Mrs. Pettigrew to harbor Vivian, somewhat deterred by memories of the old lady's expression as she departed, when Mr. Dykeman appeared at the door, suitcase in hand.

"I promised Hale I'd keep house for those fatherless boys, you know," he said. "In the meantime, you're quite welcome to use my room, Miss Elder." And he departed, her blessing going with him.

More light refreshments were now in order, Mrs. St. Cloud protesting that she wanted nothing, but finding much to praise in the delicacies set before her. Several of the other boarders drifted in, always glad of an extra bite before going to bed. Susie and Mr. Saunders returned from a walk, Morton reappeared, and Jeanne, peering sharply in, resentful of this new drain upon her pantry shelves, saw a fair, sweet-faced woman, seated at ease, eating daintily, while Miss Elder and Vivian waited upon her, and the men all gathered admiringly about. Jeanne Jeaune wagged her head. "Ah, ha, Madame!" she muttered softly, "Such as you I have met before!" Theophile she had long since sent to bed, remaining up herself to keep an eye on the continued disturbance in the front of the house. Vivian and Susie brought the dishes out, and would have washed them or left them till morning for the maids.

"Truly, no," said Jeanne Jeaune; "go you to your beds; I will attend to these."

One by one she heard them go upstairs, distant movement and soft dissuasion as two gentlemen insisted on bearing Mrs. St. Cloud's trunk into her room, receding voices and closing doors. There was no sound in the dining-room now, but still she waited; the night was not yet quiet.

Miss Elder and Susie, Vivian also, hovered about, trying to make this new guest comfortable, in spite of her graceful protests that they must not concern themselves in the least about her, that she wanted nothing—absolutely nothing. At last they left her, and still later, after some brief exchange of surprised comment and warm appreciation of Mr. Dykeman's thoughtfulness, the family retired. Vivian, when her long hair was smoothly braided for the night, felt an imperative need for water.

"Don't you want some, Susie? I'll bring you a glass." But Susie only huddled the bedclothes about her pretty shoulders and said:

"Don't bring me *anything*, until to-morrow morning!"

So her room-mate stole out softly in her wrapper, remembering that a pitcher of cool water still stood on one of the tables. The windows to the street let in a flood of light from a big street lamp, and she found her way easily, but was a bit startled for a moment to find a man still sitting there, his head upon his arms.

"Why, Morton," she said; "is that you? What are you sitting up for? It's awfully late. I'm just after some water." She poured a glassful. "Don't you want some?"

"No, thank you," he said. "Yes, I will. Give me some, please."

The girl gave him a glass, drank from her own and set it down, turning to go, but he reached out and caught a flowing sleeve of her kimono.

"Don't go, Vivian! Do sit down and talk to a fellow. I've been trying to see you for days and days."

"Why, Morton Elder, how absurd! You have certainly seen me every day, and we've talked hours this very evening. This is no time for conversation, surely."

"The best time in the world," he assured her. "All the other times there are people about—dozens—hundreds— swarms! I want to talk to just you."

There were certainly no dozens or hundreds about now, but as certainly there was one, noting with keen and disapproving interest this midnight tête-à-tête. It did not last very long, and was harmless and impersonal enough while it lasted.

Vivian sat for a few moments, listening patiently while the young man talked of his discouragements, his hopes, his wishes to succeed in life, to be worthy of her; but when the personal note sounded, when he tried to take her hand in the semi-darkness, then her New England conscience sounded also, and she rose to her feet and left him.

"We'll talk about that another time," she said. "Now do be quiet and do not wake people up."

He stole upstairs, dutifully, and she crept softly back to her room and got into bed, without eliciting more than a mild grunt from sleepy Susie. Silence reigned at last in the house. Not for long, however.

At about half past twelve Dr. Bellair was roused from a well-earned sleep by a light, insistent tap upon her door. She listened, believing it to be a wind-stirred twig; but no, it was a finger tap—quiet—repeated. She opened the door upon Jeanne in her stocking feet.

"Your pardon, Mrs. Doctor," said the visitor, "but it is of importance. May I speak for a little? No, I'm not ill, and we need not a light."

They sat in the clean little office, the swaying cotton-wood boughs making a changeful pattern on the floor.

"You are a doctor, and you can make an end to it—you must make an end to it," said Jeanne, after a little hesitation. "This young man—this nephew—he must not marry my young lady."

"What makes you think he wants to?" asked the doctor.

"I have seen, I have heard—I know," said Jeanne. "You know, all can see that he loves her. *He!* Not such as he for my young lady."

"Why do you object to him, Jeanne?"

"He has lived the bad life," said the woman, grimly.

"Most young men are open to criticism," said Dr. Bellair. "Have you anything definite to tell me—anything that you could *prove?*—if it were necessary to save her?" She leaned forward, elbows on knees.

Jeanne sat in the flickering shadows, considering her words. "He has had the sickness," she said at last.

"Can you prove that?"

"I can prove to you, a doctor, that Coralie and Anastasia and Estelle—they have had it. They are still alive; but not so beautiful."

"Yes; but how can you prove it on him?"

"I know he was with them. Well, it was no secret. I myself have seen—he was there often."

"How on earth have you managed not to be recognized?" Dr. Bellair inquired after a few moments.

Jeanne laughed bitterly. "That was eight years ago; he was but a boy—gay and foolish, with the others. What does a boy know? . . . Also, at that time I was blonde, and—of a difference."

"I see," said the doctor, "I see! That's pretty straight. You know personally of that time, and you know the record of those others. But that was a long time ago."

"I have heard of him since, many times, in such company," said Jeanne. They sat in silence for some time. A distant church clock struck a single deep low note. The woman rose, stood for a hushed moment, suddenly burst forth with hushed intensity: "You must save her, doctor—you will! I was young once," she went on. "I did not know—as she does not. I married, and—*that* came to me! It made me a devil—for awhile. Tell her, doctor—if you must; tell her about my boy!"

She went away, weeping silently, and Dr. Bellair sat sternly thinking in her chair, and fell asleep in it from utter weariness.

8

A Mixture

In poetry and painting and fiction we see
  Such praise for the Dawn of the Day,
We've long since been convinced that a sunrise must be
  All Glorious and Golden and Gay.

But we find there are mornings quite foggy and drear,
  With the clouds in a low-hanging pall;   ˎ
Till the grey light of daylight can hardly make clear
  That the sun has arisen at all.

Dr. Richard Hale left his brood of temporary orphans without really expecting for them any particular oversight from Andrew Dykeman; but the two were sufficiently close friends to well warrant the latter in moving over to The Monastery—as Jimmie Saunders called it.

Mr. Dykeman was sufficiently popular with the young men to be welcome, even if he had not had a good excuse, and when they found how super-excellent his excuse was they wholly approved.

To accommodate Miss Orella was something—all the boys liked Miss Orella. They speculated among themselves on her increasing youth and good looks, and even exchanged sagacious theories as to the particular acting cause. But when they found that Mr. Dykeman's visit was to make room for the installation of Mrs. St. Cloud, they were more than pleased.

All the unexpressed ideals of masculine youth seemed centered in this palely graceful lady; the low, sweet voice, the delicate hands, the subtle sympathy of manner, the nameless, quiet charm of dress.

Young Burns became her slave on sight, Lawson and Peters fell on the second day; not one held out beyond the third. Even Susie's attractions paled, her very youth became a disadvantage; she lacked that large considering tenderness.

"Fact is," Mr. Peters informed his friends rather suddenly, "young women are selfish. Naturally, of course. It takes some experience to—well, to understand a fellow." They all agreed with him.

Mr. Dykeman, quiet and reserved as always, was gravely polite to the newcomer, and Mr. Skee revolved at a distance, making observations. Occasionally he paid some court to her, at which times she was cold to him; and again he devoted himself to the other ladies with his impressive air, as of one bowing low and sweeping the floor with a plumed hat.

Mr. Skee's Stetson had, as a matter of fact, no sign of plumage, and his bows were of a somewhat jerky order; but his gallantry was sweeping and impressive, none the less. If he remained too far away Mrs. St. Cloud would draw him to her circle, which consisted of all the other gentlemen.

There were two exceptions. Mr. James Saunders had reached the stage where any woman besides Susie was but a skirted ghost, and Morton was by this time so deeply devoted to Vivian that he probably would not have wavered even if left alone. He was not wholly a free agent, however.

Adela St. Cloud had reached an age when something must be done. Her mysterious absent husband had mysteriously and absently died, and still she never breathed a word against him. But the Bible Class in Bainville furnished no satisfactory material for further hopes, the place of her earlier dwelling seemed not wholly desirable now, and the West had called her.

Finding herself comfortably placed in Mr. Dykeman's room, and judging from the number of his shoe-trees and the quality of his remaining toilet articles that he might be considered "suitable," she decided to remain in the half-way house for a season. So settled, why, for a thousand reasons one must keep one's hand in.

There were men in plenty, from twenty year old Archie to the uncertain decades of Mr. Skee. Idly amusing herself, she questioned that gentleman indirectly as to his age, drawing from him astounding memories of the previous century.

When confronted with historic proof that the events he described were over a hundred years passed, he would apologize, admitting that he had no memory for dates. She owned one day, with gentle candor, to being thirty-three.

"That must seem quite old to a man like you, Mr. Skee. I feel very old sometimes!" She lifted large eyes to him, and drew her filmy scarf around her shoulders.

"Your memory must be worse than mine, ma'am," he replied, "and work the same way. You've sure got ten or twenty years added on superfluous! Now me!" He shook his head; "I don't remember when I was born at all. And losin' my folks so young, *and* the family Bible—I don't expect I ever shall. But I 'low I'm all of ninety-seven."

This being palpably impossible, and as the only local incidents he could recall in his youth were quite dateless adventures among the Indians, she gave it up. Why Mr. Skee should have interested her at all was difficult to say, unless it was the appeal to his uncertainty—he was at least a game fish, if not edible.

Of the women she met, Susie and Vivian were far the most attractive, wherefore Mrs. St. Cloud, with subtle sympathy and engaging frankness, fairly cast Mr. Saunders in Susie's arms, and vice versa, as opportunity occurred.

Morton she rather snubbed, treated him as a mere boy, told tales of his childhood that were in no way complimentary—so that he fled from her.

With Vivian she renewed her earlier influence to a great degree.

With some inquiry and more intuition she discovered what it was that had chilled the girl's affection for her.

"I don't wonder, my dear child," she said; "I never told you of that—I never speak of it to anyone. . . . It was one of the—" she shivered slightly—"darkest griefs of a very dark time. . . . He was a beautiful boy. . . . I never *dreamed*—"

The slow tears rose in her beautiful eyes till they shone like shimmering stars.

"Heaven send no such tragedy may ever come into your life, dear!"

She reached a tender hand to clasp the girl's. "I am so glad of your happiness!"

Vivian was silent. As a matter of fact, she was not happy enough to honestly accept sympathy. Mrs. St. Cloud mistook her attitude, or seemed to.

"I suppose you still blame me. Many people did. I often blame myself. One cannot be *too* careful. It's a terrible responsibility, Vivian—to have a man love you."

The girl's face grew even more somber. That was one thing which was troubling her.

"But your life is all before you," pursued the older woman. "Your dream has come true! How happy—how wonderfully happy you must be!"

"I am not, not *really*," said the girl. "At least—"

"I know—I know; I understand," Mrs. St. Cloud nodded with tender wisdom. "You are not sure. Is not that it?"

That was distinctly "it," and Vivian so agreed.

"There is no other man?"

"Not the shadow of one!" said the girl firmly. And as her questioner had studied the field and made up her mind to the same end, she believed her.

"Then you must not mind this sense of uncertainty. It always happens. It is part of the morning clouds of maidenhood, my dear—it vanishes with the sunrise!" And she smiled beatifically.

Then the girl unburdened herself of her perplexities. She could always express herself so easily to this sympathetic friend.

"There are so many things that I—dislike—about him," she said. "Habits of speech—of manners. He is not—not what I—"

She paused.

"Not all the Dream! Ah! My dear child, they never are! We are given these beautiful ideals to guard and guide us; but the real is never quite the same. But when a man's soul opens to you—when he loves—these small things vanish. They can be changed—you will change them."

"Yes—he says so," Vivian admitted. "He says that he

knows that he is—unworthy—and has done wrong things. But so have I, for that matter."

Mrs. St. Cloud agreed with her. "I am glad you feel that, my dear. Men have their temptations—their vices—and we good women are apt to be hard on them. But have we no faults? Ah, my dear, I have seen good women—young girls, like yourself—ruin a man's whole life by—well, by heartlessness; by lack of understanding. Most young men do things they become ashamed of when they really love. And in the case of a motherless boy like this—lonely, away from his home, no good woman's influence about— what else could we expect? But you can make a new man of him. A glorious work!"

"That's what he says. I'm not so sure—" The girl hesitated.

"Not sure you can? Oh, my child, it is the most beautiful work on earth! To see from year to year a strong, noble character grow under your helping hand! To be the guiding star, the inspiration of a man's life. To live to hear him say:

> " 'Ah, who am I that God should bow
>   From heaven to choose a wife for me?
> What have I done He should endow
>   My home with thee?' "

There was a silence.

Vivian's dark eyes shone with appreciation for the tender beauty of the lines, the lovely thought. Then she arose and walked nervously across the floor, returning presently.

"Mrs. St. Cloud—"

"Call me Adela, my dear."

"Adela—dear Adela—you—you have been married. I have no mother. Tell me, ought not there to be more— more love? I'm fond of Morton, of course, and I do want to help him—but surely, if I loved him—I should feel happier—more sure!"

"The first part of love is often very confusing, my dear. I'll tell you how it is: just because you are a woman grown and feel your responsibilities, especially here, where you have so many men friends, you keep Morton at a distance. Then the external sort of cousinly affection you have for him rather blinds you to other feelings. But I have not forgotten—and I'm sure you have not—the memory of that hot, sweet night so long ago; the world swimming in summer moonlight and syringa sweetness; the stillness everywhere—and your first kiss!"

Vivian started to her feet. She moved to the window and stood awhile; came back and kissed her friend warmly, and went away without another word.

The lady betook herself to her toilet, and spent some time on it, for there was one of Miss Peeder's classes that night.

Mrs. St. Cloud danced with many, but most with Mr. Dykeman; no woman in the room had her swimming grace of motion, and yet, with all the throng of partners about her she had time to see Susie's bright head bobbing about beneath Mr. Saunders' down-bent, happy face, and Vivian, with her eyes cast down, dancing with Morton, whose gaze never left her. He was attention itself, he brought her precisely the supper she liked, found her favorite corner to rest in, took her to sit on the broad piazza between the dances, remained close to her, still talking earnestly, when all the outsiders had gone.

Vivian found it hard to sleep that night. All that he had said of his new hope, new power, new courage, bore out Mrs. St. Cloud's bright promise of a new-built life. And some way, as she had listened and did not forbid, the touch of his hand, the pressure of his arm, grew warmer and brought back the memories of that summer night so long ago.

He had begged hard for a kiss before he left her, and she quite had to tear herself away, as Susie drifted in, also late; and Aunt Orella said they must all go to bed right away—she was tired if they were not.

She did look tired. This dance seemed somehow less agreeable to her than had others. She took off her new prettinesses and packed them away in a box in the lower drawer.

"I'm an old fool!" she said. "Trying to dress up like a girl. I'm ashamed of myself!" Quite possibly she did not sleep well either, yet she had no room-mate to keep her awake by babbling on, as Susie did to Vivian.

Her discourse was first, last and always about Jimmie Saunders. He had said this, he had looked that, he had done so; and what did Vivian think he meant? And wasn't he handsome—and *so* clever!

Little Susie cuddled close and finally dropped off asleep, her arms around Vivian. But the older girl counted the hours; her head, or her heart, in a whirl.

Morton Elder was wakeful, too. So much so that he arose with a whispered expletive, took his shoes in his hand, and let himself softly out for a tramp in the open.

This was not the first of his love affairs, but with all his hot young heart he wished it was. He stood still, alone on the high stretches of moonlit mesa and looked up at the measureless, brilliant spaces above him.

"I'll keep straight—if I can have her!" he repeated under his breath. "I will! I will!"

It had never occurred to him before to be ashamed of the various escapades of his youth. He had done no more than others, many others. None of "the boys" he associated with intended to do what was wrong; they were quite harsh in judgment of those who did, according to their standards. None of them had been made acquainted with the social or pathological results of their amusements, and the mere "Zutritt ist Verboten" had never impressed them at all.[42]

But now the gentler influences of his childhood, even the narrow morality of Bainville, rose in pleasant colors in his mind. He wished he had saved his money, instead of spending it faster than it came in. He wished he had kept out of poker and solo and barrooms generally.[43] He wished, in a dumb, shamed way, that he could come to her as clean as she was. But he threw his shoulders back and lifted his head determinedly.

"I'll be good to her," he determined; "I'll make her a good husband."

In the days that followed his devotion was as constant as before, but more intelligent. His whole manner changed and softened. He began to read the books she liked, and to talk about them. He was gentler to everyone, more polite, even to the waitresses, tender and thoughtful of his aunt and sister. Vivian began to feel a pride in him, and in her influence, deepening as time passed.

Mrs. Pettigrew, visiting the library on one of her frequent errands, was encountered there and devotedly escorted by Mr. Skee.

"That is a most fascinating young lady who has Mr. Dykeman's room; don't you think so, ma'am?" quoth he.

"I do not," said Mrs. Pettigrew. "Young! She's not so young as you are—nothing like—never was!"

He threw back his head and laughed his queer laugh, which looked so uproarious and made so little noise.

"She certainly is a charmer, whatever her age may be," he continued.

"Glad you think so, Mr. Skee. It may be time you lost a fourth!"

"Lost a fourth? What in the—Hesperides!"[44]

"If you can't guess what, you needn't ask me!" said the lady, with some tartness. "But for my own part I prefer the Apaches. Good afternoon, Mr. Skee."

She betook herself to her room with unusual promptness, and refused to be baited forth by any kind of offered amusement.

"It's right thoughtful of Andy Dykeman, gettin' up this entertainment for Mrs. St. Cloud, isn't it, Miss Elder?" Thus Mr. Skee to Miss Orella a little later.

"I don't think it is Mr. Dykeman's idea at all," she told him. "It's those boys over there. They are all wild about her, quite naturally." She gave a little short sigh. "If Dr. Hale were home I doubt if he would encourage it."

"I'm pretty sure he wouldn't, ma'am. He's certainly down on the fair sex, even such a peacherino as this one. But with Andy, now, it's different. He is a man of excellent judgment."

"I guess all men's judgment is pretty much alike in some ways," said Miss Orella, oracularly. She seemed busy and constrained, and Mr. Skee drifted off and paid court as best he might to Dr. Bellair.

"Charmed to find you at home, ma'am," he said; "or shall I say at office?"

"Call it what you like, Mr. Skee; it's been my home for a good many years now."

"It's a mighty fine thing for a woman, livin' alone, to have a business, seems to me," remarked the visitor.

"It's a fine thing for any woman, married or single, to my mind," she answered. "I wish I could get Vivian Lane started in that kindergarten she talks about."

"There's kids enough, and goodness knows they need a gardener! What's lackin'? House room?"

"She thinks she's not really competent. She has no regular certificate, you see. Her parents would never let go of her long enough," the doctor explained.

"Some parents *are* pretty graspin', ain't they? To my mind, Miss Vivian would be a better teacher than lots of the ticketed ones. She's got the natural love of children."

"Yes, and she has studied a great deal. She just needs an impetus."

"Perhaps if she thought there was 'a call' she might be willing. I doubt if the families here realize what they're missin'. Ain't there some among your patients who could be stirred up a little?"

The doctor thought there were, and he suggested several names from his apparently unlimited acquaintance.

"I believe in occupation for the young. It takes up their minds," said Mr. Skee, and departed with serenity. He strolled over to Dr. Hale's fence and leaned upon it, watching the preparations. Mr. Dykeman, in his shirt-sleeves, stood about offering suggestions, while the young men swarmed here and there with poles and stepladders, hanging Chinese lanterns.

"Hello, Elmer; come in and make yourself useful," called Mr. Dykeman.

"I'll come in, but I'll be switched if I'll be useful," he replied, laying a large hand on the fence and vaulting his long legs over it with an agility amazing in one of his alleged years. "You all are sure putting yourself out for this occasion. Is it somebody's birthday?"

"No; it's a get-up of these youngsters. They began by wanting Mrs. St. Cloud to come over to tea—afternoon tea—and now look at this!"

"Did she misunderstand the invitation as bad as that?"

"O, no; just a gradual change of plan. One thing leads to another, you know. Here, Archie! That bush won't hold the line. Put it on the willow."

"I see," said Mr. Skee; "and, as we're quotin' proverbs, I might remark that 'While the cat's away the mice will play.' "

Mr. Dykeman smiled. "It's rather a good joke on Hale, isn't it?"

"Would be if he should happen to come home—and find this hen-party on." They both chuckled.

"I guess he's good for a week yet," said Mr. Dykeman. "Those medical associations do a lot of talking. Higher up there, George—a good deal higher."

He ran over to direct the boys, and Mr. Skee, hands behind him, strolled up and down the garden, wearing a meditative smile. He and Andrew Dykeman had been friends for many long years.

Dr. Bellair used her telephone freely after Mr. Skee's departure, making notes and lists of names. Late in the afternoon she found Vivian in the hall.

"I don't see much of you these days, Miss Lane," she said.

The girl flushed. Since Mrs. St. Cloud's coming and their renewed intimacy she had rather avoided the doctor, and that lady had kept herself conspicuously out of the way.

"Don't call me Miss Lane; I'm Vivian—to my friends."

"I hope you count me a friend?" said Dr. Bellair, gravely.

"I do, Doctor, and I'm proud to. But so many things have been happening lately," she laughed, a little nervously. "The truth is, I'm really ashamed to talk to you; I'm so lazy."

"That's exactly what I wanted to speak about. Aren't you ready to begin that little school of yours?"

"I'd like to—I should, really," said the girl. "But, somehow, I don't know how to set about it."

"I've been making some inquiries," said the doctor. "There are six or eight among my patients that you could count on—about a dozen young ones. How many could you handle?"

"Oh, I oughtn't to have more than twenty in any case. A

dozen would be plenty to begin with. Do you think I *could* count on them—really?"

"I tell you what I'll do," her friend offered; "I'll take you around and introduce you to any of them you don't know. Most of 'em come here to the dances. There's Mrs. Horsford and Mrs. Blake, and that little Mary Jackson with the twins. You'll find they are mostly friends."

"You are awfully kind," said the girl. "I wish"—her voice took on a sudden note of intensity—"I do wish I were strong, like you, Dr. Bellair."

"I wasn't very strong—at your age—my child. I did the weakest of weak things—"

Vivian was eager to ask her what it was, but a door opened down one side passage and the doctor quietly disappeared down the other, as Mrs. St. Cloud came out.

"I thought I heard your voice," she said. "And Miss Elder's, wasn't it?"

"No; it was Dr. Bellair."

"A strong character, and a fine physician, I understand. I'm sorry she does not like me."

Mrs. St. Cloud's smile made it seem impossible that anyone should dislike her.

Vivian could not, however, deny the fact, and was not diplomatic enough to smooth it over, which her more experienced friend proceeded to do.

"It is temperamental," she said gently. "If we had gone to school together we would not have been friends. She is strong, downright, progressive; I am weaker, more sensitive, better able to bear than to do. You must find her so stimulating."

"Yes," the girl said. "She was talking to me about my school."

"Your school?"

"Didn't you know I meant to have a sort of kindergarten? We planned it even before starting; but Miss Elder seemed to need me at first, and since then—things—have happened—"

"And other things will happen, dear child! Quite other and different things."

The lady's smile was bewitching. Vivian flushed slowly under her gaze.

"Oh, my dear, I watched you dancing together! You don't mind my noticing, do you?"

Her voice was suddenly tender and respectful. "I do not wish to intrude, but you are very dear to me. Come into my room—do—and tell me what to wear to-night."

Mrs. St. Cloud's clothes had always been a delight to Vivian. They were what she would have liked to wear— and never quite have dared, under the New England fear of being "too dressy." Her own beauty was kept trimly neat, like a closed gentian.[45]

Her friend was in the gayest mood. She showed her a trunkful of delicate garments and gave her a glittering embroidered scarf, which the girl rapturously admired, but declared she would never have the courage to wear.

"You shall wear it this very night," declared the lady. "Here—show me what you've got. You shall be as lovely as you *are*, for once!"

So Vivian brought out her modest wardrobe, and the older woman chose a gown of white, insisted on shortening the sleeves to fairy wings of lace, draped the scarf about her white neck, raised the soft, close-bound hair to a regal crown, and put a shining star in it, and added a string of pearls on the white throat.

"Look at yourself now, child!" she said.

Vivian looked, in the long depths of Mr. Dykeman's mirror. She knew that she had beauty, but had never seen herself so brilliantly attired. Erect, slender, graceful, the long lines of her young body draped in soft white, and her dark head, crowned and shining, poised on its white column, rising from the shimmering lace. Her color deepened as she looked, and added to the picture.

"You shall wear it to-night! You shall!" cried her admiring friend. "To please me—if no one else!"

Whether to please her or someone else, Vivian consented, the two arriving rather late at the garden party across the way.

Mr. Dykeman, looking very tall and fine in his evening clothes, was a cordial host, ably seconded by the eager boys about him.

The place was certainly a credit to their efforts, the bare rooms being turned to bowers by vines and branches

brought from the mountains, and made fragrant by piled
flowers. Lights glimmered through colored shades among
the leaves, and on the dining table young Peters, who
came from Connecticut, had rigged a fountain by means
of some rubber tubing and an auger hole in the floor. This
he had made before Mr. Dykeman caught him, and vowed
Dr. Hale would not mind. Mr. Peters' enjoyment of the
evening, however, was a little dampened by his knowledge of the precarious nature of this arrangement. He
danced attendance on Mrs. St. Cloud, with the others, but
wore a preoccupied expression, and stole in once or twice
from the lit paths outside to make sure that all was running well. It was well to and during supper time, and the
young man was complimented on his ingenuity.

"Reminds me of the Hanging Gardens of Babylon," said
Mr. Skee, sentimentally.[46]

"Why?" asked Mrs. Pettigrew.

"Oh, *why*, ma'am? How can a fellow say why?" he protested. "Because it is so—so efflorescent, I suppose."

"Reminds me of a loose faucet," said she, *sotto voce*, to
Dr. Bellair.[47]

Mr. Peters beamed triumphantly, but in the very hour of
his glory young Burns, hastening to get a cup of coffee for
his fair one, tripped over the concealed pipe, and the
fountain poured forth its contributions among the feet of
the guests.

This was a minor misadventure, however, hurting no
one's feeling but Mr. Peters', and Mrs. St. Cloud was so
kind to him in consequence that he was envied by all the
others.[48]

Mr. Dykeman was attentive to his guests, old and young,
but Mrs. Pettigrew had not her usual smile for him; Miss
Orella declined to dance, alleging that she was too tired,
and Dr. Bellair somewhat drily told him that he need not
bother with her. He was hardly to be blamed if he turned
repeatedly to Mrs. St. Cloud, whose tactful sweetness was
always ready. She had her swarm of young admirers
about her, yet never failed to find a place for her host, a
smile and a word of understanding.

Her eyes were everywhere. She watched Mr. Skee
waltzing with the youngest, providing well-chosen re-

freshments for Miss Orella, gallantly escorting Grandma to see the "Lovers' Lane" they had made at the end of the garden. Its twin lines of lights were all outside; within was grateful shadow.

Mrs. St. Cloud paced through this fragrant arbor with each and every one of the receiving party, uttering ever-fresh expressions of admiration and gratitude for their kind thoughtfulness, especially to Mr. Dykeman.

When she saw Susie and Mr. Saunders go in at the farther end, she constituted herself a sort of protective agency to keep every one else out, holding them in play with various pleasant arts.

And Vivian? When she arrived there was a little gasp from Morton, who was waiting for her near the door. She was indeed a sight to make a lover's heart leap. He had then, as it were, surrounded her. Vainly did the others ask for dances. Morton had unblushingly filled out a card with his own name and substituted it for the one she handed him.[49] She protested, but the music sounded and he whirled her away before she could expostulate to any avail.

His eyes spoke his admiration, and for once his tongue did not spoil the impression.

Half laughing and half serious, she let him monopolize her, but quite drove him away when Mr. Dykeman claimed his dance.

"All filled up!" said Morton for her, showing his card.

"Mine was promised yesterday, was it not, Miss Lane?" said the big man, smiling. And she went with him. He took her about the garden later, gravely admiring and attentive, and when Susie fairly rushed into her arms, begging her to come and talk with her, he left them both in a small rose-crowned summer-house and went back to Mrs. St. Cloud.

"Oh, Vivian, Vivian! What do you think!" Susie's face was buried on Vivian's shoulder. "I'm engaged!"

Vivian held her close and kissed her soft hair. Her joyous excitement was contagious.

"He's the nicest man in the world!" breathed Susie, "and he loves me!"

"We all supposed he did. Didn't you know it before?"

"Oh, yes, in a way; but, Vivian—he kissed me!"

"Well, child, have you never in all your little life been kissed before?"

Susie lifted a rosy, tearful face for a moment.

"Never, never, never!" she said. "I thought I had, but I haven't! Oh, I am so happy!"

"What's up?" inquired Morton, appearing with a pink lantern in his hand, in impatient search for his adored one. "Susie—crying?"

"No, I'm *not*," she said, and ran forthwith back to the house, whence Jimmie was bringing her ice cream.

Vivian started to follow her.

"Oh, no, Vivian; don't go. Wait." He dropped the lantern and took her hands. The paper cover flared up, showing her flushed cheeks and starry eyes. He stamped out the flame, and in the sudden darkness caught her in his arms.

For a moment she allowed him, turning her head away. He kissed her white shoulder.

"No! No, Morton—don't! You mustn't!"

She tried to withdraw herself, but he held her fast. She could feel the pounding of his heart.

"Oh, Vivian, don't say no! You will marry me, won't you? Some day, when I'm more worth while. Say you will! Some day—if not now. I love you so; I need you so! Say yes, Vivian."

He was breathing heavily. His arms held her motionless. She still kept her face turned from him.

"Let me go, Morton; let me go! You hurt me!"

"Say yes, dear, and I'll let you go—for a little while."

"Yes," said Vivian.

The ground jarred beside them, as a tall man jumped the hedge boundary. He stood a moment, staring.

"Well, is this my house, or Coney Island?" they heard him say. And then Morton swore softly to himself as Vivian left him and came out.

"Good evening, Dr. Hale," she said, a little breathlessly. "We weren't expecting you so soon."

"I should judge not," he answered. "What's up, anyhow?"

"The boys—and Mr. Dykeman—are giving a garden party for Mrs. St. Cloud."

"For whom?"

"For Adela St. Cloud. She is visiting us. Aren't you coming in?"

"Not now," he said, and was gone without another word.

9

Consequences

You may have a fondness for grapes that are green,
And the sourness that greenness beneath;
  You may have a right
  To a colic at night—
But consider your children's teeth!

Dr. Hale retired from his gaily illuminated grounds in too much displeasure to consider the question of dignity. One suddenly acting cause was the news given him by Vivian. The other was the sight of Morton Elder's face as he struck a match to light his cigarette.

Thus moved, and having entered and left his own grounds like a thief in the night, he proceeded to tramp in the high-lying outskirts of the town until every light in his house had gone out. Then he returned, let himself into his office, and lay there on a lounge until morning.

Vivian had come out so quickly to greet the doctor from obscure motives. She felt a sudden deep objection to being found there with Morton, a wish to appear as one walking about unconcernedly, and when that match glow made Morton's face shine out prominently in the dark shelter, she, too, felt a sudden displeasure.

Without a word she went swiftly to the house, excused herself to her grandmother, who nodded understandingly, and returned to The Cottonwoods, to her room. She felt that she must be alone and think; think of that irrevocable word she had uttered, and its consequences.

She sat at her window, rather breathless, watching the rows of pink lanterns swaying softly on the other side of the street; hearing the lively music, seeing young couples leave the gate and stroll off homeward.

182

Susie's happiness came more vividly to mind than her own. It was so freshly joyous, so pure, so perfectly at rest. She could not feel that way, could not tell with decision exactly how she did feel. But if this was happiness, it was not as she had imagined it. She thought of that moonlit summer night so long ago, and the memory of its warm wonder seemed sweeter than the hasty tumult and compulsion of to-night.

She was stirred through and through by Morton's intense emotion, but with a sort of reaction, a wish to escape. He had been so madly anxious, he had held her so close; there seemed no other way but to yield to him—in order to get away.

And then Dr. Hale had jarred the whole situation. She had to be polite to him, in his own grounds. If only Morton had kept still—that grating match—his face, bent and puffing, Dr. Hale must have seen him. And again she thought of little Susie with almost envy. Even after that young lady had come in, bubbled over with confidences and raptures, and finally dropped to sleep without Vivian's having been able to bring herself to return the confidences, she stole back to her window again to breathe.

Why had Dr. Hale started so at the name of Mrs. St. Cloud? That was puzzling her more than she cared to admit. By and by she saw his well-known figure, tall and erect, march by on the other side and go into the office.

"O, well," she sighed at last, "I'm not young, like Susie. Perhaps it *is* like this—"

Now Morton had been in no special need of that cigarette at that special moment, but he did not wish to seem to hide in the dusky arbor, nor to emerge lamely as if he had hidden. So he lit the match, more from habit than anything else. When it was out, and the cigarette well lighted, he heard the doctor's sudden thump on the other side of the fence and came out to rejoin Vivian. She was not there.

He did not see her again that night, and his meditations were such that next day found him, as a lover, far more agreeable to Vivian than the night before. He showed real understanding, no triumph, no airs of possession; took no liberties, only said: "When I am good enough I shall claim you—my darling!" and looked at her with such restrained longing that she quite warmed to him again.

He held to this attitude, devoted, quietly affectionate; till her sense of rebellion passed away and her real pleasure in his improvement reasserted itself.[50] As they read together, if now and then his arm stole around her waist, he always withdrew it when so commanded. Still, one cannot put the same severity into a prohibition too often repeated. The constant, thoughtful attention of a man experienced in the art of pleasing women, the new and frankly inexperienced efforts he made to meet her highest thoughts, to learn and share her preferences, both pleased her.

He was certainly good looking, certainly amusing, certainly had become a better man from her companionship. She grew to feel a sort of ownership in this newly arisen character; a sort of pride in it. Then, she had always been fond of Morton, since the time when he was only "Susie's big brother." That counted.

Another thing counted, too, counted heavily, though Vivian never dreamed of it and would have hotly repudiated the charge. She was a woman of full marriageable age, with all the unused powers of her woman's nature calling for expression, quite unrecognized.

He was a man who loved her, loved her more deeply than he had ever loved before, than he had even known he could love; who quite recognized what called within him and meant to meet the call. And he was near her every day.

After that one fierce outbreak he held himself well in check. He knew he had startled her then, almost lost her. And with every hour of their companionship he felt more and more how much she was to him. Other women he had pursued, overtaken, left behind. He felt that there was something in Vivian which was beyond him, giving a stir and lift of aspiration which he genuinely enjoyed.

Day by day he strove to win her full approval, and day by day he did not neglect the tiny, slow-lapping waves of little tendernesses, small affectionate liberties at well-chosen moments, always promptly withdrawing when forbidden, but always beginning again a little further on.

Dr. Bellair went to Dr. Hale's office and sat herself down solidly in the patient's chair.

"Dick," she said, "are you going to stand for this?"

"Stand for what, my esteemed but cryptic fellow-practitioner?"

She eyed his calm, reserved countenance with friendly admiration. "You are an awfully good fellow, Dick, but dull. At the same time dull and transparent. Are you going to sit still and let that dangerous patient of yours marry the finest girl in town?"

"Your admiration for girls is always stronger than mine, Jane; and I have, if you will pardon the boast, more than one patient."

"All right, Dick—if you want it made perfectly clear to your understanding. Do you mean to let Morton Elder marry Vivian Lane?"

"What business is it of mine?" he demanded, more than brusquely—savagely.

"You know what he's got."

"I am a physician, not a detective. And I am not Miss Lane's father, brother, uncle or guardian."

"Or lover," added Dr. Bellair, eyeing him quietly. She thought she saw a second's flicker of light in the deep gray eyes, a possible tightening of set lips. "Suppose you are not," she said; "nor even a humanitarian. You *are* a member of society. Do you mean to let a man whom you know has no right to marry, poison the life of that splendid girl?"

He was quite silent for a moment, but she could see the hand on the farther arm of his chair grip it till the nails were white.

"How do you know he—wishes to marry her?"

"If you were about like other people, you old hermit, you'd know it as well as anybody. I think they are on the verge of an engagement, if they aren't over it already. Once more, Dick, shall you do anything?"

"No," said he. Then as she did not add a word, he rose and walked up and down the office in big strides, turning upon her at last.

"You know how I feel about this. It is a matter of honor—professional honor. You women don't seem to know what

the word means. I've told that good-for-nothing young
wreck that he has no right to marry for years yet, if ever.
That is all I can do. I will not betray the confidence of a
patient."

"Not if he had smallpox, or scarlet fever, or the bubonic
plague? Suppose a patient of yours had the leprosy, and
wanted to marry your sister, would you betray his confidence?"

"I might kill my sister," he said, glaring at her. "I refuse
to argue with you."

"Yes, I think you'd better refuse," she said, rising. "And
you don't have to kill Vivian Lane, either. A man's honor
always seems to want to kill a woman to satisfy it. I'm glad
I haven't got the feeling. Well, Dick, I thought I'd give you
a chance to come to your senses, a real good chance. But I
won't leave you to the pangs of unavailing remorse, you
poor old goose. That young syphilitic is no patient of
mine." And she marched off to perform a difficult duty.

She was very fond of Vivian. The girl's unselfish sweetness of character and the depth of courage and power she
perceived behind the sensitive, almost timid exterior, ap-
pealed to her. If she had had a daughter, perhaps she
would have been like that. If she had had a daughter
would she not have thanked anyone who would try to save
her from such a danger? From that worse than deadly
peril, because of which she had no daughter.

Dr. Bellair was not the only one who watched Morton's
growing devotion with keen interest. To his aunt it was a
constant joy. From the time her boisterous little nephew
had come to rejoice her heart and upset her immaculate
household arrangements, and had played, pleasantly
though tyrannically, with the little girl next door, Miss Orella had dreamed this romance for him. To have it fail was
part of her grief when he left her, to have it now so visibly
coming to completion was a deep delight.

If she had been blind to his faults, she was at least vividly conscious of the present sudden growth of virtues.
She beamed at him with affectionate pride, and her manner to Mrs. Pettigrew was one of barely subdued "I told
you so." Indeed, she could not restrain herself altogether,

but spoke to that lady with tender triumph of how lovely it was to have Morton so gentle and nice.

"You never did like the boy, I know, but you must admit that he is behaving beautifully now."

"I will," said the old lady; "I'll admit it without reservation. He's behaving beautifully—now. But I'm not going to talk about him—to you, Orella." So she rolled up her knitting work and marched off.

"Too bad she's so prejudiced and opinionated," said Miss Elder to Susie, rather warmly. "I'm real fond of Mrs. Pettigrew, but when she takes a dislike—"

Susie was so happy herself that she seemed to walk in an aura of rosy light. Her Jimmie was so evidently the incarnation of every masculine virtue and charm that he lent a reflected lustre to other men, even to her brother. Because of her love for Jimmie, she loved Morton better— loved everybody better. To have her only brother marry her dearest friend was wholly pleasant to Susie.

It was not difficult to wring from Vivian a fair knowledge of how things stood, for, though reserved by nature, she was utterly unused to concealing anything, and could not tell an efficient lie if she wanted to.

"Are you engaged or are you not, you dear old thing?" demanded Susie.

And Vivian admitted that there was "an understanding." But Susie absolutely must not speak of it.

For a wonder she did not, except to Jimmie. But people seemed to make up their minds on the subject with miraculous agreement. The general interest in the manifold successes of Mrs. St. Cloud gave way to this vivid personal interest, and it was discussed from two sides among their whole circle of acquaintance.

One side thought that a splendid girl was being wasted, sacrificed, thrown away, on a disagreeable, good-for-nothing fellow. The other side thought the "interesting" Mr. Elder might have done better; they did not know what he could see in her.

They, that vaguely important They, before whom we so deeply bow, were also much occupied in their mind by speculations concerning Mr. Dykeman and two Possibilities. One quite patently possible, even probable, giving

rise to the complacent "Why, anybody could see that!"
and the other a fascinatingly impossible Possibility of a
sort which allows the even more complacent "Didn't you?
Why, I could see it from the first."

Mr. Dykeman had been a leading citizen in that new-
built town for some ten years, which constituted him almost the Oldest Inhabitant. He was reputed to be extremely wealthy, though he never said anything about it,
and neither his clothing nor his cigars reeked of affluence. Perhaps nomadic chambermaids had spread knowledge of those silver-backed appurtenances, and the long
mirror. Or perhaps it was not woman's gossip at all, but
men's gossip, which has wider base, and wider circula-
tion, too.

Mr. Dykeman had certainly "paid attention" to Miss
Elder. Miss Elder had undeniably brightened and blossomed most becomingly under these attentions. He had
danced with her, he had driven with her, he had played
piquet with her when he might have played whist. To be
sure, he did these things with other ladies, and had done
them for years past, but this really looked as if there
might be something in it.

Mr. Skee, as Mr. Dykeman's oldest friend, was even
questioned a little; but it was not very much use to question Mr. Skee. His manner was not repellant, and not in
the least reserved. He poured forth floods of information
so voluminous and so varied that the recipient was rather
drowned than fed. So opinions wavered as to Mr Dykeman's intentions.

Then came this lady of irresistible charm, and the unmarried citizens of the place fell at her feet as one man.
Even the married ones slanted over a little.

Mr. Dykeman danced with her, more than he had with
Miss Elder. Mr. Dykeman drove with her, more than he
had with Miss Elder. Mr. Dykeman played piquet with
her, and chess, which Miss Elder could not play. And Miss
Elder's little opening petals of ribbon and lace curled up
and withered away; while Mrs. St. Cloud's silken efflo-
rescence, softly waving and jewel-starred, flourished
apace.

Dr. Bellair had asked Vivian to take a walk with her;

and they sat together, resting, on a high lonely hill, a few miles out of town.

"It's a great pleasure to see this much of you, Dr. Bellair," said the girl, feeling really complimented.

"I'm afraid you won't think so, my dear, when you hear what I have to say: what I *have* to say."

The girl flushed a little. "Are you going to scold me about something? Have I done anything wrong?" Her eyes smiled bravely. "Go on, Doctor. I know it will be for my best good."

"It will indeed, dear child," said the doctor, so earnestly that Vivian felt a chill of apprehension.

"I am going to talk to you 'as man to man' as the story books say; as woman to woman. When I was your age I had been married three years."

Vivian was silent, but stole out a soft sympathetic hand and slipped it into the older woman's. She had heard of this early-made marriage, also early broken; with various dark comments to which she had paid no attention.

Dr. Bellair was Dr. Bellair, and she had a reverential affection for her.

There was a little silence. The Doctor evidently found it hard to begin. "You love children, don't you, Vivian?"

The girl's eyes kindled, and a heavenly smile broke over her face. "Better than anything in the world," she said.

"Ever think about them?" asked her friend, her own face whitening as she spoke. "Think about their lovely little soft helplessness—when you hold them in your arms and have to do *everything* for them. Have to go and turn them over—see that the little ear isn't crumpled—that the covers are all right. Can't you see 'em, upside down on the bath apron, grabbing at things, perfectly happy, but prepared to howl when it comes to dressing? And when they are big enough to love you! Little soft arms that will hardly go round your neck. Little soft cheeks against yours, little soft mouths and little soft kisses,—ever think of them?"

The girl's eyes were like stars. She was looking into the future; her breath came quickly; she sat quite still.

The doctor swallowed hard, and went on. "We mostly

don't go much farther than that at first. It's just the babies we want. But you can look farther—can follow up, year by year, the lovely changing growing bodies and minds, the confidence and love between you, the pride you have as health is established, strength and skill developed, and character unfolds and deepens.

"Then when they are grown, and sort of catch up, and you have those splendid young lives about you, intimate strong friends and tender lovers. And you feel as though you had indeed done something for the world."

She stopped, saying no more for a little, watching the girl's awed shining face. Suddenly that face was turned to her, full of exquisite sympathy, the dark eyes swimming with sudden tears; and two soft eager arms held her close.

"Oh, Doctor! To care like that and not—!"

"Yes, my dear;" said the doctor, quietly. "And not have any. Not be able to have any—ever."

Vivian caught her breath with pitying intensity, but her friend went on.

"Never be able to have a child, because I married a man who had gonorrhea. In place of happy love, lonely pain. In place of motherhood, disease. Misery and shame, child. Medicine and surgery, and never any possibility of any child for me."

The girl was pale with horror. "I—I didn't know—" She tried to say something, but the doctor burst out impatiently:

"No! You don't know. I didn't know. Girls aren't taught a word of what's before them till it's too late—not *then*, sometimes! Women lose every joy in life, every hope, every capacity for service or pleasure. They go down to their graves without anyone's telling them the cause of it all."

"That was why you—left him?" asked Vivian presently.

"Yes, I left him. When I found I could not be a mother I determined to be a doctor, and save other women, if I could." She said this with such slow, grave emphasis that Vivian turned a sudden startled face to her, and went white to the lips.

"I may be wrong," the doctor said, "you have not given me your confidence in this matter. But it is better, a thousand times better, that I should make this mistake than for you to make that. You must not marry Morton Elder."

Vivian did not admit nor deny. She still wore that look of horror.

"You think he has—That?"

"I do not know whether he has gonorrhea or not; it takes a long microscopic analysis to be sure; but there is every practical assurance that he's had it, and I know he's had syphilis."

If Vivian could have turned paler she would have, then.

"I've heard of—that," she said, shuddering.

"Yes, the other is newer to our knowledge, far commoner, and really more dangerous. They are two of the most terrible diseases known to us; highly contagious, and in the case of syphilis, hereditary. Nearly three-quarters of the men have one or the other, or both."[51]

But Vivian was not listening. Her face was buried in her hands. She crouched low in agonized weeping.

"Oh, come, come, my dear. Don't take it so hard. There's no harm done you see, it's not too late."

"Oh, it *is* too late! It is!" wailed the girl. "I have promised to marry him."

"I don't care if you were at the altar, child; you *haven't* married him, and you mustn't."

"I have given my word!" said the girl dully. She was thinking of Morton now. Of his handsome face, with its new expression of respectful tenderness; of all the hopes they had built together; of his life, so dependent upon hers for its higher interests.

She turned to the doctor, her lips quivering. "He *loves* me!" she said. "I—we—he says I am all that holds him up, that helps him to make a newer better life. And he has changed so—I can see it! He says he has loved me, really, since he was seventeen!"

The older sterner face did not relax.

"He told me he had—done wrong. He was honest about it. He said he wasn't—worthy."

"He isn't," said Dr. Bellair.

"But surely I owe some duty to him. He depends on me. And I have promised—"

The doctor grew grimmer. "Marriage is for motherhood," she said. "That is its initial purpose. I suppose you might deliberately forego motherhood, and undertake a sort of missionary relation to a man, but that is not marriage."

"He loves me," said the girl with gentle stubbornness. She saw Morton's eyes, as she had so often seen them lately; full of adoration and manly patience. She felt his hand, as she had felt it so often lately, holding hers, stealing about her waist, sometimes bringing her fingers to his lips for a strong slow kiss which she could not forget for hours.

She raised her head. A new wave of feeling swept over her. She saw a vista of self-sacrificing devotion, foregoing much, forgiving much, but rejoicing in the companionship of a noble life, a soul rebuilt, a love that was passionately grateful. Her eyes met those of her friend fairly. "And I love him!" she said.

"Will you tell that to your crippled children?" asked Dr. Bellair. "Will they understand it if they are idiots? Will they see it if they are blind? Will it satisfy you when they are dead?"

The girl shrank before her.

"You *shall* understand," said the doctor. "This is no case for idealism and exalted emotion. Do you want a son like Theophile?"

"I thought you said—they didn't have any."

"Some don't—that is one result. Another result—of gonorrhea—is to have children born blind. Their eyes may be saved, with care. But it is not a motherly gift for one's babies—blindness. You may have years and years of suffering yourself—any or all of those diseases 'peculiar to women' as we used to call them! And we pitied the men who 'were so good to their invalid wives'! You may have any number of still-born children, year after year. And every little marred dead face would remind you that you allowed it! And they may be deformed and twisted, have all manner of terrible and loathsome afflictions, they and their children after them, if they have any. And many do! Dear girl, don't you see that's wicked?"

Vivian was silent, her two hands wrung together; her whole form shivering with emotion.

"Don't think that you are 'ruining his life,' " said the doctor kindly. "He ruined it long ago—poor boy!"

The girl turned quickly at the note of sympathy.

"They don't know either," her friend went on. "What could Miss Orella do, poor little saint, to protect a lively young fellow like that! All they have in their scatter-brained heads is 'it's naughty but it's nice!' And so they rush off and ruin their whole lives—and their wives'—and their children's. A man don't have to be so very wicked, either, understand. Just one mis-step may be enough for infection."

"Even if it did break his heart, and yours—even if you both lived single, he because it is the only decent thing he can do now, you because of a misguided sense of devotion; that would be better than to commit this plain sin. Beware of a biological sin, my dear; for it there is no forgiveness."

She waited a moment and went on, as firmly and steadily as she would have held the walls of a wound while she placed the stitches.

"If you two love each other so nobly and devotedly that it is higher and truer and more lasting than the ordinary love of men and women, you might be 'true' to one another for a lifetime, you see. And all that friendship can do, exalted influence, noble inspiration—that is open to you."

Vivian's eyes were wide and shining. She saw a possible future, not wholly unbearable.

"Has he kissed you yet?" asked the doctor suddenly.

"No," she said. "That is—except—"

"Don't let him. You might catch it. Your friendship must be distant. Well, shall we be going back? I'm sorry, my dear. I did hate awfully to do it. But I hated worse to see you go down those awful steps from which there is no returning."

"Yes," said Vivian. "Thank you. Won't you go on, please? I'll come later."

An hour the girl sat there, with the clear blue sky above her, the soft steady wind rustling the leaves, the little birds that hopped and pecked and flirted their tails so near her motionless figure.

She thought and thought, and through all the tumult of

ideas it grew clearer to her that the doctor was right. She might sacrifice herself. She had no right to sacrifice her children.

A feeling of unreasoning horror at this sudden outlook into a field of unknown evil was met by her clear perception that if she was old enough to marry, to be a mother, she was surely old enough to know these things; and not only so, but ought to know them.

Shy, sensitive, delicate in feeling as the girl was, she had a fair and reasoning mind.

10

Determination[52]

You may shut your eyes with a bandage,
  The whole world vanishes soon;
You may open your eyes at a knothole
  And see the sun and moon.

It must have grieved anyone who cared for Andrew Dykeman, to see Mrs. St. Cloud's manner toward him change with his changed circumstances—she had been so much with him, had been so kind to him; kinder than Carston comment "knew for a fact," but not kinder than it surmised.

Then, though his dress remained as quietly correct, his face assumed a worn and anxious look, and he no longer offered her long auto rides or other expensive entertainment. She saw men on the piazza stop talking as he came by, and shake their heads as they looked after him; but no one would tell her anything definite till she questioned Mr. Skee.

"I am worried about Mr. Dykeman," she said to this ever-willing confidant, beckoning him to a chair beside her.

A chair, to the mind of Mr. Skee, seemed to be for pictorial uses, only valuable as part of the composition. He liked one to stand beside, to put a foot on, to lean over from behind, arms on the back; to tip up in front of him as if he needed a barricade; and when he was persuaded to sit in one, it was either facing the back, cross-saddle and bent forward, or—and this was the utmost decorum he was able to approach—tipped backward against the wall.

"He does not look well," said the lady, "you are old friends—do tell me; if it is anything wherein a woman's sympathy would be of service?"

"I'm afraid not, ma'am," replied Mr. Skee darkly. "Andy's hard hit in a worse place than his heart. I wouldn't betray a friend's confidence for any money, ma'am; but this is all over town. It'll go hard with Andy, I'm afraid, at his age."

"Oh, I'm so sorry!" she whispered. "So sorry! But surely with a man of his abilities it will be only a temporary reverse!—"

"Dunno 'bout the abilities—not in this case. Unless he has ability enough to discover a mine bigger'n the one he's lost! You see, ma'am, it's this way," and he sunk his voice to a confidential rumble. "Andy had a bang-up mine, galena ore—not gold, you understand, but often pays better.[53] And he kept on putting money it made back into it to make more. Then, all of a sudden, it petered out! No more eggs in that basket. 'Course he can't sell it—now. And last year he refused half a million. Andy's sure down on his luck."

"But he will recover! You western men are so wonderful! He will find another mine!"

"O yes, he *may!* Certainly he *may*, ma'am. Not that he found this one—he just bought it."

"Well—he can buy another, there are more, aren't there?"

"Sure there are! There's as good mines in the earth as ever was salted—that's my motto! But Andy's got no more money to buy any mines. What he had before he inherited. No, ma'am," said Mr. Skee, with a sigh. "I'm afraid it's all up with Andy Dykeman financially!"

This he said more audibly; and Miss Elder and Mrs. Pettigrew, sitting in their parlor, could not help hearing. Miss Elder gave a little gasp and clasped her hands tightly, but Mrs. Pettigrew arose, and came outside.

"What's this about Mr. Dykeman?" she questioned abruptly. "Has he had losses?"

"There now," said Mr. Skee, remorsefully, "I never meant to give him away like that. Mrs. Pettigrew, ma'am, I must beg you not to mention it further. I was only satisfyin' this lady here, in answer to sympathetic anxiety, as to what was making Andrew H. Dykeman so down in the mouth. Yes'm—he's lost every cent he had in the world, or is likely to have. Of course, among friends, he'll get a job fast enough, bookkeepin', or something like that—though he's not a brilliant man, Andy isn't. You needn't to feel worried, Mrs. Pettigrew; he'll draw a salary all right, to the end of time; but he's out of the game of Hot Finance."

Mrs. Pettigrew regarded the speaker with a scintillating eye. He returned her look with unflinching seriousness. "Have a chair, ma'am," he said. "Let me bring out your rocker. Sit down and chat with us."

"No, thanks," said the old lady. "It seems to me a little— chilly, out here. I'll go in."

She went in forthwith, to find Miss Orella furtively wiping her eyes.

"What are you crying about, Orella Elder! Just because a man's lost his money? That happens to most of 'em now and then."

"Yes, I know—but you heard what he said. Oh, I can't believe it! To think of his having to be provided for by his friends—and having to take a small salary—after being so well off! I am so sorry for him!"

Miss Elder's sorrow was increased to intensity by noting Mrs. St. Cloud's changed attitude. Mr. Dykeman made no complaint, uttered no protest, gave no confidences; but it soon appeared that he was working in an office; and furthermore that his position was given him by Mr. Skee.

That gentleman, though discreetly reticent as to his own affairs, now appeared in far finer raiment than he had hitherto affected; developed a pronounced taste in fobs and sleeve buttons; and a striking harmony in socks and scarfs.[54]

Men talked openly of him; no one seemed to know anything definite, but all were certain that "Old Skee must have struck it rich."

Mr. Skee kept his own counsel; but became munificent in gifts and entertainments. He produced two imposing presents for Susie; one a "betrothal gift," the other a conventional wedding present.

"This is a new one to me," he said when he offered her the first; "but I understand it's the thing. In fact I'm sure of it—for I've consulted Mrs. St. Cloud and she helped me to buy 'em."

He consulted Mrs. St. Cloud about a dinner he proposed giving to Mr. Saunders—"one of these Farewell to Egypt affairs," he said.[55] "Not that I imagine Jim Saunders ever was much of a—Egyptian—but then—!"

He consulted her also about Vivian—did she not think the girl looked worn and ill? Wouldn't it be a good thing to send her off for a trip somewhere?

He consulted her about a library; said he had always wanted a library of his own, but the public ones were somewhat in his way. How many books did she think a man ought really to own—to spend his declining years among. Also, and at considerable length he consulted her about the best possible place of residence.

"I'm getting to be an old man, Mrs. St. Cloud," he remarked meditatively; "and I'm thinking of buying and building somewhere. But it's a ticklish job. Lo! these many years I've been perfectly contented to live wherever I was at; and now that I'm considering a real Home— blamed if I know where to put it! I'm distracted between A Model Farm, and A Metropolitan Residence. Which would you recommend, ma'am?"

The lady's sympathy and interest warmed to Mr. Skee as they cooled to Mr. Dykeman, not with any blameworthy or noticeable suddenness, but in soft graduations, steady and continuous. The one wore his new glories with an air of modest pride; making no boast of affluence; and the other accepted that which had befallen him without rebellion.

Miss Orella's tender heart was deeply touched. As fast as Mrs. St. Cloud gave the cold shoulder to her friend, she extended a warm hand; when they chatted about Mr. Skee's visible success, she spoke bravely of the beauty of limited means; and when it was time to present her weekly bills to the boarders, she left none in Mr. Dykeman's room. This he took for an oversight at first; but when he found the omission repeated on the following week, he stood by his window smiling thoughtfully for some time, and then went in search of Miss Orella.

She sat by her shaded lamp, alone, knitting a silk tie which was promptly hidden as he entered. He stood by the door looking at her in spite of her urging him to be seated, observing the warm color in her face, the graceful lines of her figure, the gentle smile that was so unfailingly attractive. Then he came forward, calmly inquiring, "Why haven't you sent me my board bill?"

She lifted her eyes to his, and dropped them, flushing. "I—excuse me; but I thought—"

"You thought I couldn't conveniently pay it?"

"O please excuse me! I didn't mean to be—to do anything you wouldn't like. But I did hear that you were—temporarily embarrassed. And I want you to feel sure, Mr. Dykeman, that to your real friends it makes no difference in the *least*. And if—for a while that is—it should be a little more convenient to—to defer payment, please feel perfectly at liberty to wait!"

She stood there blushing like a girl, her sweet eyes wet with shining tears that did not fall, full of tender sympathy for his misfortune.

"Have you heard that I've lost all my money?" he asked.

She nodded softly.

"And that I can't ever get it back—shall have to do clerk's work at a clerk's salary—as long as I live?"

Again she nodded.

He took a step or two back and forth in the quiet parlor, and returned to her.

"Would you marry a poor man?" he asked in a low tender voice. "Would you marry a man not young, not clever, not rich, but who loved you dearly? You are the sweetest woman I ever saw, Orella Elder—will you marry me?"

She came to him, and he drew her close with a long sigh of utter satisfaction. "Now I am rich indeed," he said softly.

She held him off a little. "Don't talk about being rich. It doesn't matter. If you like to live here—why this house will keep us both. If you'd rather have a little one—I can live *so* happily—on *so* little! And there is my own little home in Bainville—perhaps you could find something to do there. I don't care the least in the world—so long as you love me!"

"I've loved you since I first set eyes on you," he answered her. "To see the home you've made here for all of us was enough to make any man love you. But I thought awhile back that I hadn't any chance—you weren't jealous of that Artificial Fairy, were you?"

And conscientiously Miss Orella lied.

Carston society was pleased, but not surprised at Susie's engagement; it was both pleased and surprised when Miss Elder's was announced. Some there were who protested that they had seen it from the beginning; but disputatious friends taxed them with having prophesied quite otherwise.

Some thought Miss Elder foolish to take up with a man of full middle age, and with no prospects; and others attributed the foolishness to Mr. Dykeman, in marrying an old maid. Others again darkly hinted that he knew which side his bread was buttered—"and first-rate butter, too." Adding that they "did hate to see a man sit around and let his wife keep boarders!"

In Bainville circles the event created high commotion. That one of their accumulated maidens, part of the Virgin Sacrifice of New England, which finds not even a Minotaur—had thus triumphantly escaped from their ranks and achieved a husband; this was flatly heretical.[56] The fact that he was a poor man was the only mitigating circumstance, leaving it open to the more captious to criticize the lady sharply.

But the calm contentment of Andrew Dykeman's face, and the decorous bliss of Miss Elder's were untroubled by what anyone thought or said.

Little Susie was delighted, and teased for a double wedding; without success. "One was enough to attend to, at one time," her aunt replied.

* * * *

In all this atmosphere of wooings and weddings, Vivian walked apart, as one in a bad dream that could never end. That day when Dr. Bellair left her on the hill, left her alone in a strange new horrible world, was still glaring across her consciousness, the end of one life, the bar to any other. Its small events were as clear to her as those which stand out so painfully on a day of death; all that led up to the pleasant walk, when an eager girl mounted the breezy height, and a sad-faced woman came down from it.

She had waited long and came home slowly, dreading to see a face she knew, dreading worst of all to see Morton. The boy she had known so long, the man she was beginning to know, had changed to an unbelievable horror; and the love which had so lately seemed real to her recoiled upon her heart with a sense of hopeless shame.

She wished—eagerly, desperately, she wished—she need never see him again. She thought of the man's resource of running way—if she could just *go*, go at once, and write to him from somewhere.

Distant Bainville seemed like a haven of safety; even the decorous, narrow monotony of its dim life had a new attraction. These terrors were not in Bainville, surely. Then the sickening thought crept in that perhaps they were—only they did not know it. Besides, she had no money to go with. If only she had started that little school sooner! Write to her father for money she would not. No, she must bear it here.

The world was discolored in the girl's eyes. Love had become a horror and marriage impossible. She pushed the idea from her, impotently, as one might push at a lava flow.

In her wide reading she had learned in a vague way of "evil"—a distant undescribed evil which was in the world, and which must be avoided. She had known that there was such a thing as "sin," and abhorred the very thought of it.

Morton's penitential confessions had given no details; she had pictured him only as being "led astray," as being "fast," even perhaps "wicked." Wickedness could be forgiven; and she had forgiven him, royally. But wickedness was one thing, disease was another. Forgiveness was no cure.

The burden of new knowledge so distressed her that she avoided the family entirely that evening, avoided Susie, went to her grandmother and asked if she might come and sleep on the lounge in her room.

"Surely, my child, glad to have you," said Mrs. Pettigrew affectionately. "Better try my bed—there's room a-plenty."

The girl lay long with those old arms about her, crying

quietly. Her grandmother asked no questions, only patted her softly from time to time, and said, "There! There!" in a pleasantly soothing manner. After some time she remarked, "If you want to say things, my dear, say 'em—anything you please."

In the still darkness they talked long and intimately; and the wise old head straightened things out somewhat for the younger one.

"Doctors don't realize how people feel about these matters," said Mrs. Pettigrew. "They are so used to all kinds of ghastly things they forget that other folks can't stand 'em. She was too hard on you, dearie."

But Vivian defended the doctor. "Oh, no, Grandma. She did it beautifully. And it hurt her so. She told me about her own—disappointment."

"Yes, I remember her as a girl, you see. A fine sweet girl she was too. It was an awful blow—and she took it hard. It has made her bitter, I think, perhaps; that and the number of similar cases she had to cope with."

"But, Grandma—is it—*can* it be as bad as she said? Seventy-five per cent! Three-quarters of—of everybody!"

"Not everybody, dear; thank goodness. Our girls are mostly clean, and they save the race, I guess."

"I don't even want to *see* a man again!" said the girl with low intensity.

"Shouldn't think you would, at first. But, dear child—just brace yourself and look it fair in the face! The world's no worse than it was yesterday—just because you know more about it!"

"No," Vivian admitted, "but it's like uncovering a charnel house!" she shuddered.[57]

"Never saw a charnel house myself," said the old lady, "even with the lid on. But now see here, child; you mustn't feel as if all men were Unspeakable Villains. They are just ignorant boys—and nobody ever tells 'em the truth. Nobody used to know it, for that matter. All this about gonorrhea is quite newly discovered—it has set the doctors all by the ears. Having women doctors has made a difference too—lots of difference."

"Besides," she went on after a pause, "things are changing very fast now, since the general airing began. Dr.

Prince Morrow in New York, with that society of his—(I can never remember the name—makes me think of tooth-brushes) has done much; and the popular magazines have taken it up.[58] You must have seen some of those articles, Vivian."

"I have," the girl said, "but I couldn't bear to read them—ever."

"That's it!" responded her grandmother, tartly; "we bring up girls to think it is not proper to know anything about the worst danger before them. Proper!—Why my dear child, the young girls are precisely the ones *to* know! It's no use to tell a woman who has buried all her chil-dren—or wishes she had!—that it was all owing to her ignorance, and her husband's. You have to know before-hand if it's to do you any good."

After awhile she continued: "Women are waking up to this all over the country, now. Nice women, old and young. The women's clubs and congresses are taking it up, as they should. Some states have passed laws requiring a medical certificate—a clean bill of health—to go with a li-cense to marry. You can see that's reasonable! A man has to be examined to enter the army or navy, even to get his life insured; Marriage and Parentage are more important than those things! And we are beginning to teach children and young people what they ought to know. There's hope for us!"

"But Grandma—it's so awful—about the children."

"Yes, dear, yes. It's pretty awful. But don't feel as if we were all on the brink of perdition. Remember that we've got a whole quarter of the men to bank on. That's a good many, in this country. We're not so bad as Europe—not yet—in this line. Then just think of this, child. We have lived, and done splendid things all these years, even with this load of disease on us. Think what we can do when we're rid of it! And that's in the hands of woman, my dear—as soon as we know enough. Don't be afraid of knowledge. When we all know about this we can stop it! Think of that. We can religiously rid the world of all these—'undesirable citizens.' "

"How, Grandma?"

"Easy enough, my dear. By not marrying them."

There was a lasting silence.

Grandma finally went to sleep, making a little soft whistling sound through her parted lips; but Vivian lay awake for long slow hours.

* * * *

It was one thing to make up her own mind, though not an easy one, by any means; it was quite another to tell Morton.

He gave her no good opportunity. He did not say again, "Will you marry me?" So that she could say, "No," and be done with it. He did not even say, "When will you marry me?" to which she could answer "Never!" He merely took it for granted that she was going to, and continued to monopolize her as far as possible, with all pleasant and comfortable attentions.

She forced the situation even more sharply than she wished, by turning from him with a shiver when he met her on the stairs one night and leaned forward as if to kiss her.

He stopped short.

"What is the matter, Vivian—are you ill?"

"No—" She could say nothing further, but tried to pass him.

"Look here—there *is* something. You've been—different—for several days. Have I done anything you don't like?"

"Oh, Morton!" His question was so exactly to the point; and so exquisitely inadequate! He had indeed.

"I care too much for you to let anything stand between us, now," he went on. "Come, there's no one in the upper hall—come and 'tell me the worst.' "

"As well now as ever," thought the girl. Yet when they sat on the long window seat, and he turned his handsome face toward her, with that newer, better look on it, she could not believe that this awful thing was true.

"Now then—What is wrong between us?" he said.

She answered only, "I will tell you the worst, Morton. I cannot marry you—ever."

He whitened to the lips, but asked quietly, "Why?"

"Because you have—Oh, I *cannot* tell you!"

"I have a right to know, Vivian. You have made a man of

me. I love you with my whole heart. What have I done—
that I have not told you?"

Then she recalled his contrite confessions; and con-
trasted what he had told her with what he had not; with
the unspeakable fate to which he would have consigned
her—and those to come; and a sort of holy rage rose
within her.

"You never told me of the state of your health, Morton."

It was done. She looked to see him fall at her feet in
utter abashment, but he did nothing of the kind. What he
did do astonished her beyond measure. He rose to his
feet, with clenched fists.

"Has that damned doctor been giving me away?" he demanded. "Because if he has I'll kill him!"

"He has not," said Vivian. "Not by the faintest hint,
ever. And is *that* all you think of?—

"Good-bye."

She rose to leave him, sick at heart.

Then he seemed to realize that she was going; that she
meant it.

"Surely, surely!" he cried, "you won't throw me over
now! Oh, Vivian! I told you I had been wild—that I wasn't
fit to touch your little slippers! And I wasn't going to ask
you to marry me till I felt sure this was all done with. All
the rest of my life was yours, darling—is yours. You have
made me over—surely you won't leave me now!"

"I must," she said.

He looked at her despairingly. If he lost her he lost not
only a woman, but the hope of a life. Things he had never
thought about before had now grown dear to him; a home,
a family, an honorable place in the world, long years of
quiet happiness.

"I can't lose you!" he said. "I *can't!*"

She did not answer, only sat there with a white set face
and her hands tight clenched in her lap.

"Where'd you get this idea anyhow?" he burst out again.
"I believe it's that woman doctor! What does she know!"

"Look here, Morton," said Vivian firmly. "It is not a
question of who told me. The important thing is that it's—
true! And I cannot marry you."

"But Vivian—" he pleaded, trying to restrain the inten-

sity of his feeling; "men get over these things. They do,
really. It's not so awful as you seem to think. It's very common. And I'm nearly well. I was going to wait a year or two
yet—to make sure—. Vivian! I'd cut my hand off before I'd
hurt you!"

There was real agony in his voice, and her heart smote
her; but there was something besides her heart ruling the
girl now.

"I am sorry—I'm very sorry," she said dully. "But I will
not marry you."

"You'll throw me over—just for that! Oh, Vivian don't—
you can't. I'm no worse than other men. It seems so terrible to you just because you're so pure and white. It's only
what they call—wild oats, you know. Most men do it."

She shook her head.

"And will you punish me—so cruelly—for that? I can't
live without you, Vivian—I won't!"

"It is not a question of punishing you, Morton," she said
gently. "Nor myself. It is not the sin I am considering. It is
the consequences!"

He felt something high and implacable in the gentle
girl; something he had never found in her before. He
looked at her with despairing eyes. Her white grace, her
stately little ways, her delicate beauty, had never seemed
so desirable.

"Good God, Vivian. You can't mean it. Give me time.
Wait for me. I'll be straight all the rest of my life—I mean
it. I'll be true to you, absolutely. I'll do anything you say—
only don't give me up!"

She felt old, hundreds of years old, and as remote as far
mountains.

"It isn't anything you can do—in the rest of your life, my
poor boy! It is what you have done—in the first of it! . . .
Oh, Morton! It isn't right to let us grow up without knowing! You never would have done it *if* you'd known—would
you? Can't you—can't we—do something to—stop this
awfulness!"

Her tender heart suffered in the pain she was inflicting,
suffered too in her own loss; for as she faced the thought
of final separation she found that her grief ran back into
the far-off years of childhood. But she had made up her

mind with a finality only the more absolute because it
hurt her. Even what he said of possible recovery did not
move her—the very thought of marriage had become impossible.

"I shall never marry," she added, with a shiver; thinking
that he might derive some comfort from the thought; but
he replied with a bitter derisive little laugh. He did not
rise to her appeal to "help the others." So far in life the
happiness of Morton Elder had been his one engrossing
care; and now the unhappiness of Morton Elder assumed
even larger proportions.

That bright and hallowed future to which he had been
looking forward so earnestly had been suddenly withdrawn from him; his good resolutions, his "living
straight" for the present, were wasted.

"You women that are so superior," he said, "that'll turn
a man down for things that are over and done with—that
he's sorry for and ashamed of—do you know what you
drive a man to! What do you think's going to become of me
if you throw me over!"

He reached out his hands to her in real agony. "Vivian!
I love you! I can't live without you! I can't be good without
you! And you love me a little—don't you?"

She did. She could not deny it. She loved to shut her
eyes to the future, to forgive the past, to come to those out-
stretched arms and bury everything beneath that one
overwhelming phrase—"I love you!"

But she heard again Dr. Bellair's clear low accusing
voice—"Will you tell that to your crippled children?"

She rose to her feet. "I cannot help it, Morton. I am
sorry—you will not believe how sorry I am! But I will
never marry you."

A look of swift despair swept over his face. It seemed
to darken visibly as she watched. An expression of bitter
hatred came upon him; of utter recklessness.[59]

All that the last few months had seemed to bring of
higher better feeling fell from him; and even as she pitied
him she thought with a flicker of fear of how this might
have happened—after marriage.

"Oh, well!" he said, rising to his feet. "I wish you could

have made up your mind sooner, that's all. I'll take myself off now."

She reached out her hands to him.

"Morton! Please!—don't go away feeling so hardly! I am—fond of you—I always was.—Won't you let me help you—to bear it—! Can't we be—friends?"

Again he laughed that bitter little laugh. "No, Miss Lane," he said. "We distinctly cannot. This is good-bye— You won't change your mind—again?"

She shook her head in silence, and he left her.

11
Thereafter

If I do right, though heavens fall,
  And end all light and laughter;
Though black the night and ages long,
  Bitter the cold—the tempest strong—
If I do right, and brave it all—
  The sun shall rise thereafter!

The inaccessibility of Dr. Hale gave him, in the eye of Mrs. St. Cloud, all the attractiveness of an unscaled peak to the true mountain climber. Here was a man, an unattached man, living next door to her, whom she had not even seen. Her pursuance of what Mr. Skee announced to his friends to be "one of these Platonic Friendships," did not falter; neither did her interest in other relations less philosophic. Mr. Dykeman's precipitate descent from the class of eligibles was more of a disappointment to her than she would admit even to herself; his firm, kind friendliness had given a sense of comfort, of achieved content that her restless spirit missed.

But Dr. Hale, if he had been before inaccessible, had now become so heavily fortified, so empanoplied in armor offensive and defensive, that even Mrs. Pettigrew found it difficult to obtain speech with him.

That his best friend, so long supporting him in cheerful bachelorhood, should have thus late laid down his arms, was bitterly resented. That Mr. Skee, free lance of years standing, and risen victor from several "stricken fields," should show signs of capitulation, annoyed him further. Whether these feelings derived their intensity from another, which he entirely refused to acknowledge, is a matter for the psychologist, and Dr. Hale avoided all psychologic self-examination.

With the boys he was always a hero. They admired his quiet strength and the unbroken good nature that was always presented to those about him, whatever his inner feelings.

Mr. Peters burst forth to the others one day, in tones of impassioned admiration.

"By George, fellows," he said, "you know how nice Doc was last night?"

"Never saw him when he wasn't," said Archie.

"Don't interrupt Mr. Peters," drawled Percy. "He's on the brink of a scientific discovery. Strange how these secrets of nature can lie unrevealed about us so long—and then suddenly burst upon our ken!"

Mr. Peters grinned affably. "That's all right, but I maintain my assertion; whatever the general attraction of our noble host, you'll admit that on the special occasion of yesterday evening, which we celebrated to a late hour by innocent games of cards—he was—as usual—the soul of—of—"

"Affability?" suggested Percy.

"Precisely!" Peters admitted. "If there is a well-chosen word which perfectly describes the manner of Dr. Richard Hale—it is affable! Thank you, sir, thank you. Well, what I wish to announce, so that you can all of you get down on your knees at once and worship, is that all last evening he—had a toothache—a bad toothache!"

"My word!" said Archie, and remained silent.

"Oh, come now," Percy protested, "that's against nature. Have a toothache and not *mention* it? Not even mention it—without exaggeration! Why Archimedes couldn't do that! Or—Sandalphon—or any of them!"[60]

"How'd you learn the facts, my son? Tell us that."

"Heard him on the 'phone making an appointment. 'Yes;' 'since noon yesterday,' 'yes, pretty severe.' '11:30? You can't make it earlier? All right.' I'm just mentioning it to convince you fellows that you don't appreciate your opportunities. There was some exceptional Female once—they said 'to know her was a liberal education.' What would you call it to live with Dr. Hale?"

And they called it every fine thing they could think of;

for these boys knew better than anyone else, the effect of that association.

His patients knew him as wise, gentle, efficient, bringing a sense of hope and assurance by the mere touch of that strong hand; his professional associates in the town knew him as a good practitioner and friend, and wider medical circles, readers of his articles in the professional press had an even higher opinion of his powers.

Yet none of these knew Richard Hale. None saw him sitting late in his office, the pages of his book unturned, his eyes on the red spaces of the fire. No one was with him on those night tramps that left but an hour or two of sleep to the long night, and made that sleep irresistible from self-enforced fatigue. He had left the associations of his youth and deliberately selected this far-off mountain town to build the life he chose; and if he found it unsatisfying no one was the wiser.

His successive relays of boys, young fellows fresh from the East, coming from year to year and going from year to year as business called them, could and did give good testimony as to the home side of his character, however. It was not in nature that they should [not] speculate about him. As they fell in love and out again with the facility of so many Romeos, they discoursed among themselves as to his misogyny.

"He certainly has a grouch on women," they would admit. "That's the one thing you can't talk to him about—shuts up like a clam. Of course, he'll let you talk about your own feelings and experiences, but you might as well talk to the side of a hill. I wonder what did happen to him?"

They made no inquiry, however. It was reported that a minister's wife, a person of determined character, had had the courage of her inquisitiveness, and asked him once, "Why is it that you have never married, Dr. Hale?" And that he had replied, "It is owing to my dislike of the meddlesomeness of women." He lived his own life, unquestioned, now more markedly withdrawn than ever, coming no more to The Cottonwoods.

Even when Morton Elder left, suddenly and without warning, to the great grief of his aunt and astonishment of his sister, their medical neighbor still "sulked in his tent"—or at least in his office.

Morton's departure had but one explanation; it must be that Vivian had refused him, and she did not deny it.

"But why, Vivian, why? He has improved so—it was just getting lovely to see how nice he was getting. And we all thought you were so happy." Thus the perplexed Susie. And Vivian found herself utterly unable to explain to that happy little heart, on the brink of marriage, why she had refused her brother.

Miss Orella was even harder to satisfy. "It's not as if you were a foolish changeable young girl, my dear. And you've known Morton all your life—he was no stranger to you. It breaks my heart, Vivian. Can't you reconsider?"

The girl shook her head.

"I'm awfully sorry, Miss Orella. Please believe that I did it for the best—and that it was very hard for me, too."

"But, Vivian! What can be the reason? I don't think you understand what a beautiful influence you have on the boy. He has improved so, since he has been here. And he was going to get a position here in town—he told me so himself—and really settle down. And now he's *gone*. Just off and away, as he used to be—and I never shall feel easy about him again."

Miss Orella was frankly crying; and it wrung the girl's heart to know the pain she was causing; not only to Morton, and to herself, but to these others.

Susie criticised her with frankness.

"I know you think you are right, Vivian, you always do—you and that conscience of yours. But I really think you had gone too far to draw back, Jimmie saw him that night he went away—and he said he looked awfully. And he really was changed so—beginning to be so thoroughly nice. Whatever was the matter? I think you ought to tell me, Vivian, I'm his sister, and—being engaged and all—perhaps I could straighten it out."

And she was as nearly angry as her sunny nature allowed, when her friend refused to give any reason, beyond that she thought it right.

Her aunt did not criticise, but pleaded. "It's not too late, I'm sure, Vivian. A word from you would bring him back in a moment. Do speak it, Vivian—do! Put your pride in your pocket, child, and don't lose a lifetime's happiness for some foolish quarrel."

Miss Orella, like Susie, was at present sure that marriage must mean a lifetime's happiness. And Vivian looked miserably from one to the other of these loving womenfolk, and could not defend herself with the truth.

Mrs. Pettigrew took up the cudgels for her. She was not going to have her favorite grandchild thus condemned and keep silence. "Anybody'd think Vivian had married the man and then run away with another one!" she said tartly. "Pity if a girl can't change her mind before marrying—she's held down pretty close afterward. An engagement isn't a wedding, Orella Elder."

"But you don't consider the poor boy's feelings in the least, Mrs. Pettigrew."

"No, I don't," snapped the old lady. "I consider the poor girl's. I'm willing to bet as much as you will that his feelings aren't any worse than hers. If *he'd* changed his mind and run off and left *her*, I warrant you two wouldn't have been so hard on him."

Evading this issue, Miss Orella wiped her eyes, and said: "Heaven knows where he is now. And I'm afraid he won't write—he never did write much, and now he's just heartbroken. I don't know as I'd have seen him at all if I hadn't been awake and heard him rushing downstairs. You've no idea how he suffers."

"I don't see as the girl's to blame that he hadn't decency enough to say good-bye to the aunt that's been a mother to him; or to write to her, as he ought to. A person don't need to forget *all* their duty because they've got the mitten."[61]

Vivian shrank away from them all. Her heart ached intolerably. She had not realized how large a part in her life this constant admiration and attention had become. She missed the outward agreeableness, and the soft tide of affection, which had risen more and more warmly about her. From her earliest memories she had wished for affection—affection deep and continuous, tender and with full expression. She had been too reserved to show her feeling, too proud by far to express it, but under that delicate reticence of hers lay always that deep longing to love and be loved wholly.

Susie had been a comfort always, in her kittenish affection and caressing ways, but Susie was doubly lost, both in her new absorption and now in this estrangement.

Then, to bring pain to Miss Orella, who had been so kind and sweet to her from earliest childhood, to hurt her so deeply, now, to mingle in her cup of happiness this grief and anxiety, made the girl suffer keenly. Jimmie, of course, was able to comfort Susie. He told her it was no killing matter anyhow, and that Morton would inevitably console himself elsewhere. "He'll never wear the willow for any girl, my dear. Don't you worry about him."

Also, Mr. Dykeman comforted Miss Orella, not only with wise words, but with his tender sympathy and hopefulness. But no one could comfort Vivian.

Even Dr. Bellair seemed to her present sensitiveness an alien, cruel power. She had come like the angel with the flaming sword to stand between her and what, now that it was gone, began to look like Paradise.[62]

She quite forgot that she had always shrunk from Morton when he made love too warmly, that she had been far from wholly pleased with him when he made his appearance there, that their engagement, so far as they had one, was tentative—"sometime, when I am good enough" not having arrived. The unreasoning voice of the woman's nature within her had answered, though but partially, to the deep call of the man's; and now she missed more than she would admit to herself the tenderness that was gone.

She had her intervals of sharp withdrawal from the memory of that tenderness, of deep thanksgiving for her escape; but fear of a danger only prophesied, does not obliterate memory of joys experienced.

Her grandmother watched her carefully, saying little. She forced no confidence, made no comment, was not obtrusively affectionate, but formed a definite decision and conveyed it clearly to Dr. Bellair.

"Look here, Jane Bellair, you've upset Vivian's dish, and quite right; it's a good thing you did, and I don't know as you could have done it easier."

"I couldn't have done it harder—that I know of," the

doctor answered. "I'd sooner operate on a baby—without an anaesthetic—than tell a thing like that—to a girl like that. But it had to be done; and nobody else would."

"You did perfectly right. I'm thankful enough, I promise you; if you hadn't I should have had to—and goodness knows what a mess I'd have made. But look here, the girl's going all to pieces. Now we've got to do something for her, and do it quick."

"I know that well enough," answered her friend, "and I set about it even before I made the incision. You've seen that little building going up on the corner of High and Stone Streets?"

"That pretty little thing with the grass and flowers round it?"

"Yes—they got the flowers growing while the decorators finished inside. It's a first-rate little kindergarten. I've got a list of scholars all arranged for, and am going to pop the girl into it so fast she can't refuse. Not that I think she will."

"Who did it?" demanded Mrs. Pettigrew. "That man Skee?"

"Mr. Skee has had something to do with it," replied the doctor, guardedly; "but he doesn't want his name mentioned."

"Huh!" said Mrs. Pettigrew.

Vivian made no objection, though she was too listless to take up work with enthusiasm.

As a prescription nothing could have worked better. Enough small pupils were collected to pay the rent of the pretty place, and leave a modest income for her.

Dr. Bellair gathered together the mothers and aunts for a series of afternoon talks in the convenient building, Vivian assisting, and roused much interest among them. The loving touch of little hands, the pleasure of seeing the gay contentment of her well-ordered charges, began to lighten the girl's heart at last. They grew so fond of her that the mothers were jealous, but she played with and taught them so wisely, and the youngsters were so much improved by it, that no parent withdrew her darling.

Further than that, the new interest, the necessary reading and study, above all the steady hours of occupation acted most beneficently, slowly, but surely steadying the nerves and comforting the heart.

There is a telling Oriental phrase describing sorrow: "And the whole world became strait unto him." The sense of final closing down of life, of a dull, long, narrow path between her and the grave, which had so oppressed the girl's spirit, now changed rapidly. Here was room to love at least, and she radiated a happy and unselfish affection among the little ones. Here was love in return, very sweet and honest, if shallow. Here was work; something to do, something to think about; both in her hours with the children and those spent in study. Her work took her out of the house, too; away from Susie and her aunt, with their happy chatter and endless white needlework, and the gleeful examination of presents.

Never before had she known the blessed relief of another place to go to.

When she left The Cottonwoods, as early as possible, and placed her key in the door of the little gray house sitting among the roses, she felt a distinct lightening of the heart. This was hers. Not her father's, not Miss Elder's; not anybody's but hers—as long as she could earn the rent.

She paid her board, too, in spite of deep and pained remonstrance, forcing Miss Elder to accept it by the ultimatum "would you rather make me go away and board somewhere else?" She could not accept favors where she was condemned.

This, too, gave her a feeling hitherto inexperienced, deep and inspiring. She began to hold her graceful head insensibly higher, to walk with a freer step. Life was not ended after all, though Love had gone. She might not be happy, but she might be useful and independent.

Then Dr. Bellair, who had by quiet friendliness and wise waiting, regained much of her former place with the girl, asked her to undertake, as a special favor to her, the care of a class of rather delicate children and young girls, in physical culture.

"Of course, Johanna Johnson is perfectly reliable and an excellent teacher. I don't know a better; but their mothers will feel easier if there's someone they know on the spot. You keep order and see that they don't overdo. You'll have to go through their little exercises with them, you see. I can't pay you anything for it; but it's only part of two afternoons in the week—and it won't hurt you at any rate."

Vivian was more than glad to do something for the doctor, as well as to extend her friendship among older children; also glad of anything to further fill her time. To be alone and idle was to think and suffer.

Mrs. Pettigrew came in with Dr. Bellair one afternoon to watch the exercises.

"I don't see but what Vivian does the tricks as well as any of them," said her grandmother.

"She does beautifully," the doctor answered. "And her influence with the children is just what they needed. You see there's no romping and foolishness, and she sets the pace—starts them off when they're shy. I'm extremely obliged to her."

Mrs. Pettigrew watched Vivian's rhythmic movements, her erect carriage and swinging step, her warm color and sparkling eyes, as she led the line of happy youngsters, and then turned upon the doctor.

"Huh!" she said.

At Susie's wedding, her childhood's friend was so far forgiven as to be chief bridesmaid, but seeing the happiness before her opened again the gates of her own pain.

When it was all over, and the glad young things were safely despatched upon their ribboned way, when all the guests had gone, when Mrs. St. Cloud felt the need of air and with the ever-gallant Mr. Skee set forth in search of it, when Dr. Bellair had returned to her patients, and Miss Orella to her own parlor, and was there consoled by Mr. Dykeman for the loss of her niece, then Vivian went to her room—all hers now, looking strangely large and empty— and set down among the drifts of white tissue paper and scattered pins—alone.

She sank down on the bed, weary and sad at heart, for an hour of full surrender long refused; meaning for once to let her grief have its full way with her. But, just as on the night of her hurried engagement she had been unable to taste to the full the happiness expected, so now, surren-

der as she might, she could not feel the intensity of expected pain.

She was lonely, unquestionably. She faced a lonely life.
Six long, heavy months had passed since she had made
her decision.

"I am nearly twenty-seven now," she thought, resign-
edly. "I shall never marry," and she felt a little shiver of
the horror of last year.

But, having got this far in melancholy contemplation,
her mind refused to dwell upon it, but filled in spite of her
with visions of merry little ones, prancing in wavering circles, and singing their more wavering songs. She was
lonely and a single woman—but she had something to do;
and far more power to do it, more interest, enthusiasm,
and skill, than at the season's beginning.

She thought of Morton—of what little they had heard
since his hurried departure. He had gone farther West;
they had heard of him in San Francisco, they had heard
of him, after some months, in the Klondike region, then
they had heard no more. He did not write. It seemed hard
to so deeply hurt his aunt for what was no fault of hers;
but Morton had never considered her feelings very
deeply, his bitter anger, his hopelessness, his desperate
disappointment, blinding him to any pain but his own.

But her thoughts of him failed to rouse any keen distinc-
tive sorrow. They rambled backward and forward, from
the boy who had been such a trouble to his aunt, such a
continuous disappointment and mortification; to the man
whose wooing, looked back upon at this distance, seemed
far less attractive to the memory than it had been at the
time. Even his honest attempt at improvement gave her
but a feeling of pity, and though pity is akin to love it is
not always a near relation.

From her unresisting descent into wells of pain, which
proved unexpectedly shallow, the girl arose presently
and quietly set to work arranging the room in its new capacity as hers only.

From black and bitter agony to the gray tastelessness of
her present life was not an exciting change, but Vivian
had more power in quiet endurance than in immediate

resistance, and set herself now in earnest to fulfill the tasks before her.

This was March. She was planning an extension of her classes, the employment of an assistant. Her work was appreciated, her school increased. Patiently and steadily she faced her task, and found a growing comfort in it. When summer came, Dr. Bellair again begged her to help out in the plan of a girls' camp she was developing.

This was new work for Vivian, but her season in Mrs. Johnson's gymnastic class had given her a fresh interest in her own body and the use of it. That stalwart instructress, a large-boned, calm-eyed Swedish woman, was to be the manager of the camp, and Vivian this time, with a small salary attached, was to act as assistant.

"It's a wonderful thing the way people take to these camps," said Dr. Bellair. "They are springing up everywhere. Magnificent for children and young people."

"It is a wonderful thing to me," observed Mrs. Pettigrew. "You go to a wild place that costs no rent; you run a summer hotel without any accommodations; you get a lot of parents to pay handsomely for letting their children be uncomfortable—and there you are."

"They are not uncomfortable!" protested her friend, a little ruffled. "They like it. And besides liking it, it's good for them. It's precisely the roughing it that does them good."

It did do them good; the group of young women and girls who went to the high-lying mountain lake where Dr. Bellair had bought a piece of wild, rough country for her own future use, and none of them profited by it more than Vivian.

She had been, from time to time, to decorous "shore places," where one could do nothing but swim and lie on the sand; or to the "mountains," those trim, green, modest, pretty-picture mountains, of which New England is so proud; but she had never before been in an untouched wilderness.

Often in the earliest dawn she would rise from the springy, odorous bed of balsam boughs and slip out alone for her morning swim. A run through the pines to a little rocky cape, with a small cave she knew, and to glide, naked, into that glass-smooth water, warmer than the sunless air, and swim out softly, silently, making hardly a ripple, turn on her back and lie there—alone with the sky—this brought peace to her heart. She felt so free from every tie to earth, so like a soul in space, floating there with the clean, dark water beneath her, and the clear, bright heaven above her; and when the pale glow in the east brightened to saffron, warmed to rose, burst into a level blaze of gold, the lake laughed in the light, and Vivian laughed, too, in pure joy of being alive and out in all that glittering beauty.

She tramped the hills with the girls; picked heaping pails of wild berries, learned to cook in primitive fashion, slept as she had never slept in her life, from dark to dawn, grew brown and hungry and cheerful.

After all, twenty-seven was not an old age.

She came back at the summer-end, and Dr. Bellair clapped her warmly on the shoulder, declaring, "I'm proud of you, Vivian! Simply proud of you!"

Her grandmother, after a judicious embrace, held her at arm's length and examined her critically.

"I don't see but what you've stood it first rate," she admitted. "And if you *like* that color—why, you certainly are looking well."

She was well, and began her second year of teaching with a serene spirit.

In all this time of slow rebuilding Vivian would not have been left comfortless if masculine admiration could have pleased her. The young men at The Cottonwoods, now undistracted by Susie's gay presence, concentrated much devotion upon Vivian, as did also the youths across the way. She turned from them all, gently, but with absolute decision.

Among her most faithful devotees was young Percy Watson, who loved her almost as much as he loved Dr. Hale, and could never understand, in his guileless, boyish heart, why neither of them would talk about the other.

They did not forbid his talking, however, and the earnest youth, sitting in the quiet parlor at The Cottonwoods, would free his heart to Vivian about how the doctor worked too hard—sat up all hours to study—didn't give himself any rest—nor any fun.

"He'll break down some time—I tell him so. It's not natural for any man to work that way, and I don't see any real need of it. He says he's working on a book—some big medical book, I suppose; but what's the hurry? I wish you'd have him over here oftener, and make him amuse himself a little, Miss Vivian."

"Dr. Hale is quite welcome to come at any time—he knows that," said she.

Again the candid Percy, sitting on the doctor's shadowy piazza, poured out his devoted admiration for her to his silent host.

"She's the finest woman I ever knew!" the boy would say. "She's so beautiful and so clever, and so pleasant to everybody. She's *square*—like a man. And she's kind—like a woman, only kinder; a sort of motherliness about her. I don't see how she ever lived so long without being married. I'd marry her in a minute if I was good enough—and if she'd have me."

Dr. Hale tousled the ears of Balzac, the big, brown dog whose head was so often on his knee, and said nothing.[63] He had not seen the girl since that night by the arbor.

Later in the season he learned, perforce, to know her better, and to admire her more.

Susie's baby came with the new year, and brought danger and anxiety. They hardly hoped to save the life of the child. The little mother was long unable to leave her bed. Since her aunt was not there, but gone, as Mrs. Dykeman, on an extended tour—"part business and part honeymoon," her husband told her—and since Mrs. Pettigrew now ruled alone at The Cottonwoods, with every evidence of ability and enjoyment, Vivian promptly installed herself in the Saunders home, as general housekeeper and nurse.

She was glad then of her strength, and used it royally, comforting the wretched Jim, keeping up Susie's spirits, and mothering the frail tiny baby with exquisite devotion.

Day after day the doctor saw her, sweet and strong and patient, leaving her school to the assistant, regardless of losses, showing the virtues he admired most in women.

He made his calls as short as possible; but even so, Vivian could not but note how his sternness gave way to brusque good cheer for the sick mother, and to a lovely gentleness with the child.

When that siege was over and the girl returned to her own work, she carried pleasant pictures in her mind, and began to wonder, as had so many others, why this man, who seemed so fitted to enjoy a family, had none.

She missed his daily call, and wondered further why he avoided them more assiduously than at first.

12

Achievements

There are some folk born to beauty,
  And some to plenteous gold,
Some who are proud of being young,
  Some proud of being old.

Some who are glad of happy love,
  Enduring, deep and true,
And some who thoroughly enjoy
  The little things they do.

Upon all this Grandma Pettigrew cast an observant eye, and meditated sagely thereupon. Coming to a decision, she first took a course of reading in some of Dr. Bellair's big books, and then developed a series of perplexing symptoms, not of a too poignant or perilous nature, that took her to Dr. Hale's office frequently.

"You haven't repudiated Dr. Bellair, have you?" he asked her.

"I have never consulted Jane Bellair as a physician," she replied, "though I esteem her much as a friend."

The old lady's company was always welcome to him; he liked her penetrating eye, her close-lipped, sharp remarks, and appreciated the real kindness of her heart.

If he had known how closely she was peering into the locked recesses of his own, and how much she saw there, he would perhaps have avoided her as he did Vivian, and if he had known further that this ingenious old lady, pursuing long genealogical discussions with him, had finally unearthed a mutual old-time friend, and had forthwith started a correspondence with that friend, based on this common acquaintance in Carston, he might have left that city.

The old-time friend, baited by Mrs. Pettigrew's innocent comment on Dr. Hale's persistence in single blessed-
ness, poured forth what she knew of the cause with no
more embellishment than time is sure to give.

"I know why he won't marry," wrote she. "He had reason
good to begin with, but I never dreamed he'd be obstinate
enough to keep it up sixteen years. When he was a boy in
college here I knew him well—he was a splendid fellow,
one of the very finest. But he fell desperately in love with
that beautiful Mrs. James—don't you remember about
her? She married a St. Cloud later, and he left her, I think.
She was as lovely as a cameo—and as hard and flat. That
woman was the saintliest thing that ever breathed. She
wouldn't live with her husband because he had done
something wrong; she wouldn't get a divorce, nor let him,
because that was wicked—and she always had a string of
boys round her, and talked about the moral influence she
had on them.

"Young Hale worshipped her—simply worshipped
her—and she let him. She let them all. She had that much
that was godlike about her—she loved incense. You need
not ask for particulars. She was far too 'particular' for
that. But one light-headed chap went and drowned himself—that was all hushed up, of course, but some of us felt
pretty sure why.[64] He was a half-brother to Dick Hale, and
Dick was awfully fond of him. Then he turned hard and
hateful all at once—used to talk horridly about women.
He kept straight enough—that's easy for a misogynist, and
studying medicine didn't help him any—doctors and ministers know too much about women. So there you are. But
I'm astonished to hear he's never gotten over it; he always
was obstinate—it's his only fault. They say he swore never
to marry—if he did, that accounts. Do give my regards if
you see him again."

Mrs. Pettigrew considered long and deeply over this information, as she slowly produced a jersey striped with
Roman vividness. It was noticeable in this new life in Carston that Mrs. Pettigrew's knitted jackets had grown
steadily brighter in hue from month to month. Whereas,
in Bainville, purple and brown were the high lights, and
black, slate and navy blue the main colors; now her wor-

steds were as a painter's palette, and the result not only cheered, but bade fair to inebriate.

"A pig-headed man," she said to herself, as her needle prodded steadily in and out; "a pig-headed man, with a pig-headedness of sixteen years' standing. His hair must 'a turned gray from the strain of it. And there's Vivian, biddin' fair to be an old maid after all. What on *earth!*" She appeared to have forgotten that marriages are made in heaven, or to disregard that saying. "The Lord helps those that help themselves," was one of her favorite mottoes. "And much more those that help other people!" she used to add.

Flitting in and out of Dr. Hale's at all hours, she noted that he had a fondness for music, with a phenomenal incapacity to produce any. He encouraged his boys to play on any and every instrument the town afforded, and to sing, whether they could or not; and seemed never to weary of their attempts, though far from satisfied with the product.

"Huh!" said Mrs. Pettigrew.

Vivian could play, "Well enough to know better," she said, and seldom touched the piano. She had a deep, full, contralto voice, and a fair degree of training. But she would never make music unless she felt like it—and in this busy life, with so many people about her, she had always refused.

Grandma meditated.

She selected an evening when most of the boarders were out at some entertainment, and selfishly begged Vivian to stay at home with her—said she was feeling badly and wanted company. Grandma so seldom wanted anything that Vivian readily acquiesced; in fact, she was quite worried about her, and asked Dr. Bellair if she thought anything was the matter.

"She has seemed more quiet lately," said the astute lady, "and I've noticed her going in to Dr. Hale's during office hours. But perhaps it's only to visit with him."

"Are you in any pain, Grandma?" asked the girl, affectionately. "You're not sick, are you?"

"O, no—I'm not sick," said the old lady, stoutly. "I'm just—well, I felt sort of lonesome to-night—perhaps I'm homesick."

As she had never shown the faintest sign of any feeling for their deserted home, except caustic criticism and unfavorable comparison, Vivian rather questioned this theory, but she began to think there was something in it when her grandmother, sitting by the window in the spring twilight, began to talk of how this time of year always made her think of her girlhood.

"Time for the March peepers at home. It's early here, and no peepers anywhere that I've heard.[65] 'Bout this time we'd be going to evening meeting. Seems as if I could hear that little organ—and the singing!"

"Hadn't I better shut that window," asked Vivian. "Won't you get cold?"

"No, indeed," said her grandmother, promptly. "I'm pretty warm—I've got this little shawl around me. And it's so soft and pleasant out."

It was soft and pleasant, a delicious May-like night in March, full of spring scents and hints of coming flowers. On the dark piazza across the way she could make out a still figure sitting alone, and the thump of Balzac's heel as he struggled with his intimate enemies told her who it was.

"Come Ye Disconsolate," she began to hum, most erroneously. "How does that go, Vivian? I was always fond of it, even if I can't sing any more'n a peacock."

Vivian hummed it and gave the words a low voice.

"That's good!" said the old lady. "I declare, I'm kinder hungry for some of those old hymns. I wish you'd play me some of 'em, Vivian."

So Vivian, glad to please her, woke the yellow keys to softer music than they were accustomed to, and presently her rich, low voice, sure, easy, full of quiet feeling, flowed out on the soft night air.

Grandma was not long content with the hymns. "I want some of those old-fashioned songs—you used to know a lot of 'em. Can't you do that 'Kerry Dance' of Molloy's, and 'Twickenham Ferry'—and 'Lauriger Horatius?' "

Vivian gave her those, and many another, Scotch ballads, English songs and German Lieder—glad to please her grandmother so easily, and quite unconscious of a dark figure which had crossed the street and come silently to sit on the farthest corner of their piazza.[66]

Grandma, meanwhile, watched him, and Vivian as well, and then, with the most unsuspected suddenness, took to her bed. Sciatica, she said.[67] An intermittent pain that came upon her so suddenly she couldn't stand up. She felt much better lying down. And Dr. Hale must attend her unceasingly.

This unlooked for overthrow of the phenomenally active old lady was a great blow to Mr. Skee; he showed real concern and begged to be allowed to see her.

"Why not?" said Mrs. Pettigrew. "It's nothing catching."

She lay, high-pillowed, as stiff and well arranged as a Knight Templar on a tombstone, arrayed for the occasion in a most decorative little dressing sack and ribbony night-cap.[68]

"Why, ma'am," said Mr. Skee, "it's highly becomin' to you to be sick. It leads me to hope it's nothin' serious."

She regarded him enigmatically. "Is Dr. Hale out there, or Vivian?" she inquired in a low voice.

"No, ma'am—they ain't," he replied after a glance in the next room.

Then he bent a penetrating eye upon her. She met it unflinchingly, but as his smile appeared and grew, its limitless widening spread contagion, and her calm front was broken.

"Elmer Skee," said she, with sudden fury, "you hold your tongue!"

"Ma'am!" he replied, "I have said nothin'—and I don't intend to. But if the throne of Europe was occupied by you, Mrs. Pettigrew, we would have a better managed world."

He proved a most agreeable and steady visitor during this period of confinement, and gave her full accounts of all that went on outside, with occasional irrelevant bursts of merriment which no rebuke from Mrs. Pettigrew seemed wholly to check.

He regaled her with accounts of his continuous consultations with Mrs. St. Cloud, and the wisdom and good taste with which she invariably advised him.

"Don't you admire a Platonic Friendship, Mrs. Pettigrew?"

"I do not!" said the old lady, sharply. "And what's more
I don't believe you do."

"Well, ma'am," he answered, swaying backward and forward on the hind legs of his chair, "there are moments
when I confess it looks improbable."

Mrs. Pettigrew cocked her head on one side and turned
a gimlet eye upon him. "Look here, Elmer Skee," she said
suddenly, "how much money have you really got?"

He brought down his chair on four legs and regarded
her for a few moments, his smile widening slowly. "Well,
ma'am, if I live through the necessary expenses involved
on my present undertaking, I shall have about two thousand a year—if rents are steady."

"Which I judge you do not wish to be known?"

"If there's one thing more than another I have always
admired in you, ma'am, it is the excellence of your judgment. In it I have absolute confidence."

Mrs. St. Cloud had some time since summoned Dr. Hale
to her side for a severe headache, but he had merely sent
word that his time was fully occupied, and recommended
Dr. Bellair.

Now, observing Mrs. Pettigrew's tactics, the fair invalid
resolved to take the bull by the horns and go herself to his
office. She found him easily enough. He lifted his eyes as
she entered, rose and stood with folded arms regarding
her silently. The tall, heavy figure, the full beard, the
glasses, confused even her excellent memory. After all it
was many years since they had met, and he had been but
one of a multitude.

She was all sweetness and gentle apology for forcing
herself upon him, but really she had a little prejudice
against women doctors—his reputation was so great—he
was so temptingly near—she was in such pain—she had
such perfect confidence in him—

He sat down quietly and listened, watching her from
under his bent brows. Her eyes were dropped, her voice
very weak and appealing; her words most perfectly
chosen.

"I have told you," he said at length, "that I never treat women for their petty ailments, if I can avoid it."

She shook her head in grieved acceptance, and lifted large eyes for one of those penetrating sympathetic glances so frequently successful.

"How you must have suffered!" she said.

"I have," he replied grimly. "I have suffered a long time from having my eyes opened too suddenly to the brainless cruelty of women, Mrs. James."

She looked at him again, searchingly, and gave a little cry. "Dick Hale!" she said.

"Yes, Dick Hale. Brother to poor little Joe Medway, whose foolish young heart you broke, among others; whose death you are responsible for."

She was looking at him with widening wet eyes. "Ah! If you only knew how I, too, have suffered over that!" she said. "I was scarce more than a girl myself, then. I was careless, not heartless. No one knew what pain I was bearing, then. I liked the admiration of those nice boys—I never realized any of them would take it seriously. That has been a heavy shadow on my life, Dr. Hale—the fear that I was the thoughtless cause of that terrible thing. And you have never forgiven me. I do not wonder."

He was looking at her in grim silence again, wishing he had not spoken.

"So that is why you have never been to The Cottonwoods since I came," she pursued. "And I am responsible for all your loneliness. O, how dreadful!"

Again he rose to his feet.

"No, madam, you mistake. You were responsible for my brother's death, and for a bitter awakening on my part, but you are in no way responsible for my attitude since. That is wholly due to myself. Allow me again to recommend Dr. Jane Bellair, an excellent physician and even more accessible."

He held the door for her, and she went out, not wholly dissatisfied with her visit. She would have been far more displeased could she have followed his thoughts afterward.

"What a Consummate Ass I have been all my life!" he was meditating. "Because I met this particular type of sex parasite, to deliberately go sour—and forego all chance of happiness. Like a silly girl. A fool girl who says, 'I will never marry!' just because of some quarrel.*** But the girl never keeps her word. A man must."

The days were long to Vivian now, and dragged a little, for all her industry.

Mrs. St. Cloud tried to revive their former intimacy, but the girl could not renew it on the same basis. She, too, had sympathized with Mr. Dykeman, and now sympathized somewhat with Mr. Skee. But since that worthy man still volubly discoursed on Platonism, and his fair friend openly agreed in this view, there seemed no real ground for distress.

Mrs. Pettigrew remained ailing and rather captious. She had a telephone put at her bedside, and ran her household affairs efficiently, with Vivian as lieutenant, and the ever-faithful Jeanne to uphold the honor of the cuisine. Also she could consult her physician, and demanded his presence at all hours.

He openly ignored Mrs. St. Cloud now, who met his rude treatment with secret, uncomplaining patience.

Vivian spoke of this. "I do not see why he need be so rude, Grandma. He may hate women, but I don't see why he should treat her so shamefully."

"Well, I do," replied the invalid, "and what's more I'm going to show you; I've always disliked that woman, and now I know why. I'd turn her out of the house if it wasn't for Elmer Skee. That man's as good as gold under all his foolishness, and if he can get any satisfaction out of that meringue he's welcome. Dr. Hale doesn't hate women, child, but a woman broke his heart once—and then he made an idiot of himself by vowing never to marry."

She showed her friend's letter, and Vivian read it with rising color. "O, Grandma! Why that's worse than I ever thought—even after what Dr. Bellair told us. And it was his brother! No wonder he's so fond of boys. He tries to warn them, I suppose."

"Yes, and the worst of it is that he's really got over his grouch; and he's in love—but tied down by that foolish oath, poor man."

"Is he, Grandma? How do you know? With whom?"

"You dear, blind child!" said the old lady, "with you, of course. Has been ever since we came."

The girl sat silent, a strange feeling of joy rising in her heart, as she reviewed the events of the last two years. So that was why he would not stay that night. And that was why. "No wonder he wouldn't come here!" she said at length. "It's on account of that woman. But why did he change?"

"Because she went over there to see him. He wouldn't come to her. I heard her 'phone to him one evening." The old lady chuckled. "So she marched herself over there—I saw her, and I guess she got her needin's. She didn't stay long. And his light burned till morning."

"Do you think he cares for her, still?"

"Cares for her!" The old lady fairly snorted her derision. "He can't bear the sight of her—treats her as if she wasn't there. No, indeed. If he did she'd have him fast enough, now. Well! I suppose he'll repent of that foolishness of his all the days of his life—and stick it out! Poor man."

Mrs. Pettigrew sighed, and Vivian echoed the sigh. She began to observe Dr. Hale with new eyes; to study little matters of tone and manner—and could not deny her grandmother's statement. Nor would she admit it—yet.

The old lady seemed weaker and more irritable, but positively forbade any word of this being sent to her family.

"There's nothing on earth ails me," she said. "Dr. Hale says there's not a thing the matter that he can see—that if I'd only eat more I'd get stronger. I'll be all right soon, my dear. I'll get my appetite and get well, I have faith to believe."

She insisted on his coming over in the evening, when not too busy, and staying till she dropped asleep, and he seemed strangely willing to humor her; sitting for hours in the quiet parlor, while Vivian played softly, and sang her low-toned hymns.

So sitting, one still evening, when for some time no fretful "not so loud" had come from the next room, he turned suddenly to Vivian and asked, almost roughly—"Do you hold a promise binding?—an oath, a vow—to oneself?"

She met his eyes, saw the deep pain there, the long combat, the irrepressible hope and longing.

"Did you swear to keep your oath secret?" she asked.

"Why, no," he said, "I did not. I will tell you. I did not swear never to tell a woman I loved her. I never dreamed I should love again. Vivian, I was fool enough to love a shallow, cruel woman, once, and nearly broke my heart in consequence. That was long years ago. I have never cared for a woman since—till I met you. And now I must pay double for that boy folly."

He came to her and took her hand.

"I love you," he said, his tense grip hurting her. "I shall love you as long as I live—day and night—forever! You shall know that at any rate!"

She could not raise her eyes. A rich bright color rose to the soft border of her hair. He caught her face in his hands and made her look at him; saw those dark, brilliant eyes softened, tear-filled, asking, and turned sharply away with a muffled cry.

"I have taken a solemn oath," he said in a strained, hard voice, "never to ask a woman to marry me."

He heard a little gasping laugh, and turned upon her. She stood there smiling, her hands reached out to him.

"You don't have to," she said.

* * * *

A long time later, upon their happy stillness broke a faint voice from the other room:

"Vivian, I think if you'd bring me some bread and butter—and a cup of tea—and some cold beef and a piece of pie—I could eat it."

* * * *

Upon the rapid and complete recovery of her grandmother's health, and the announcement of Vivian's engagement, Mr. and Mrs. Lane decided to make a visit to their distant mother and daughter, hoping as well that Mr. Lane's cough might be better for a visit in that altitude. Mr. and Mrs. Dykeman also sent word of their immediate return.

Jeanne, using subtle powers of suggestion, caused Mrs. Pettigrew to decide upon giving a dinner, in honor of these events. There was the betrothed couple, there were the honored guests; there were Jimmie and Susie, with or without the baby; there were the Dykemans; there was Dr. Bellair, of course; there was Mr. Skee, an even number.

"I'm sorry to spoil that table, but I've got to take in Mrs. St. Cloud," said the old lady.

"O, Grandma! Why! It'll spoil it for Dick."

"Huh!" said her grandmother. "He's so happy you couldn't spoil it with a mummy. If I don't ask her it'll spoil it for Mr. Skee."

So Mrs. St. Cloud made an eleventh at the feast, and neither Mr. Dykeman nor Vivian could find it in their happy hearts to care.

Mr. Skee arose, looking unusually tall and shapely in immaculate every-day dress, his well-brushed hair curling vigorously around the little bald spots; his smile wide and benevolent.

"Ladies and Gentlemen, both Domestic and Foreign, Friends and Fellowtownsmen and Women—Ladies, God Bless 'em; also Children, if any: I feel friendly enough to-night to include the beasts of the fields—but such would be inappropriate at this convivial board—among these convivial boarders.

"This is an occasion of great rejoicing. We have many things to rejoice over, both great *and* small. We have our healths; all of us, apparently. We are experiencing the joys of reunion—in the matter of visiting parents that is, and long absent daughters.

"We have also the Return of the Native, in the shape of my old friend Andy—now become a Benedict—and seeming to enjoy it.[69] About this same Andy I have a piece of news to give you which will cause you astonishment and gratification, but which involves me in a profuse apology—a most sincere and general apology.

"You know how a year or more ago it was put about in this town that Andrew Dykeman was a ruined man?" Mrs. St. Cloud darted a swift glance at Mr. Dykeman, but his eyes rested calmly on his wife; then at Mr. Skee—but he was pursuing his remorseful way.

"I do not wish to blame my friend Andy for his reticence—but he certainly did exhibit reticence on this occasion—to beat the band! *He* never contradicted this rumor—not once. He just went about looking kind o' down in the mouth for some reason or other, and when for the sake o' Auld Lang Syne I offered him a job in my office—the cuss took it![70] I won't call this deceitful, but it sure was reticent to a degree.

"Well, Ladies—and Gentlemen—the best of us are liable to mistakes, and I have to admit—I am glad to humble myself and make this public admission—I was entirely in error in this matter.

"It wasn't so. There was nothing in it. It was rumor, pure and simple. Andy Dykeman never lost no mine, it appears; or else he had another up his sleeve concealed from his best friends. Anyhow, the facts are these; not only that A. Dykeman as he sits before you is a prosperous and wealthy citizen, but that he has been, for these ten years back, and we were all misled by a mixture of rumor and reticence. If he has concealed these facts from the wife of his bosom I submit that that is carrying reticent too far!" Again Mrs. St. Cloud sent a swift glance at the reticent one, and again caught only his tender apologetic look toward his wife, and her utter amazement.

Mr. Dykeman rose to his feet.

"I make no apologies for interrupting my friend," he said. "It is necessary at times. He at least can never be accused of reticence. Neither do I make apologies for letting rumor take its course—a course often interesting to observe. But I do apologize—in this heartfelt and public manner, to my wife, for marrying her under false pretenses. But any of you gentlemen who have ever had any experience in the attitude of," he hesitated mercifully, and said, "the World, toward a man with money, may understand what it meant to me, after many years of bachelorhood, to find a heart that not only loved me for myself alone, but absolutely loved me better because I'd lost my money—or she thought I had. I have hated to break the charm. But now my unreticent friend here has stated the facts, and I make my confession. Will you forgive me, Orella?"

"Speech! Speech!" cried Mr. Skee. But Mrs. Dykeman could not be persuaded to do anything but blush and smile and squeeze her husband's hand under the table, and Mr. Skee arose once more.

"This revelation being accomplished," he continued cheerfully; "and no one any the worse for it, as I see," he was not looking in the direction of Mrs. St. Cloud, whose slippered foot beat softly under the table, though her face wore its usual sweet expression, possibly a trifle strained; "I now proceed to a proclamation of that happy event to celebrate which we are here gathered together. I allude to the Betrothal of Our Esteemed Friend, Dr. Richard Hale, and the Fairest of the Fair! Regarding the Fair, we think she has chosen well. But regarding Dick Hale, his good fortune is so clear, so evidently undeserved, and his pride and enjoyment thereof so ostentatious, as to leave us some leeway to make remarks.

"Natural remarks, irresistible remarks, as you might say, and not intended to be acrimonious. Namely, such as these: It's a long lane that has no turning; There's many a slip 'twixt the cup and the lip; The worm will turn; The pitcher that goes too often to the well gets broken at last; Better Late than Never. And so on and so forth. Any other gentleman like to make remarks on this topic?"

Dr. Hale rose, towering to his feet.

"I think I'd better make them," he said. "No one else could so fully, so heartily, with such perfect knowledge point out how many kinds of a fool I've been for all these years. And yet of them all there are only two that I regret—this last two in which if I had been wiser, perhaps I might have found my happiness sooner. As that cannot be proven, however, I will content myself with the general acknowledgment that Bachelors are Misguided Bats, I myself having long been the worst instance; women, in general, are to be loved and honored; and that I am proud and glad to accept your congratulations because the sweetest and noblest woman in the world has honored me with her love."

"I never dreamed you could put so many words together, Doc—and really make sense!" said Mr. Skee, genially, as he rose once more. "You certainly show a proper spirit at last, and all is forgiven. But now, my friends; now

if your attention is not exhausted, I have yet another
Event to confide to you."

Mr. and Mrs. Lane wore an aspect of polite interest.
Susie and Jim looked at each other with a sad but re-
signed expression. So did Mrs. Dykeman and her husband. Vivian's hand was in her lover's and she could not
look unhappy, but they, too, deprecated this last announcement, only too well anticipated. Only Mrs. St.
Cloud, her fair face bowed in gentle confusion, showed
anticipating pleasure.

Mr. Skee waved his hand toward her with a large and
graceful gesture.

"You must all of you have noticed the amount of Platonic Friendship which has been going on for some time
between my undeserving self and this lovely lady here.
Among so many lovely ladies perhaps I'd better specify
that I refer to the one on my left.

"What she has been to me, in my lonely old age, none of
you perhaps realize." He wore an expression as of one
long exiled, knowing no one who could speak his language.

"She has been my guide, counsellor and friend; she has
assisted me with advice most wise and judicious; she has
not interfered with my habits, but has allowed me to
enjoy life in my own way, with the added attraction of her
companionship.

"Now, I dare say, there may have been some of you who
have questioned my assertion that this friendship was
purely Platonic. Perhaps even the lady herself, knowing
the heart of man, may have doubted if my feeling toward
her was really friendship."

Mr. Skee turned his head a little to one side and regarded her with a tender inquiring smile.

To this she responded sweetly: "Why no, Mr. Skee, of
course, I believed what you said."

"There, now," said he admiringly. "What is so noble as
the soul of woman? It is to this noble soul in particular,
and to all my friends here in general, that I now confide
the crowning glory of a long and checkered career,
namely, and to wit, that I am engaged to be married to that
Peerless Lady, Mrs. Servilla Pettigrew, of whose remark-

able capacities and achievements I can never sufficiently express my admiration."

A silence fell upon the table. Mr. Skee sat down smiling, evidently in cheerful expectation of congratulations. Mrs. Pettigrew wore an alert expression, as of a skilled fencer preparing to turn any offered thrusts. Mrs. St. Cloud seemed to be struggling with some emotion, which shook her usual sweet serenity. The others, too, were visibly affected, and not quick to respond.

Then did Mr. Saunders arise with real good nature and ever-ready wit; and pour forth good-humored nonsense with congratulations all around, till a pleasant atmosphere was established, in which Mrs. St. Cloud could so far recover as to say many proper and pretty things; sadly adding that she regretted her imminent return to the East would end so many pleasant friendships.

NOTES

1. Dr. Prince Albert Morrow, *Social Diseases and Marriage, Social Prophylaxis* (New York and Philadelphia: Lea Brothers and Co., 1904); and Lavinia Dock, *Hygiene and Morality* (1910; reprint in *A Lavinia Dock Reader*, ed. J. W. James [New York: Garland Publishing, 1985]). See the introduction to this volume for more discussion of Morrow (32, 65–66 n.77 and n.78) and Dock (28, 29).

2. A syringa is a type of fragrant, ornamental shrub.

3. An ell is an archaic English unit of measurement equal to 45 inches.

4. *Kinetescope* might refer to "kinetoscope," the trademark name for a device that produces the illusion of a moving image on film. Its magnifying lens, light source, and moving shutter allow the viewer to advance a band of film, producing a quick succession of images that appears as continuous movement. Gilman may equally be referring, however, to the "Kinescope" (also a trademark name), a motion picture produced by an image on a picture tube.

5. A shuttlecock is the conical, lightweight object, with a rounded nose, that is volleyed back and forth in badminton.

6. For the single-volume edition, Gilman changed Vivian's mother's name from Martha to Laura.

7. A kitchen-midden is a heap of refuse, especially that marking a site of prehistoric habitation.

8. As Rebecca suggests, the word that Josie mispronounces here is pedagogy, the study and practice of teaching.

9. The *Centurion* is either a fictional magazine or an allusion to the

Century, a popular quarterly illustrated magazine in print between 1870 and 1930. Gilman reviewed the *Century* periodically while editing the *Impress* and *The Forerunner.*

10. Abydos was a city in ancient Egypt whose ruins include temples and a burial ground.

11. Worsted is twisted yarn made of wool.

12. A darning egg is an egg-shaped object held under a tear or hole in clothing while it is mended (or darned).

13. Quince is a kind of pickled fruit.

14. Lester Ward was a well-known sociologist and leading voice of Reform Darwinism; his theories of evolution, which granted women primacy in the human species and held that humanity was capable of directing its own evolution in an enlightened manner, underlay his advocacy of a variety of social reforms. For discussion of Ward's influence on Gilman, see the introduction, 39, and 69 n.112.

15. The Reverend R. J. Campbell's *The New Theology* (New York: Macmillan, 1907) treated doctrinal theology, while *The New Theology and the Socialist Movement* (Stockport, UK: Socialist Publishing Co., 1908) discussed Christian socialism.

16. A palimpsest is a writing surface that has been used two or more times, the old inscription being erased each time to make room for the new.

17. *Arthritis deformans* is a form of chronic arthritis that deforms the joints.

18. Women gained the right to vote in Colorado in 1893.

19. For a comparison of the ratio of men to women in Massachusetts and Colorado, see the introduction, 69–70 n.114.

20. In the theories of Charles Darwin and other evolutionary scientists, the term "arrested development" refers to the failure of an organism to reach full maturity.

21. For a discussion of the significance of pockets for women in Gilman's thought, see the introduction, 19, and 60 n.25.

22. A fret is an ornamental band that can appear in a variety of patterns; Greek frets are often composed of straight lines intersecting one another at right angles.

23. Hack is short for "hackney," a hired carriage or coach.

24. A Pullman is a specially-furnished railroad passenger car equipped for overnight travel.

25. Used in the past for medical and cosmetic purposes, court plaster (so called because it was worn at court by royal ladies) is an adhesive plaster composed of glycerin and gelatin. It was often used to attach a patch of silk to the face or neck. A troche is a soothing lozenge.

26. Legal cap is ruled paper designed for use by lawyers, approximately 8 inches wide and 13–14 inches long.

27. For the single-volume edition, Gilman changed the length of Dr. Hale's residence in Colorado from ten years to nine.

28. This extremely racist portrayal of Chinese immigrants is, unfortunately, in keeping with much of Gilman's work. Elsewhere in the

novel, for example, she is grossly insensitive to the plights of working-class characters (particularly "The Cottonwoods"' cook, Jeanne Jeaune), Native Americans (who are erased from her Western narrative except as "savages" known for scalping white settlers), and the disabled (a case in point being Jeaune's brain-damaged son, Theophile, whom Gilman describes in demeaning, subhuman terms; see *Crux* 154ff.). For more discussion of this issue, see the introduction 32–33, 41–42, and 66 n.80.

29. A settle is a wooden bench with a high back, solid arms, and an enclosed space for storage underneath the seat.

30. A jimcrack is a trifling object or knickknack.

31. In the *Forerunner* edition, this sentence begins with "Vivian" rather than "The girls." It is not clear why Gilman changed the subject from Vivian to the two young women, since the following sentence and subsequent dialogue have a singular subject—Vivian. Further, the subject portrayed in this first sentence clearly fits the characterization of Vivian, but not that of Susie, who surely would not be oblivious to the attentions of Hale's young male boarders.

32. The ruins of Persepolis, an ancient capital of Persia, are in what is now southern Iran, and they contain lions among other images carved in relief. The "other lion-and-ruin thing" is likely a reproduction of Giovanni Battista Piranesi's *The Lion Bas-Relief* (c. 1761), an etching in his series called *Carceri di Invenzione (Imaginary Prisons)*, which pictures an ancient, crumbling palace with lions in bas-relief along with a scene of victorious Roman soldiers and their bound captive. Like the other etchings in this collection, *The Lion Bas-Relief* is a gloomy, menacing image busy with crumbling beams and arches, flights of stairs leading nowhere, and human figures engulfed by the enormity of these structures. Saint Jerome (c. 347–419/420 c.e.), the Church Father and biblical translator, spent two lonely, difficult years living as a hermit in the desert of Chalcis, and is conventionally symbolized by a lion. The biblical hero Daniel was cast into a den of lions for continuing to pray to his own god after the conquest of Jerusalem by the Babylonians; he was then divinely delivered from danger. Circe is a mythological enchantress who, in Homer's *Odyssey*, turns the companions of Odysseus (or Ulysses) into swine, and thus threatens the hero's completion of his journey. The significance of "Island of Death" is uncertain; it may be a reference to Hades, the underworld of Greek mythology, which was said to be separated from the land of the living by five rivers. Sir Edward Coley Burne-Jones (1833–1898) was a highly regarded English painter who used the Pre-Raphaelite style in his mystical, romantic images, often touching on medieval chivalry.

33. Marcus Aurelius (121–180 c.e.) was a Stoic philosopher and writer, as well as Emperor of Rome. The Greek Epictetus (c. 60–c. 120 c.e.) was a Stoic teacher and philosopher. Plato (427–347 b.c.e.) was a Greek philosopher. Ralph Waldo Emerson (1803–1882) was an American poet, essayist, and philosopher. And Thomas Carlyle (1795–1881), to whom Gilman refers as "Carlisle," was a Scottish-born English

prose writer, whose interest in heroic individualism strongly influenced Emerson's belief in the divine power of the individual. Not surprisingly, Gilman is known to have read and/or owned works by all of these philosophers. See Gary Scharnhorst and Denise D. Knight, "Charlotte Perkins Gilman's Library: A Reconstruction," *Resources for American Literary Study* 23.2 (1997): 181–219.

34. A prairie schooner is a type of covered wagon used by the pioneers for cross-country travel.

35. In the *Forerunner* edition of the novel, the first line of this introductory poem reads: "There is hope till life is through, my dear!"

36. A transom is a crosspiece, in this case likely made of wood, separating a door from the small window above it.

37. Whist is a card game using fifty-two cards and played usually by two teams of two players each. One point is earned for each trick made in excess of six. Long whist has ten points to a game.

38. "Stay me with flagons, comfort me with apples: for I am sick of love," Song of Sol. 2:5. In this context, "flagon" is an archaic term for a raisin cake, and the speaker is saying that he is sick with love for his god.

39. In Scottish parlance, "bonny" means pretty, and "een" means eyes.

40. A gadder is someone who moves about aimlessly, usually with little purpose other than gossip or curiosity.

41. Horace Fletcher (1849–1919) was an American nutritionist; to Fletcherize is to chew one's food thoroughly and slowly, as he advocated.

42. "Zutritt ist Verboten" is German for "access is forbidden" or "keep out."

43. Solo is any type of card game in which one plays alone against others, rather than as part of a team.

44. Mr. Skee's exclamation ("the—Hesperides") refers to islands that, in classical mythology, are located at the western-most edge of the world, featuring a garden with golden apples. The souls of great heroes were thought to be transported there after death. "Hesperides" is also the name for the nymphs who supposedly guarded this fabled garden.

45. A gentian is a type of plant with red, yellow, white, or, most often, blue flowers.

46. The Hanging Gardens of Babylon, one of the Seven Wonders of the World, were roof gardens said to have been erected in the royal palace at Babylon (in what is now southern Iraq) between the eighth and sixth centuries B.C.E. They supposedly were irrigated with water from the Euphrates River. In the Judeo-Christian tradition, Babylon has been associated with excess and impiety.

47. In this context, *sotto voce* means "under her breath."

48. In revising the novel from *The Forerunner* to the single-volume edition, Gilman excised a paragraph that would have followed here. It read:

"The music was so placed that they could dance in the double parlors, on the piazza or even on the lawn if they chose, and those who did not choose to dance might stroll under the lucent pink lanterns, or into green shades quite lanternless."

49. It formerly was customary that women attending a dance would obtain a card, called a "dance-card," on which to list their prospective partners.

50. In revising the novel from *The Forerunner* to the single-volume edition, Gilman removed the word "sincere" from its place before "devoted" in the list of adjectives describing Morton's improved attitude.

51. For a discussion of sexually transmitted disease at the turn of the century, see the introduction, 26–35.

52. This chapter was not given a title in the *Forerunner* edition.

53. Galena is a bluish-gray mineral, the principal ore of lead.

54. A fob is a short, ornamented chain or ribbon by which a pocket-watch is attached to a pocket.

55. The significance of a "Farewell to Egypt affair" is unclear; it may be obscure slang for bachelor party.

56. In Greek mythology, the Minotaur was a monster with a bull's head on a man's body. It was kept in the Labyrinth (or maze) on the island of Crete, where every nine years until its death it was fed fourteen youths and maidens (or female virgins).

57. A charnel house is a structure containing the bodies and bones of the dead.

58. Dr. Prince Morrow was the founder of the American Society for Sanitary and Moral Prophylaxis. His book, *Social Diseases and Marriage*, likely inspired many of Gilman's assertions about sexually transmitted diseases in the novel: for example, he argues that 75 percent of American men had at some time had gonorrhea, many of whom also had had syphilis; he details the effects on children of parents with such diseases (especially blindness); and he asserts that preventing such diseases from being introduced into marriage was a duty to society and to the preservation of the (white) "race." Morrow founded the American Society for Sanitary and Moral Prophylaxis in 1905 to prevent the spread of sexually transmitted diseases; Gilman herself addressed this group in 1910. See Gilman, "In Its Sociological Aspects," *Transactions of the American Society for Sanitary and Moral Prophylaxis* 3 (1910): 141–44.

59. Before this last clause in the *Forerunner* edition, Gilman had included another: "of scornful indifference."

60. Archimedes (c. 287–212 B.C.E.) was a Greek mathematician and physicist renowned for his ingenious inventions (though Percy seems to associate him with stoicism, this is incorrect). There was no such person as Sandalphon; *Sandal-on* is the ancient Greek word for sandal, and *phon* is associated with the term "phonic." Thus, the joke is on Percy, whose fictional Sandalphon actually means "sandal-sound." I am grateful to Tricia Gilson for her assistance with this translation.

61. In archaic usage, a man is said to have "gotten the mitten" if his proposal of marriage is refused.

62. "And the Lord God said, Behold, the man is become as one of us, to know good and evil: and now, lest he put forth his hand, and take also of the tree of life, and eat, and live for ever: Therefore the Lord God sent him forth from the garden of Eden, ... So he drove out the man; and he placed at the east of the garden of Eden Cherubims, and a flaming sword which turned every way, to keep the way of the tree of life." Gen. 3:22–24.

63. Hale has named his dog after the prolific French novelist Honoré de Balzac (1799–1850), whose coarse prose combined realism with romanticism.

64. It is likely that this love-struck young man, Dick Hale's half-brother, who drowned himself over Mrs. St. Cloud (then Mrs. James), is St. Cloud's disappointed "acolyte" who is said in chapter 3 to have shot himself out of unrequited love for her (*Crux* 114). The time pressures of serial publishing under which Gilman first composed the novel might easily explain such an inconsistency. It is not entirely surprising that she neglected to clarify this when she revised the text, since she published the single-volume edition of the novel during that same year.

65. A peeper is any of several frogs emitting a peeping sound, prevalent in the spring.

66. German *Lieder* ("songs"), from the nineteenth century, were written in the German vernacular.

67. Sciatica is the term for pain along the sciatic nerve, usually extending from the hip to the back of the thigh.

68. The Knights Templar were an order of knights who united originally to protect pilgrims during the Crusades. They were often portrayed on tombstones in a seated position.

69. Skee calls Andrew Dykeman a "Benedict" because Dykeman, formerly a confirmed bachelor, is now newly married (the term derives from Benedick, a character in William Shakespeare's *Much Ado About Nothing*).

70. Auld Lang Syne is Scots for "the good old days."